Swiftly Ruth tore herself from the overpowering pull of his smouldering grey eyes.

The gentle banter between them had transformed into something far more deadly serious. She turned her head, frowned in confusion. Clayton was flirting outrageously with her, making her think unsuitable thoughts, making her feel emotions she didn't want to feel…

Foolishly she'd encouraged the attention of a notorious rake in the belief she could match his sophisticated skill in a trifling game. For an interminable moment she refused to meet his eyes whilst a riot of thoughts whirled in her head. She must cede him his victory in their verbal duel but not let him know how greatly he'd unsettled her.

She might be unworldly and wearing a tired-looking dress, but she'd not crumple beneath the sensual challenge he'd thrown down…

Author Note

The path of true love never runs smooth, so the old saying goes, and I have written a duet of novels with those wise words in mind. In the first book, THE VIRTUOUS COURTESAN, it was certainly a fitting adage! The heroine, Sarah Marchant, had suffered a traumatic childhood. When her future was cruelly bound to that of Gavin Stone—something neither of them wanted—it seemed matters must only get worse…or would they?

This second story, THE RAKE'S DEFIANT MISTRESS, features Ruth Hayden as the heroine. Widowed when very young, she has also endured a great deal of heartache in her early years. Then Sir Clayton Powell arrives. He's a man she wants to refuse, but a scandal results in their engagement. Can a marriage without love survive?

May you enjoy them both to the full.

THE RAKE'S DEFIANT MISTRESS

Mary Brendan

All the characters in this book have no existence outside the imagination of the author, and have no relation whatsoever to anyone bearing the same name or names. They are not even distantly inspired by any individual known or unknown to the author, and all the incidents are pure invention.

First published in Great Britain 2009
Harlequin Mills & Boon Limited,
Eton House, 18-24 Paradise Road, Richmond, Surrey TW9 1SR

ISBN: 978 0 263 86767 1

Set in Times Roman 10¾ on 13½ pt.
04-0309-64772

Printed and bound in Spain
by Litografia Rosés S.A., Barcelona

THE RAKE'S DEFIANT MISTRESS

Mary Brendan was born in North London, but now lives in rural Suffolk. She has always had a fascination with bygone days, and enjoys the research involved in writing historical fiction. When not at her word processor, she can be found trying to bring order to a large overgrown garden, or browsing local fairs and junk shops for that elusive bargain.

Recent novels by this author:

WEDDING NIGHT REVENGE*
THE UNKNOWN WIFE*
A SCANDALOUS MARRIAGE*
THE RAKE AND THE REBEL*
A PRACTICAL MISTRESS†
THE WANTON BRIDE†
THE VIRTUOUS COURTESAN**

**The Meredith Sisters*
†The Hunter Brothers
**linked to THE RAKE'S DEFIANT MISTRESS

Chapter One

'I think I must ask you to leave, sir.'

The lady received no response to her firm request. The gentleman she had attempted to eject from her small sitting room continued to pace across the rug, stamping a deeper trench into its tired pile.

'Doctor Bryant!' Ruth Hayden's suffocated plea held a hint of irritation. 'I beg I will not have to again ask you to go.'

The fellow halted, exasperatedly planting his hands on to his hips. 'I cannot believe you will not hear me out, Mrs Hayden.' A grimace stressed his bewilderment. 'Why will you not at least let me fully explain to you the benefits—?'

'I need no full explanation, sir,' Ruth Hayden interrupted him briskly. 'I have the gist of your proposal and it is enough for me to want to spare you…spare us both…the embarrassment of any further mention of it. I am conscious of the honour you do me, but I cannot marry you. Now I must bid you good day.' Ruth walked swiftly to the sitting-room door and pointedly opened it.

As he realised he was being summarily dismissed, the look of surprise quit Dr Ian Bryant's features to be replaced by one of anger.

In the rural town of Willowdene he was an eminent member of society and not used to receiving such a set down. The woman delivering the snub was barely tolerated in company hereabouts and that made her attitude to his proposal the more unexpected. As his wife she would once more be welcomed into the fold.

He was a ruggedly good-looking man in his middle thirties with nothing exceptional or objectionable in his demeanour. He was moderately broad of shoulder and quite tall. Now he drew himself even higher in his shoes before stalking towards the exit.

'Had you not once given me reason to hope that you would welcome my attentions, madam, I would not be here at all.' His lips curled in satisfaction as he noticed how that barb unsettled her.

High spots of colour burned on Ruth's slanting cheekbones as she recalled the incident to which he referred. But she tilted her head to a proud angle and squarely met his eyes. 'I think on that occasion too, sir, you presumed too much,' she rejoined coolly. 'I was in need of a little comfort when my father died suddenly. I again thank you for giving it to me. Now there is no more to be said.' She opened the door a mite wider, but still he seemed reluctant to go. Eyes that were unwavering settled on her face as Dr Bryant relentlessly studied the object of his desire.

Ruth Hayden was beautiful rather than fashionably pretty. She was not blessed with delicate features and her complexion was not fair enough for what was considered nice in a genteel lady. Her thick dark brown hair had resisted sleek confinement in the pleat at her nape and glossy locks wisped untidily against her cheeks. Beneath defined brows were large chocolate-coloured eyes that were far too direct and steady for a modest female of gentle birth. The womanly trait he normally found alluring, flirtatiousness, was absent from her character. Today she might have blushed and lowered her eyelashes before him, but that was due to her being disconcerted, not playful. Yet in mocking contrast to her strait-laced attitude was the curvaceous body he had once—far too briefly—felt moulding to his. His eyes were drawn to it now: full high breasts and rounded hips that were separated by a divinely tiny waist he ached to girdle with his hands.

Her unequivocal rejection had astonished him as well as dented his pride. A woman in her unenviable position ought to have jumped at the chance to improve her status and prospects. But she had thwarted not only his desire to bed her, but to have her mother his infant son. Ian was abruptly jolted from his brooding thoughts by a polite reminder that he was outstaying his welcome.

'I have much to do, sir; I must insist you leave and again bid you good day.'

Without another word Ian strode out. Within a moment Ruth closed her eyes in relief as she heard the bolts being slid home. Her maid appeared on the threshold to the sitting room. 'Shall I put on the kettle, Mrs Hayden?' the girl asked in concern.

Ruth gave Cissie a small smile and a grateful nod. So Cissie knew she was in need of a little comfort! She did not believe Cissie to be an intentional eavesdropper. Her maid had sensed rather than heard the delicate nature of the conversation that had taken place moments ago between her and Dr Bryant. Cissie would have deduced from the doctor's grim expression that she'd declined his proposal. Now the girl was curious to know her reasons for turning down an offer of marriage from an eligible gentleman.

One only needed to glance about the sitting room to realise that Mrs Hayden lived frugally. The fresh herby atmosphere that wafted throughout the spotless cottage could not improve furniture that was shabby or furnishings that had seen far better days. If one were to venture into the kitchen and investigate the larders, similar proof of want would be found. The obvious conclusion to be drawn was that this widow's lot in life would improve dramatically were she to marry a rich widower.

And Dr Bryant was such a fellow—so everyone hereabouts thought. He had a fine home and income and had increased his wealth on marriage. Therefore it was reasoned that his worthy profession was a philanthropic vocation rather than necessary toil.

As Cissie went off to prepare the tea Ruth sank into a chair. She turned her head to frown over the bright budding gardens and wondered why she had, with so little thought given to the certain benefits she was rejecting, turned down Dr Bryant. She might have asked him for a little time to mull over becoming his wife. It was an accepted response by a lady startled by a marriage proposal.

When she'd been a gauche eighteen-year-old, Paul Hayden had taken her by surprise and asked her to marry him. In her tender innocence she had guessed it might be deemed vulgar, after so short an acquaintance, to seem too keen too soon, so had given him a blurted prevarication. A private smile curved her mouth at the sweet memory of it. But by the time he had reached the door and turned to take his leave, her overwhelming happiness had prompted her to fly to him and insist that she'd like nothing better than to be his wife. She had loved him too much to make him unnecessarily suffer her indecision.

Doctor Bryant did not stir any such passionate longing in her. But she had thought him to be her friend until the day he had ruined it all by asking her to become his mistress. Now he had lost his wife in childbed, he had improved his offer to her.

Was she simply a silly fool to yearn to fall in love with a man before she'd consider the advantages to be had in matrimony?

'You're becoming tiresomely repetitive, my dear,' the gentleman told the pouting brunette who was lounging, naked, amid rumpled silk sheets.

Undeterred by her lover's softly spoken reprimand, Lady Loretta Vane smoothed the sulky expression from her pretty face and rolled on to her belly in a flash of lissom white limbs. Satisfied with her seductive pose, she raised long dusky lashes to reveal limpid blue eyes. Triumphantly she noticed his flinty gaze drop to her lush breasts alluringly presented on an artfully plumped pillow.

Sir Clayton Powell stopped buttoning his shirt and sauntered back towards the four-poster where his mistress excitedly awaited his approach. As soon as he came within reach Loretta stretched out elegant fingers to curve on his thigh, her hard oval nails pressing indents in the material covering solid muscle.

'Come back to bed,' she invited huskily. 'Perhaps I might change your mind and show you what you will soon be missing if you don't make an honest woman of me.'

Clayton leaned towards her, planted a hand on the mattress either side of her slender figure. Sinuously she flipped on to her back and coiled her arms about his neck, dragging him close.

'Think what beautiful children we would have,' she whispered urgently against his mouth. 'A little girl with blonde hair like you and a boy…your heir…dark like me.'

Clayton smiled against her lips. 'And what does your fiancé think to bigamy and bastards?'

Loretta threw back her head and chuckled, deliberately tempting his lips to an alluring column of milky skin. She wriggled delightedly as a moist caress moved on her smooth white throat. 'He would be most put out…but it does not signify. You know I would drop Pomfrey tomorrow and take you in his stead.'

'Yes…I know you would,' Clayton said and lifted his head to look at her with slate-grey eyes. He touched his mouth to hers in an oddly passionless salute.

Just a short while ago the bed had been the scene of torrid lovemaking. Now his response to Loretta Vane's seductive teasing had cooled considerably. His change of attitude was not simply caused by his irritation at her constant marriage proposals. He'd no quarrel with the Honourable Ralph Pomfrey and had no intention of becoming embroiled in one because Loretta had now pinned her ambitions to net a wealthy husband on him.

It had recently come to light, when Pomfrey unwisely approached Claude Potts—a known blabbermouth—for a loan, that he might not be quite as flush as was generally thought. In fact, it was rumoured that Loretta's bank balance might be healthier than was Pomfrey's following a disastrous run of luck he'd had backing nags.

Thus, it had become more obvious why this pleasant fellow of impeccable lineage would propose marriage to a woman who, although a lady by name, was a courtesan by nature.

Loretta had been left a tidy sum by her late husband, Lord John Vane. She had already frittered away a good portion of it. Doubtless she was now fretting that, far from improving her prospects by marrying the Earl of Elkington's youngest son, she might put in jeopardy what remained of her little nest egg. It was surely no coincidence that her enthusiasm for the match had waned with Pomfrey's luck.

Worried by her lover's lack of response, Loretta tugged at Clayton's shirt front and slid her tongue on his lips to tempt him to kiss her properly.

'Pomfrey is your fiancé,' Clayton reminded her lightly, holding her by the wrists away from him. 'You will make a good couple. He is the right husband for you.' He released her as he said that and, collecting his jacket from the velvet *chaise longue*, pushed his arms into the sleeves.

'You are the right husband for me!' Loretta fiercely objected. Realising he was about to go before giving a satisfactory answer, she sprang upright and swung two shapely legs off the bed. Her honed features were no longer softened by sensuality, but set in determined lines that set aslant her full mouth and dark brows.

'I'm not the right husband for any woman...trust me on that,' Clayton returned with a wry smile as he negligently stuffed his cravat into a pocket. 'Do you want to go to the opera tomorrow evening?' he asked idly, his hand on the doorknob.

'Marry me!' Loretta demanded. 'It's *you* I want. It's always been you I want. *We* make a good couple. I swear if you do not, Clayton...if you do not...' she repeated, playing for time to rally enough courage to issue the ultimatum.

'If I do not?' Clayton prompted. He leaned back against the door to watch her, while shooting two pristine shirt cuffs out of his jacket. A steady dark gaze was levelled on her flushing face. 'Come, tell me what you plan to do to punish me.'

'I will finish it between us,' she stated in a brittle tone and tilted her chin to an obstinate angle. 'I will go ahead and marry Ralph Pomfrey as soon as maybe and once I am his wife I will not cuckold him. I will sleep with only my husband.'

A spontaneous laugh broke in Clayton's throat. 'I'm impressed. You're going to be a faithful spouse. That's most unusual for the *ton* and most certainly novel for you, my dear. I'm sure your late departed husband would be miffed to know you've reformed rather too late for him to gain any benefit. I hope Pomfrey appreciates your sacrifice.'

Ralph Pomfrey was aware—as was the whole of the *ton*—that he'd proposed marriage to the woman who had been Clayton Powell's mistress for over six months. The knowledge that his betrothed was continuing to sleep with another man seemed not to trouble Pomfrey. Naturally, it was assumed that once the nuptials were imminent the liaison would end, at least until Loretta had done her duty and provided her husband with a legitimate son and heir.

'You won't find it all so amusing when I turn you away,' Loretta said with a choke of annoyance. She had used her ace and had it immediately trumped. Now she wished she had saved it for another time, but could not withdraw it. 'You won't find another woman to please you as well as I do.'

In Clayton's view, that petulant afterthought *was* her ace and it kept him loitering by the door while he gave both it and her his attention. Without doubt Loretta Vane was an enthusiastic and uninhibited bed partner.

A slow appraisal roamed over the naked young woman provocatively posing on the edge of the bed. Her figure was undeniably lush and perfectly proportioned. But it wasn't just Loretta's physical charms that made men keen to win her favours. She'd gained a reputation as a wanton with an appetite she'd been previously unashamed to sate in adulterous affairs during her first marriage. If she'd meant what she said about staying true to Pomfrey once they were wed, it would indeed be an odd union. Polite society was, for the most part, composed of people untroubled by discreet promiscuity within marriage, once the nursery was full.

Clayton tilted Loretta a wry smile that hinted at his capitulation. He approached her, noticing sultry triumph glittering in her eyes as she rose gracefully from the bed to sway towards him.

'How do you know you please me very well?' he asked and pressed a kiss to the pulse bobbing beneath the porcelain skin of her throat. 'I've never told you so.'

'You don't need to say. I know I do,' she said huskily. An ardent gleam was darkening her blue eyes as she peeped up at him. 'Shall I make you say it?'

'Do you think you can?'

'I *know* I can,' she promised and flicked her small tongue to curl on his ear.

'Well…in that case I suppose it would be rude to decline the challenge,' Clayton said before his lips hardened on hers, parting her mouth wide so he could immediately plunge inside. He gasped a laugh as her nimble fingers immediately opened the buttons covering the magnificent bulge straining the material at his groin. They slipped inside to slide with skilful rhythm until he growled at her to cease. She did so and instead lithely dropped to her knees in front of him.

With blood pounding through his veins, Clayton curved long fingers over the dark head rocking efficiently in front of his hips. With a groaning oath he tensed and drew her up. Swinging Loretta in to his arms, he carried her back to bed.

At six in the morning Clayton again shrugged in to his coat and approached the door of Loretta's boudoir. As she softly called his name he turned to smile at the dishevelled sight of her. Her half-open eyes were glazed in torpor.

'I know I pleased you,' she purred. 'Deny it if you can…'

'You pleased me. Without doubt you make an excellent paramour.'

Sensual languor was still drugging her mind, but Loretta frowned at the amusement in his tone. 'I'll make a far better wife than mistress. I meant what I said, Clayton,' she whispered throatily.

He shot her a grin. 'So did I,' he said and went out, quietly shutting the door.

A nebulous March morning was moistening the cobbles as Clayton emerged into the street. He turned in the direction of Belgravia Place, a leafy square hemmed by elegant town houses, the largest of which was his home.

John Vane had left his young widow her own apartment conveniently situated in the heart of town. Thus it was just a short time later, and with a weak dawn light at his back, that Clayton was taking the stone steps to his mansion two at a time.

On entering the hallway he was surprised to see Hughes, his butler, striding towards him as though anticipating his arrival. The elderly servant had been in the army in his heyday and, being sprightly for his years, still strutted about as though on parade.

'An urgent post arrived, Sir Clayton,' he told his master and held out the tray on which reposed a parchment. If he deemed it odd to see his master arrive home at daybreak with his cravat trailing from a pocket and the remainder of his clothes in a state likely to give his valet an attack, he gave no outward sign.

Clayton took the letter while issuing an order. 'Arrange for hot water for a bath, please, and coffee and toast.'

'At once, sir,' Hughes said with a crisp nod and marched off.

Clayton took a proper look at the writing on the

note he held. A grin split his face. He recognised the hand as that of his good friend Viscount Tremayne. He guessed that, as the post was urgent, Gavin was already on his way to Mayfair from his estate in Surrey. Clayton dropped into his chair in his study and read the very welcome news that Gavin Stone was due in town today.

Chapter Two

'Oh! You have not brought him for me to cuddle!'

'You may cuddle me instead!' Viscountess Tremayne teasingly replied and proceeded to give Ruth a warm hug. 'I have missed you,' she said fiercely.

'And I have missed you,' Ruth said simply, tightening her arms about her best friend. 'I am longing to hear more wonderful news about Surrey. But first tell me—where is that darling baby boy?'

'He has been snuffling a little bit and I thought it best to leave him in the warm with his nurse as the weather has turned so bitter cold.' Sarah gave Ruth an expressive look. 'James is teething and I fret that he might take a chill.' A soft maternal smile preceded, 'He is a darling little chap, the image of his papa, and at times I feel I will die for love of him.'

Ruth linked arms with Sarah and led the way to the sitting room. Once her visitor had shed her hat and gloves, they sat in comfortable fireside chairs. Logs were crackling valiantly in the grate, keeping at bay the draughts. Outside was weak spring sunlight, but the March winds were strong enough to infiltrate the casements and stir the curtains.

Ruth poured tea from the prepared tray that sat on a table close to the hearth. Once they had sipped at the warming brew their conversation was resumed with a fluency that mocked the long months and miles that had separated them. To an observer they might have been dear sisters, so affectionate and natural were they as they chatted and warmed their palms on the china cups.

'How long will you stay at Willowdene Manor?'

'Until Michaelmas…if I have my way,' Sarah said with a grin.

Ruth cocked an eyebrow at her friend. 'And I imagine you have a tendency to get your own way.' She sighed in *faux* sympathy. 'Poor Gavin!'

'Poor Gavin, indeed!' Sarah mocked, but her expression softened as she named her beloved husband. 'He likes it very well when I get my own way, I assure you he does,' she added saucily.

'Hussy!' Ruth chided and clucked her tongue.

'Indeed I am,' Sarah agreed with an impish look from beneath her lashes. 'And ever was…as you know…'

An amicable quiet settled on the room for a

moment while they dwelled on the events Sarah had alluded to and how, subsequently, her life had improved so wonderfully.

Just a year ago Lady Tremayne had been Sarah Marchant, a kept woman, shunned by the locals as a brazen harlot. Following her lover's untimely death, she had been living frugally in the rural town of Willowdene when she met and fell in love with Gavin Stone, new master of Willowdene Manor. A few months after their wedding in the chapel at the Manor, Sarah had moved with her husband to his magnificent estate in Surrey to take up her new life as Viscountess Tremayne.

Now Sarah was a fine lady, with an adorable baby son. Once the two women had been united in living quietly, ostracised by the townsfolk. Now a chasm had opened between their positions. Sarah's status as the wife of a distinguished peer of the realm meant her company was highly sought by everyone, especially the hypocritical. But far from resenting her friend's astonishing good fortune, Ruth was glad that Sarah had been so blessed.

'You're very happy,' Ruth stated with quiet contentment. 'I knew you would be. Gavin is a fine gentleman and all that gossip about his roguish ways was piffle.'

'Not quite…' Sarah demurred. 'Besides, roguish ways have their benefits,' she said archly. 'Gavin says he now has too many responsibilities to rake around town. He leaves that to his friend, Sir Clayton Powell, who, by all accounts, still does it very well.'

Ruth lowered her teacup and cocked her head to one side. 'I remember him. He came to Willowdene and stayed for a short while when Gavin was here chasing after you.'

'He did, indeed.'

'Would it worry you if soon you saw Sir Clayton again?' Sarah recalled that Ruth had been rather wary of her husband's best friend. 'One of the reasons we are back in Willowdene—apart from to see you, of course—is to make arrangements to have James christened at the Manor's chapel.' She placed down her cup to continue. 'I so wanted to have the ceremony here where we were married and where my best friend is. I can't deny that the chapel at Tremayne Park is much finer than the one at Willowdene Manor, but it won't do.' She paused. 'And we very much want you to agree to be James's godmother. Please say you will.'

'I would be most happy to accept,' Ruth said huskily. Spontaneous tears glossed her eyes at the great honour and privilege being bestowed upon her.

'That is good!' Sarah exclaimed in delight. 'Clayton is to be godfather. Gavin says he must be asked, for beneath the heart of a scoundrel beats one of pure gold.' She gestured in emphasis. 'Gavin says he takes his responsibilities most seriously. His heir—his nephew that is, for there were no children from his own marriage—is being educated at Clayton's vast expense.'

'He is married?' Ruth spluttered, faintly amused. 'And still he rakes around town as if a bachelor?'

'Oh, he *was* married.' Sarah inclined her head to impart, 'Apparently it was a long time ago and a very great *mésalliance* that lasted barely a year. His wife, Priscilla, led him a merry dance, then defected with a foreign count! I do not know all the ins and outs, but I know the marriage was annulled and Clayton was, from Gavin's report, very bitter over it all at the time.' A sigh stressed her sadness. 'Clayton has vowed never again to wed and that is why he is grooming his nephew to take the role his own son ought to have occupied.'

'Perhaps I need not have worried that he might have dug into my past and found skeletons.' Ruth raised her dark brows. 'It seems he has a scandal of his own to keep buried. So to answer your question: I do not mind if I meet him again.'

'You needn't worry over him asking impertinent questions. I've come to know him a little, and to like him a lot. He is most charming and mannerly.' After a brief pause Sarah said firmly, 'You must agree to dine with us both this evening. It is all arranged,' she insisted as she glimpsed her friend preparing to object from good manners and the fear of playing gooseberry. 'Gavin is not yet home. He had to break his journey in the City as he had business to attend to. But he is due to arrive by six and in time to dine. We both said how nice it would be for you to join us this evening and celebrate our return to the Manor. And of course you will see baby James.' That last was added in a cajoling tone that made Ruth smile as she guessed its purpose.

'In that case, I would be delighted to join you both.' Ruth accepted with a dip of her dark head.

Sarah grasped Ruth's hands and gave them an affectionate squeeze. 'Good,' she breathed. 'Now, tell me what I have been missing in Willowdene? I thought I might die laughing when you wrote to me about Rosamund Pratt's fall from grace! And with an ostler at the Red Lion, too!' Sarah chuckled as heartily as she had on first learning that the respectable matron who had been particularly mean to them both had been caught rolling in hay with a tavern groom young enough to be her son. 'I want all the latest tattle, you know!'

Ruth, too, had been savouring the memory of Mrs Pratt's come-uppance, but now her amusement faded. 'Well, you have arrived at the right time to be the first to know some gossip. I imagine by the end of the week the rumour mill will be grinding in Willowdene.'

That information was delivered in such an odd tone that Sarah immediately begged to know more.

'I have recently received a marriage proposal from Dr Bryant. I turned him down.'

Sarah's eyes grew round and her lips parted in astonishment. She knew that the doctor had propositioned Ruth over a year ago. She knew, too, from a letter she'd received from Ruth, that later that year Ian Bryant's wife had tragically died in childbed. 'How did he take it?' she eventually blurted.

'Not very well, I'm afraid. He seemed astounded by my answer. I had to ask him more than once to leave. Eventually he did go, wearing a thunderous expression.'

'He assumed you would accept.' Sarah sat back in her chair.

'He assumed I would be very grateful.' Ruth's small teeth worried at her lower lip. 'He did not say so, but I could tell from his attitude.' A humourless little laugh preceded, 'Of course, the whole of Willowdene will join him in thinking me a fool to reject him.' She shot a frown at Sarah. 'He turned up without warning and I would never have guessed what had prompted his visit. But why did I turn him down with so little consideration given the benefits attached to what he offered?'

'Because you don't love him?' Sarah gently advanced.

'No, I don't love him…but is that reason enough to decline a nice home and financial security?'

'I can't answer that for you,' Sarah replied. 'But instinctively you thought it was. You adored Paul and I can understand why you would again want to have a husband to love.'

'It is rather vexing to have been indulged in a love match,' Ruth wryly complained. 'It is equally irksome to have a friend who is blissfully happy with her rich, handsome lord.' Ruth gave Sarah a mock-stern look. 'Now I constantly berate fate for not being equally kind to me.'

'If it is of help, I too would often pray fate might be kind to me, just a little bit.' Sarah clasped Ruth's hands in comfort. 'And eventually it was.'

'How long must I wait for that little bit?' Ruth asked with wry gravity. 'After nine years as a widow perhaps it is time I was sensible and stopped pining for heroes on white chargers to happen by.' She gave a sigh. 'I have to admit that if I were to be given a list of all the available gentlemen hereabouts and told I must pick from it a husband, Dr Bryant would probably be the most appealing to me.'

'Yet instinctively you refused him,' Sarah gently reminded Ruth. 'So we must widen your circle of gentlemen acquaintances forthwith. If you were to socialise in London, you would attract suitors like bees to a honeypot.'

'I doubt that an impecunious widow of twenty-eight years…soon to be twenty-nine…who has forgotten how to dance and flirt will seem very sweet to our drones,' Ruth said ruefully.

'I can teach you how to dance and how to flirt,' Sarah offered impishly. 'Not that I think you will need much reminding on the latter once the right gentleman comes along.'

Ruth rested back into the sofa and gave her friend a tranquil smile. 'You always cheer me up. Thank you. I now feel much less sorry for myself. Things are not so drear. I have this cottage and a few investments Papa left to help me get by. I think I will settle on waiting in Willowdene for my knight in shining armour. After all, there are far worse places to be—Almack's wallflower corner for a start!' She gave an exaggerated shudder on mentioning the renowned matchmaking venue in London. As a débutante of seventeen she had been there regularly and danced with young bucks in the market for a suitable wife. In the event she had met her future husband, Paul Hayden, at her aunt's house. But she could quite clearly recall the alcove in Almack's ballroom where the more mature single ladies—who acted as chaperons and companions to the débutantes—would congregate. The thought of ever joining their number was as depressing now as it had been then.

'Come, I shall wait while you get ready and we will return to the Manor together in the landau. There is still time to cuddle James before he is put to bed. And there is so much more I want to tell you about Tremayne Park. When we return to Surrey you must come too.'

'I imagine your husband might want to take you on honeymoon now you are well enough to travel,' Ruth protested laughingly. She got to her feet to get ready to go out. The thought of a very pleasant evening spent with her friends, and her first sight of their darling baby boy, cheered her enormously.

'I've always liked the silver-grey silk, but the plum satin is pretty too.'

'The silver-grey it is,' Ruth said and put the other gown away.

'Do you think Dr Bryant is sufficiently rebuffed or might he return to try again?' Sarah asked as Ruth went about her *toilette* quite unconcerned by her friend's observation or her uninvited assistance in closing buttons or pinning curls that were hard to reach.

'I think he is too indignant to be persistent,' Ruth answered. She stood up from the stool, pleased with her appearance. She had collected her warm coat and hat before she concluded, 'I think I have heard the last from him on that score. When he left he looked as though his pride had taken a hefty dent.'

'You've dented her pride and a woman scorned is best avoided for as long as possible.'

'Amen to that,' Clayton agreed, scowling at his friend's wry philosophy. His black humour didn't subdue Viscount Tremayne's amusement. As his friend chuckled beneath his breath, Clayton leaned back into the sumptuous squabs of the splendid travelling coach that bore the crest of the Tremayne clan and was presently heading, at breakneck speed in the hope of outrunning the snow clouds, towards Willowdene Manor.

Clayton was glad to be spending time with his good friend and glad to be away from the metropolis for a while. Yet niggling at his conscience was a feeling that he was fleeing from an unpleasant situation and he never usually did that. Beneath his breath he cursed Loretta Vane for having managed to spoil his long-awaited reunion with Gavin and his family.

Shortly after Gavin had arrived at Clayton's home that afternoon a letter from his mistress had been delivered. It had conveyed the outrageous news that Loretta expected him to arrange for their betrothal to be immediately gazetted. In anticipation of his submitting to that action, she had written to Pomfrey to warn him of his jilting. Loretta had also found the gall to infer that she'd dropped Pomfrey at Clayton's behest… as though Clayton had browbeaten her into it.

After Clayton had spent an incredulous few moments rereading the unsubtle blackmail, he had been vacillating between laughing out loud and swearing at the ceiling. Seething anger had triumphed and he had screwed the perfumed paper in a fist and hurled it as far as he could while fighting down the need to storm straight to her house and shake some sense into the scheming minx.

He knew he would never allow himself to be coerced into marrying her, no matter how devious her strategies. A curt, unequivocal note had been despatched to tell her that. It had also made it clear that their relationship was at an end and that shortly his lawyer would contact her regarding a settlement.

Aware of his friend's steady gaze on him, Clayton turned his head aside to stare at the dusky passing landscape. The first fat flakes of snow drifted past the carriage window, but still Clayton's simmering fury at Loretta's scheming preoccupied his mind. 'The vixen is intent on stirring up trouble between Pomfrey and me,' he remarked, almost to himself.

'Don't rise to the bait.'

'I've no intention of doing so. But Pomfrey might. He won't want to be made a laughing stock over this. He might feel obliged to act on it simply to protect his family's good name.'

'You think he might call for pistols at dawn?' Gavin asked with a sardonic smile. He knew very well—as did the whole of the *ton*—that his friend was an excellent shot and unlikely to be challenged by a sane man to a duel. 'Pomfrey has his pockets to let, not his attic. He won't allow her to pull his strings any more than will you.'

'She is extremely adept at pulling the strings of gentlemen.'

'I'm sure,' Gavin said on a dry chuckle. 'Let's hope Pomfrey is able to resist her persuasion as well as you can.'

Clayton stretched out his long legs comfortably in front of him and a slow grin softened his features. 'You'd best tell the driver to slow down. The bad weather's caught up with us.'

Gavin whipped his head about to frown at the falling snow. The urgent need to be reunited with his beloved wife and baby son made him reluctant to issue the order. With a sigh he realised he risked never seeing them again if they continued to drive at reckless speed on roads that would soon be treacherous. Having taken Clayton's good advice and instructed the driver to rein in and take extreme care negotiating the road, he settled back into the seat and turned his mind again to his friend's unfortunate plight.

'It could all be a bluff, in any case,' Gavin reasoned. 'Lady Vane might not have sent Pomfrey a letter yet. She might be hedging her bets. I'll warrant she won't drop Pomfrey until she accepts it's all over with you.'

'I'm inclined to agree on that,' Clayton said reflectively. 'If she doesn't understand plain English, as soon as I get back to town I'll make sure she knows that I mean what I say.'

'There is one certain way to make her accept you

mean what you say and that you'll never have her as your wife.'

'And that is…?' Clayton asked with lazy interest.

'Marry someone else,' Gavin said.

Chapter Three

'I do hope Gavin has put up for the night somewhere. It would be foolhardy to travel on in such dreadful weather.'

Ruth gently settled baby James in his crib before turning her attention to the boy's mother. Sarah had spoken in a voice sharpened by anxiety and with her melancholy gaze directed through the nursery window.

Inside the Manor all was cosy and warm, but sloping away from the house the lawns, that this afternoon had been murky green, appeared icy white. It was after eight o'clock in the evening and more than two hours since the time of Gavin's expected arrival. The snow had stopped falling and the sky had become the darkest shade of blue, threatening a night of perilous frost lay ahead. A pale, hard moon had escaped from a scrap of cloud and beneath its faint light the snow scintillated back at the stars.

'It is possible Gavin has not yet set out at all,' Ruth soothingly reminded. 'I expect he has sensibly remained in London if the snow has come from that direction.' It was a valid reassurance, given more than once since the snow started, yet it did little to erase the look of strain from the Viscountess's features. Sarah's small teeth continued to nip ferociously at her lower lip. Forlornly she peered at the long driveway that led to the house as though willing her husband's carriage to hove into view.

When they had travelled together from the hamlet of Fernlea, where Ruth lived, the air had held a cruel effervescence. But the breeze had kindly whipped the heavy clouds before it, giving them no chance to hover and shed their load. Within an hour of their arrival at the Manor the elements had turned against them. The wind had dropped, leaving the heavens concealed behind an unmoving blanket of sullen grey. The first gentle flurries had seemed harmless, but inexorably the dainty flakes had thickened and settled on the ground. Sarah and Ruth had taken turns at the window to report on the creeping progress of the frosting on the grass. Now the two women stood side by side, silently surveying the treacherous white landscape that stretched as far as the eye could see.

'There is the tavern at Woodville.' Ruth quickly attempted to comfort her friend. Sarah's countenance had become as still and pale as the scenery they gazed upon. 'If Gavin was close to home when the weather took a turn for the worse, I expect he instructed his coachman to pull in there.' Again the suggestion was valid: Woodville was a small town situated about seventeen miles south of Willowdene and the King's Head was a well-known stopping point for travellers going to and from London.

'Yes, I'm sure he would have done that.' Sarah managed a constrained little smile. 'Gavin would not be foolish enough to carry on regardless simply to get home to us…would he?'

'Of course not,' Ruth reassured fraudulently and drew her friend away from the window and back into the room. 'Little James is a contented soul. His nurse must dote on him,' she said, trying to divert Sarah's attention to something pleasant as they sat down by the cot.

A moment after they had settled into their chairs to watch James peacefully dozing, Sarah suddenly cocked her head, then leaped to her feet. In a trice she had flown back to the window and was craning her neck to peer out. 'He is here!' she sobbed out at the glass. She whirled about to gulp at Ruth, 'The carriage is here.'

Quickly Ruth joined her at the window and was instantly enveloped in Sarah's hug. 'Oh, thank Heavens! He is safely home.' Sarah snuffled back tears of blessed joy, her eyes glistening with the strength of her relief.

'You must go and welcome him.' Ruth was well aware that Sarah yearned to do so. 'I shall be quite happy to stay here with this darling boy if I may.'

'Gavin will think me quite a nincompoop to get in such a state.' Sarah knuckled away the wet that dewed her lashes. But she was soon at the door, leaving Ruth to gaze down, soft-eyed, at the infant left in her care. James was sleeping soundly, his cherubic face turned away from her. Carefully, so as not to disturb him, Ruth drew the covers closer about him, then stroked a tiny curled palm. Reflexively the baby clutched at her finger. Ruth felt her chest constrict and an ache surged up her throat at the memory of another baby—one whose delicate fingers had remained cold and unresponsive to her loving touch.

Ruth went to sit close by the fire. She eased back gratefully into the comfy chair, realising that she was quite enervated. In truth she, too, had begun to feel extremely concerned for Gavin's safety as nightfall came with no sign of a thaw or the arrival of the master of the house. Feeling now relaxed and quite cosy, she allowed her weary eyelids to fall.

The baby's whimpering woke her. Immediately Ruth looked at the fire; it had burned low in the grate. She then glanced at the clock on the mantel. It was approaching nine o'clock. Jumping to her feet, she quickly went to peer in the cot. From his scrunched, angry face and drawn-up knees, and from female intuition, Ruth guessed that colic was the culprit.

Having lifted the fretful baby to her shoulder, she began murmuring soothingly to him. Rhythmically she rubbed at his back in the hope of easing his cramps while walking towards the door. The corridor was deserted. The baby's nurse had earlier been dismissed for the afternoon so Sarah and Ruth could chat and enjoy each other's company in private. With no idea where she might find James's nurse, and guessing Sarah and Gavin might be in the small salon, Ruth headed off in that direction.

'Mrs Hayden?'

Ruth had traversed many yards of quiet, carpeted corridor and was close to the top of the majestic staircase when she heard her name called in a cultured baritone voice.

Turning about, she stared, astonished, at a tall blond gentleman who was strolling towards her. She recognised him at once and that was odd, she obliquely realised, for after their brief introduction—which could not have lasted more than a few minutes—she had never again seen Sir Clayton Powell. It was equally odd that he should remember her after that meeting in Willowdene over a year ago. Or perhaps Sarah or Gavin had informed him she was a guest this evening.

'I had no idea you were staying at Willowdene Manor,' he said pleasantly as he came closer and executed a polite bow. 'Our hosts made no mention of it.'

'I had no idea you would be here either, sir,' Ruth said quickly. So her presence had not been mentioned, yet he *had* recognised her. 'And I am not staying here. I received an invitation to dine this evening with the Viscount and Viscountess.'

'Do you live close by?' Clayton asked with a frown. 'The roads are now virtually impassable. I doubt you will get home tonight.'

That thought had already occurred to Ruth. She had guessed that Sarah would kindly offer her a bed for the night. And Ruth would have accepted, despite having no night things with her. She would never contemplate putting at risk a coach and driver by insisting on going home through miles of lanes blocked by snow. A short while ago the thought of staying a day or two while they waited for a thaw had not presented a problem. Now, for some odd reason, the thought of sleeping beneath the same roof as this gentleman made her feel awkward.

'You have both arrived safely, if a little tardy,' Ruth pointed out rather lamely.

'Gavin would have moved heaven and earth to do so.'

'I imagined he would,' Ruth replied wryly. 'And so did Sarah. It worried her half to death that he would take risks to get here.'

'The power of love,' Clayton muttered exceedingly drily, but he cast a fond look at the baby boy fidgeting on Ruth's shoulder. 'Should he not be abed?'

'I think he should,' Ruth answered politely, yet rather indignant on hearing him sound so cynical. He might have been embittered by a bad marriage, but he had no right to scoff at her dear friends' wedded bliss. 'His nurse was given the afternoon off and I'm just on my way to find Sarah,' Ruth informed him briskly and took a step towards the head of the stairs. 'I think he might have a pain…or perhaps it has passed,' she said as quite an embarrassing noise and unpleasant smell issued from the little boy's rump.

Clayton grinned. 'I imagine young James is feeling much better now.'

An involuntary giggle escaped Ruth, despite her cheeks having turned pink. 'Still, I shall look for Sarah and hand him over. We were in the nursery when she heard the coach arrive and she rushed off to greet Gavin. I was on my way to the small salon. They might have gone there. I expect they have much news to catch up on.'

'Indeed,' Clayton drawled, amusement far back in his slate-grey eyes. 'But I doubt you'll find them in there yet.' He paused as though mentally phrasing his next words. 'I believe Gavin went to his chamber to freshen up after the journey. Sarah accompanied him.'

'Oh…I see,' Ruth said and averted her face to hide

her blushing confusion. She felt quite silly for not having guessed that the two lovebirds would find an opportunity to have some time alone on being safely reunited.

While Ruth composed herself by fussing over the baby, Clayton began to subtly study her with a very male eye. He'd been attracted to her when they had briefly met in Willowdene town despite the fact she had been garbed head to toe in mourning clothes. She'd been capably driving a little pony and trap through the High Street and, from their short conversation that day, he'd learned that she wore weeds because her father had recently died. He'd also learned that she was related by marriage to one of his commanding officers, Colonel Hayden. It was a while later that he'd learned from Gavin that Ruth Hayden had been a widow for many years.

Clayton's roving appraisal continued and he knew he'd been right in instinctively sensing that beneath the dreary bombazine that had been shrouding her body on that occasion, and the dark bonnet brim that had made sallow her complexion, was a woman of rare beauty.

On first glance Ruth Hayden's features might appear rather severe, yet on finer appraisal were undoubtedly exquisite. Her deep brown eyes were fringed by lengthy black lashes and topped by delicate brows that looked soft as sable. Her nose was thin, her mouth asymmetrical with a lower lip that was fuller than the curving cupid's bow on top. She was petite, her smooth peachy cheek barely reached his shoulder, and fragile wrist bones were in his line of vision as she cuddled James close to her. But her figure was generously curvaceous in all the right places. The weight of the baby pressing on her chest had accentuated a satiny ivory cleavage swelling above her bodice. His hooded eyes lingered a moment too long on silver silk straining enticingly across her bosom.

Feeling once more adequately self-possessed, Ruth looked up and immediately her cheeks regained a vivid bloom as she noticed Sir Clayton eyeing her breasts. On the previous occasion when they had conversed she had sensed he found her interesting, and not just because he'd discovered he was acquainted with her in-laws. At the time she'd dismissed the idea he was attracted to her as fanciful and scoffed at her conceit. Yet there was no denying that she'd just caught him regarding her lustfully. Knowing that he found her desirable caused a peculiar mixture of uneasiness and excitement to tumble her insides.

It might have been many years since she had lain with her husband, or even been kissed, but she could recognise the signs that a man wanted her. She had seen the same smouldering intensity at the back of Ian Bryant's eyes just a couple of days ago when he proposed to her. She had known for a year or more that

Ian wanted to bed her. But the doctor didn't possess skill enough to neutralise a tense situation, or his passion, as it seemed this man could.

Sir Clayton didn't look in the least disconcerted at being caught out. He raised a long finger, stroked the baby's soft cheek and lightly remarked, 'There's a young maid hovering at the end of the corridor.' He gave Ruth a nonchalant smile. 'Perhaps she has come to see to James.'

Ruth slowly expelled her pent-up breath. She pivoted about, grateful for the distraction, and gave young Rosie a beseeching look. At the signal the nursemaid immediately hastened to them and dipped a curtsy.

'Beggin' your pardon, ma'am…sir…' she began in her lilting Irish way, 'but the mistress did tell me to come to settle the little lad down sooner. When I said to her that I'd found you was asleep and so was little James, she said to leave it for a while and not to disturb you at all.'

Ruth gave the nervous girl a smile. She could tell that Rosie was in awe of the handsome gentleman by the way she kept sliding glances at Sir Clayton, then blushing and shuffling on the spot.

Ruth handed over her precious burden. 'I think he might need some urgent attention,' she told the girl and gently patted at the baby's bottom.

Rosie took the baby carefully and with natural

fondness immediately smoothed the fair down on his head. 'Come on then, me little lad,' she crooned against his warm cheek. 'Let's get you seen to.'

Once the maid had disappeared with her charge, and Ruth and Clayton were left alone at the top of the stairs, they both attempted to immediately breach the quiet with conversation.

'I thought we had left this behind us…'

'Are you staying long in Willowdene…?'

They had spoken simultaneously and fell silent at the same time too.

'Please do finish what you were saying, sir,' Ruth blurted.

'It was nothing important, just a remark about the unseasonal weather. I thought we had left the snow behind us in the winter months. Only last week we were enjoying fine spring sunshine in town.'

'Indeed, it was glorious in the countryside too,' Ruth responded quickly. The weather was always an easy topic to discuss and she eagerly picked up the thread he'd dangled. 'But it is not so unusual to have snow at this time of the year,' Ruth spun out the dialogue. 'I recall my mother telling me that it was snowing in March in the year of my birth. The doctor had quite a journey through the blizzard and was almost late for my arrival.'

'So…you've had a birthday recently, Mrs Hayden,' Clayton observed with a smile.

'No...not yet...it is my birthday next week,' Ruth admitted, suddenly wishing she had kept that particular anecdote private. Into the expectant pause she said with a hint of defensiveness, 'I shall be nine and twenty on the twenty-fifth of March.'

'Will you indeed?' Clayton said, gently amused, but genuinely surprised. She certainly did not appear to be so close to thirty. 'You're still a youngster, then,' he added charmingly. 'In November of this year I shall turn thirty-five.'

A small smile from Ruth rewarded him for his gallantry. 'Then you must be either born under the sign of Scorpio or Sagittarius,' she remarked, gladly turning the focus on to him.

'Very possibly,' he admitted on a chuckle, 'but I have little interest in stargazing or what it all means.'

'I find the study of the heavens quite pleasing,' Ruth said.

'Whereas I prefer to concentrate on earthly pleasures.'

Ruth felt herself blush, but shot back rather acidly, 'Sagittarians are often hedonistic. I would hazard a guess that your birthday falls at the end of the month of November.'

He gave her a smile, but no further information. Instead he said easily, 'I interrupted you earlier. I believe you were enquiring how long I intended to stay in Willowdene.'

'I…yes…I did…' Ruth admitted, while hoping he did not think she cared if he was soon to leave.

'You asked from courtesy rather than curiosity, I take it,' Clayton remarked.

The note of mockery in his voice made Ruth bristle and tilt her chin. 'Indeed, and I expect we might need to find some more polite topics of conversation while we wait for our hosts.'

Clayton's slow smile turned to a chuckle. 'I expect we shall; and probably quite a few of them. I wouldn't be surprised if the fond couple are occupied…catching up on news…for some while yet.'

This time Ruth refused to turn away in embarrassment despite sensing heat fizzing beneath her cheeks. Her earthy dark eyes clashed with his in a way that deepened his smile.

'Shall we go to the library?' Clayton extended an elegant arm. 'When I arrived there was a good fire in there and plenty of weighty tomes to peruse, in the event that we run out of polite chitchat while we wait for our supper to be served.'

After a barely discernible pause Ruth extended a hand to hover on his arm. As they descended the stairs together she was again impressed by the way he could dissolve tension between them. He looked down at her with engaging grin. 'I'm feeling ravenous, actually. I hope a good dinner is waiting for us. And plenty of it.'

'Sarah is a very competent hostess,' Ruth championed her friend. 'And the last time I dined here—just before they left for Surrey—there were fourteen courses.'

'Ah! That should just about fill me up,' he said contentedly. 'It is a shame you missed their marriage,' Clayton remarked as they gained the hallway and turned towards the library.

Ruth nodded her shiny dark head and sent him a glancing smile. 'Yes, it was,' she softly agreed, recalling her sadness at having turned down Sarah's invitation to be her matron of honour. 'But at that time my papa had only recently been buried and, much as I would have loved to be part of the celebrations, it would not have been appropriate. Etiquette must be observed,' she said ruefully.

'Etiquette can be a damnable nuisance,' Clayton returned and slid her a look. 'I had hoped to see you that day.'

That blunt admission surprised Ruth to such a degree that for a moment she was unable to tear her gaze from his. 'Well…I think our dinner will be worth waiting for,' she blurted and swung her face towards the green baize door that led to the kitchens. 'Something smells exceedingly good.'

Clayton sniffed at air that was thick with a tantalising savoury aroma. 'Beef and horseradish,' he guessed.

'I would say chicken…or perhaps goose.' Ruth was

sure she could discern the tang of sage-and-onion stuffing wafting in the atmosphere.

'A wager?' Clayton carelessly challenged.

'Of course,' she accepted with a gay laugh. 'And I know exactly what I claim as my prize. If I am right, I must insist you demand we play cards later when Sarah suggests I entertain the company by playing the pianoforte. She will have it that I can sing in key. I assure you that I cannot and you won't want to listen to me prove it.'

Clayton chuckled. 'Agreed. But what if I win…?'

Ruth tossed him a smile. 'Oh, if you win, I shall allow you to beat me just the once at piquet. I'm very good, you know.'

'Are you, indeed?' Clayton murmured. 'Most of the ladies I know are very bad…'

Ruth turned her head, the knot of excitement within tightening. He was a practised flirt, she told herself—a man with a reputation as a womaniser. Nevertheless she felt quite elated that, after an inauspicious start, they seemed to have established a fragile rapport.

Chapter Four

'Would you like something to drink?' Clayton asked, having escorted Ruth to a chair close to the fire.

A console table was dotted with sparkling crystal and he picked up each decanter then, following a brief inspection, knowledgeably identified its contents for her to choose which she would like.

'A small sherry would be nice, thank you,' Ruth said quickly on noticing Clayton was still awaiting her answer.

Clayton approached to hand over her drink and then took the chair opposite. Ruth watched surreptitiously as he stretched out his long legs in front of him and turned his head towards the mesmerising dance in the fire.

His lean profile was softened by the warm glow, his blond hair burnished to an autumn sheen. In his long fingers a brandy balloon gently oscillated. Far from being interested in continuing to flirt with her, or to engage in a little more light-hearted banter, he seemed to Ruth to have forgotten she existed and to have plunged deep into his own thoughts. Perhaps he thought to pay her back for her preoccupation moments ago. Thus, confident she was unobserved, she deemed it safe to slowly study him.

Ruth knew that a good deal of the gentlemen of the *ton* favoured bright colours and all manner of fobs and trinkets as personal adornments. This man was no dandified peacock. He was elegantly rather than fashionably clothed in a dark tailcoat and trousers and his person seemed devoid of jewellery. Then she noticed a heavy gold signet ring as it winked on a finger of the hand that was swinging the glass. Her eyes slipped on and a glint of gold could be seen where a watch reposed low in a waistcoat pocket.

She lifted her eyes from his lap and immediately her face flooded with blood. Unwisely she took a swift gulp of her sherry, then tried to quell the burning in her throat with fingers that flew to press her mouth. How long had he been watching her look him over in so vulgar a fashion?

'Would you like another?' Clayton asked with soft mockery and a deliberate glance at her depleted glass.

'No…no, thank you. I was looking…that is, you seem rather melancholy, sir. I didn't mean to stare.'

'I'm sure you didn't…or rather, you didn't mean me to see you at it.'

Ruth's dark eyes flashed dangerously at him. 'As you didn't mean to be caught eyeing me earlier?'

Just before Clayton despatched his cognac in a single swallow he said, 'I've no objection at all in you knowing I think you attractive.'

For a long moment Ruth simply sat quite still, her eyes on the fire. Would it be best to thank him briefly for the compliment? Or should she ignore what he'd said as simple flattery from a notorious philanderer? Just a short while ago she'd learned from Sarah that Sir Clayton Powell was an incorrigible rake.

'Perhaps we should think of something else to talk about,' Ruth suggested calmly. 'You know a little about my family history—would you tell me a little about yours?'

A humourless noise issued from Clayton's throat. 'I take it you would like to discover why I'm no longer married?'

Astonishment kept Ruth momentarily speechless, her eyes captured by his, her soft lips quivering and slightly parted. Sir Clayton Powell was certainly a bluff individual! Or perhaps he reserved such shocking candour for women he deemed to be too inquisitive? She had not wanted to pry into his personal life. She'd hoped, as he knew she had lost her father, they might have an innocent chat about his parents or his siblings. A slow anger burned in Ruth, boosting her determination to regain her composure and give him the answer he deserved.

'On the contrary, sir, I have no interest in your marital status,' she snapped icily.

'Have you not?' he enquired. 'Well, you must be the only female of my acquaintance under fifty who has not.'

'And you must be the only gentleman of my acquaintance who has the arrogance to suppose I might care to know whether or not he has a wife.' That fierce declamation came after quite a pause and in a voice suffocated with indignation. How quickly he could change from charming companion to cynical churl.

'So you didn't know that I'm divorced?' Clayton challenged softly, his eyes fixed pitilessly on her face.

A betraying flush began to creep under Ruth's skin. She *did* know. Just today she had discovered from Sarah that Clayton had once been married. She wished she could honestly say she was ignorant of his *mésalliance* with Priscilla and had no interest in knowing of it. But, in truth, while quietly sitting with him, she *had* pondered on why a handsome and wealthy aristocrat would make a disastrous match. And, had Sarah not already told her, she could have easily deduced from his attitude that his divorce had left him extremely bitter.

Clayton watched Ruth fidget and blush beneath his

gaze and his lips slanted in a hard smile. It seemed he'd touched on a nerve. He had agreed to journey to Willowdene on the spur of the moment after Gavin suggested he distance himself from Loretta and her pathetic scheming. Perhaps his invitation to spend a little time in the country with the Tremaynes hadn't been as impromptu or philanthropic as it had seemed. Had Sarah given Gavin instructions to persuade him to come because she had an ulterior motive?

He liked Sarah very much. He envied Gavin for having such a lovely wife. But that didn't alter the fact that every society hostess of his acquaintance had made it her business at least once to try to pair him off with a nubile friend or relative.

'Did the Viscountess tell you I would be invited to dine here this evening?' he asked bluntly.

Finally, Ruth understood what was prompting his sardonic questions. He was not so much bothered that she knew he had lost his wife as that she might have designs on replacing her. Her lips tightened as a ferocious anger bubbled inside. The nerve of the man! He seriously believed she might have collaborated with Sarah to trap him! No doubt he also believed she'd schemed at having this time alone with him. 'I believe I've already said I didn't know you would be coming from London with the Viscount,' Ruth reminded him in a frigid tone. 'And when I mentioned your family it was not with the intention of discovering if you were a husband or a father. You know my father died because we briefly spoke about it when last you were in Willowdene. I was simply making a polite enquiry as to the health of your kin.' With no table close to hand, Ruth put down her empty glass on the hearthstone and stood up. 'I had hoped our hosts' unexpected absence might not become an ordeal for either of us. Unfortunately, it has...'

The thought of staying here, alone, with this conceited swine was now unbearable to Ruth. She didn't want to upset Sarah by leaving, but if the snow had cleared—even just a little bit—she would go home. In truth, she wished she'd not agreed to come at all. And that angered her, for her longed-for reunion with Sarah had been spoiled through no fault of her own.

Swiftly she went to the long window that looked out on to the grounds of the Manor. She twitched back the heavy velvet curtain, then folded back the shutter just enough to peep at the night. The whiteness glistened back at her; lifting her eyes to the heavens, she saw small sparkling droplets defiantly descending. With heavy heart and a soundless sigh of regret she turned back in to the library.

Clayton had also left his chair and was refilling his glass from the decanter. He tossed back the brandy and his blond head remained tilted towards the ceiling for some time before he addressed Ruth.

'I'm sorry,' he said quietly. 'I don't know why I said

what I did.' His hands plunged into his pockets, withdrew almost immediately. 'Well, perhaps I do, but, whatever my mood, I had no right to make my problems yours. I behaved with unforgivable rudeness just now. Unfortunately, my manners seem to be sadly lacking this evening.'

'It's heartening to know that you believe you possess some,' Ruth responded coolly, only a little mollified by his apology.

A small noise issued from Clayton's throat that could have been a mirthless laugh. 'I take it from your disappointed expression that the snow hasn't melted enough for you to flee my boorish company and allow you to go home.'

'You're very perceptive, sir,' Ruth replied and slid a book from a shelf to peruse the cover.

'Come...sit down again, please,' Clayton invited. 'It's impossible for either of us to make our escape and I wouldn't want a bad atmosphere to ruin our evening with our friends.'

'No more would I,' Ruth answered with some asperity, yet she didn't give him the courtesy of a glance. Busily she turned the pages of the book, though she saw not a single word or picture on the fluttering pages.

'Come back to the fire,' Clayton urged gently. 'It looks to be quite draughty over there.'

Immediately Ruth ceased rubbing absently at an arm to warm it. But she wouldn't give him the satisfaction of knowing he was correct or that he could make her do his bidding.

'Gavin and Sarah will join us soon,' Clayton said persuasively. 'I promise you I shall be returning to town tomorrow, whatever the weather.'

'There is no need for you to risk such a journey,' Ruth said briskly and deposited the book back on the shelf. 'I haven't so far to go. I shall go home in the morning.' Ruth prayed inwardly that she might be able to do just that. From what she had seen through the window a moment ago, it seemed unlikely that the conditions would improve overnight. The snow had started to fall again, very lightly, but if it settled the condition of the roads might be yet more hazardous.

'Well, let's not squabble over who insists on leaving first,' Clayton said with a return to rueful humour. 'It's enough that we've both seen fit to offer to do so.'

Inwardly Clayton was cursing himself to the devil. He had been enjoying Ruth's company. There was a quiet grace about her that he found as enchanting as her physical beauty. Yet, despite his fascination with his lovely companion, he couldn't quite block from his mind the memory of his minx of a mistress.

Loretta's plotting had prompted him to take up Gavin's offer of a sojourn in the country. Even at a distance she was constantly infiltrating his mind as he pondered on whether he ought to have stayed in Mayfair and sorted out the mischief she seemed determined to concoct. He had no reason to apologise to Pomfrey. He'd done nothing wrong. His relationship with Loretta had been established when Pomfrey asked her to marry him. And now it was over. Yet he felt as though he ought to make contact with the man and reassure him that, whatever Loretta said, he didn't want her as his wife, now or ever.

'Ah! There you are, Ruth. I'm sorry I abandoned you,' Sarah happily chirped, entering the room in a shimmy of pretty lemon silk. 'When Rosie said you were taking a nap it seemed wrong to wake you.' Her sparkling eyes settled on Clayton. 'Good! You have had Sir Clayton to keep you company. Have you been having a nice chat?' Sarah sent a winsome smile to her husband, a few paces behind, to include him in her chatter.

A protracted pause was breached by Clayton saying lazily, 'Mrs Hayden has been diverting company. She told me you appreciate listening to her sing and play the piano.'

A look of startled disbelief froze Ruth's features. An expressive glance demanded he say no more on the subject. He returned her an easy smile that promised nothing.

'Ruth *is* very accomplished,' Sarah said with a proud look at her friend. 'And she is far too modest. It takes a lot of persuasion to get her to perform even one song.'

Gavin appeared rather more perceptive to the frost in the atmosphere than did his vivacious spouse. He sent his friend a penetrating look that terminated in a slight, quizzical elevation of dark brows.

'I'm famished and I expect our guests must be too.' Gavin took his wife's dainty fingers and placed them on his arm. 'Come, we can talk at the table. Let us go in to dine.'

'Oh, you must stay here tonight, Ruth. I can lend you whatever you need. It's impossible to travel even a short distance in such atrocious weather.' Sarah gaily sent that instruction back over an elegant shoulder as she allowed her husband to steer her towards their dinner.

With elaborate courtesy Clayton extended a hand to Ruth. After giving him a sharp glance, she lifted five stiff fingers on to his sleeve. She wanted to berate him for bringing musical entertainment to Sarah's attention. She guessed that was what he wanted her to do, so she swallowed the reprimand. In silence they followed their friends towards the dining room.

After several courses of fine food and several glasses of mellow ruby wine, Ruth had relaxed enough to overcome her annoyance and allow her eyes to meet Clayton's. Throughout the meal so far she'd often sensed him looking at her. On the few occasions he'd addressed her directly there had been no hint of challenge or mockery in his polite conversation and she imagined he had consciously made an effort to leave behind in the library his conceit and irascibility.

Their hosts were indeed fine company and there had been no lapse in genial chatter. They had discussed the start of the Season in London and, more lengthily, matters closer to home. Clayton had been interested to know how the unexpected snowfall might affect people in the villages obtaining necessary supplies and going about their business. His own country estate lay far to the south-west of the country, he'd explained to Ruth, where such bad weather was uncommon. He had added that he rarely visited it—being too fond of town living—so had thus far never been inconvenienced by the vagaries of the seasons. What a boon and a curse could be the weather! It had provided an ample source of neutral conversation, yet it also had trapped her here!

'Do you spend time in London during the Season, Mrs Hayden?'

Ruth placed down her spoon and gave Clayton a rather startled glance. She hadn't been expecting such a leading question. 'I don't, sir. I haven't been to London since I lived there as a child.'

'And whereabouts did you live?'

'Close to Chelsea, in Willoughby Street,' Ruth supplied and gave her attention to her pudding, taking a dainty mouthful of syllabub.

'Ah...I know it,' Clayton said pleasantly, undeterred by her hint that the subject was closed. 'A friend of mine, Keith Storey, lived there with his parents until he took a wife.'

Ruth gave a spontaneous smile at being reminded of the family. 'I knew them; my parents were friendly with Mr. and Mrs Storey.'

'And did you move to the country while still young?'

'No, sir.' Ruth again placed down her spoon, feeling a little miffed. He had no hesitation in interrogating her over her past, yet had become unpleasant at the first mention of discussing his. 'My parents moved to Fernlea after my marriage. I moved here to live with my father nine years ago; he was by then a widower.' Ruth turned quickly to her right and said to Sarah the first thing that came into her head. 'Little James had a pain earlier. I think the poor mite had colic.'

'He does suffer with it,' Sarah answered, well aware of her friend's wish to curtail a conversation with Clayton that must lead eventually to her late husband and perhaps the manner of his death. 'Mrs Plover,' she named the housekeeper, 'has a remedy for it. Just a small spoonful of the stuff seems to put him to rights. She's quite a marvel with her pills and potions. And she's of enormous help with planning extravagant menus and so on.'

'On which note, I must thank you for a delicious dinner,' Ruth said graciously, indicating she'd eaten her fill.

A polite murmur of assent came from Clayton as he too laid aside his cutlery.

'Well…shall we leave the gentlemen to their port?' Sarah suggested.

Ruth gave her a grateful smile. She could always rely on Sarah to sense her mood. Her friend knew very well she was keen to escape any further of Clayton's probing questions.

'If James is abed, we can bid him goodnight even if he is asleep.'

As the door closed on the two strikingly attractive ladies—one very fair, one very dark—Gavin gave his friend a wry glance and a measure of port he'd dispensed from the decanter. 'I take it you're glad you came.'

'What makes you say that?'

'I'd need to be a blind man not to notice you're smitten by Mrs Hayden.'

'And I'd need to be a cynic to think that perhaps you're glad of that. As we both know, I'm a cynic.'

Gavin grimaced bemusement. 'I'm not good with riddles. What's that supposed to mean?'

'Did you know that Mrs Hayden would be here when you asked me to come home with you?'

'Of course I did,' Gavin said and lounged contentedly back in to his chair. 'Sarah was keen to see her best friend straight away. I still don't see…' A look of amused enlightenment crossed his rugged features.

'Ah, you think Sarah has some maggot in her head about matchmaking the two of you.'

'It wouldn't be the first, or the hundredth, time a lady had arranged a dinner party for just that purpose. So, am I correct?'

'No,' Gavin said bluntly and sipped at his port. 'You might have designs on Ruth, but, not to put too fine a point on it, my friend, I doubt she has any interest in you.' Gavin gave Clayton a cautionary look. 'She's no man's mistress...not even yours, no matter how generous you're feeling. Take my word on it.'

Clayton sat back in his chair and fondled the stem of his glass with long fingers. His slate-grey eyes watched the crystal as it performed a balletic twirl. 'Is she spoken for?'

'Sarah told me earlier this evening that Ruth's recently received a proposal of marriage.' Gavin refilled his glass and pushed the decanter towards Clayton. 'Her suitor is by all accounts a pillar of society here in Willowdene. Don't ask more,' he said ruefully. 'I've been indiscreet as it is. Sarah adores Ruth, and with good reason. Ruth was a loyal friend and a support when Sarah was very much alone and in need of help,' he explained gruffly. 'I'd hate Ruth to think I'd spoken out of turn.'

Clayton nodded acceptance of that. 'He's a lucky chap, whoever he is.'

'Indeed,' Gavin murmured. He sent a subtle look at

his brooding friend and amusement tipped his lips upwards.

He knew, of course, that Clayton was a hardened cynic where women were concerned. Clayton's wife had made a complete fool of him by acting like a seasoned trollop throughout their short marriage. Since his divorce ambitious women had constantly thrown themselves at him, hoping to take her place. He was mercilessly hounded by every mama with aspirations of marrying her débutante daughter to a man of great wealth and lineage—when Clayton's octogenarian grandfather died he would take a clutch of titles to add to the baronetcy he already had.

It seemed the longer Sir Clayton Powell remained stubbornly single, the more of a challenge the hostesses seemed to find him. Gavin knew that wagers had been laid amongst the *ton*'s *grandes dames* as to which of them might finally snare him for a favoured niece or goddaughter.

Clayton knew of their scheming too, and their ulterior motives. He knew he was wanted at their balls for what he had rather than himself. The more desperate they became to have him attend their functions, the more reluctant he became to turn up. The fact that his friend would choose to spend his evenings at the theatre with a demi-rep, or gambling with male friends, rather than socialise with women of his own class, spoke volumes about his friend's attitude to courtship and marriage. In fact, Gavin mused, he would not be at all surprised to learn that Clayton had badly misjudged the situation tonight and treated Ruth as though she were some mercenary temptress with an eye on his wallet. It would certainly explain the frost he'd sensed in the atmosphere when he and Sarah had joined them in the library.

A soundless laugh tickled Gavin's throat. He imagined from Clayton's rather mystified expression that he was still wondering why Mrs Hayden had refused to flutter her eyelashes and gaze adoringly at him, as did every other single woman of his acquaintance. He could have told his friend that, in fact, Mrs Hayden had turned down the doctor's proposal, but for some reason he had not. And it was not just because in another respect he'd told Clayton the truth.

Ruth would undoubtedly be better off financially as a rich man's paramour, but in Gavin's opinion she would hold out for a man to love, and to love her, before she slept with him.

Chapter Five

'No! Please don't say anything,' Ruth begged. 'Sir Clayton has apologised and been charm personified since his odd outburst.'

'And so he ought to improve his behaviour!' Sarah responded pithily.

After they had settled down into chairs beside the crib to chat and listen to James's gentle snores, Ruth had quite naturally told Sarah she had clashed with her gentleman guest. They had long been kindred spirits and didn't have secrets. But Sarah's reaction to knowing that her husband's friend had been rather insulting to *her* friend had been stronger than Ruth had anticipated. She'd immediately said that she'd tell Gavin to speak to Clayton about his manners.

'How dare he suppose we might plot to get him to marry you!' Sarah hissed beneath her breath so as not to wake her son.

'Now I think on it,' Ruth commented ruefully, 'I'm not sure marriage entered his mind.' The more indignant Sarah became, the more her own annoyance receded and she saw a farcical side to it all. 'I'm a widow, unattached, of limited means,' she listed out her fair-game status. 'It's possible he believed I harboured no such high aspirations and was angling for a less formal arrangement with him.' On seeing Sarah's anger re-igniting, she made a small dismissive gesture. 'No doubt he is used to women fawning over him. He is handsome…rich too, I expect.'

'Oh, yes!' Sarah stressed, nodding her head vigorously and setting her blonde ringlets dancing. 'He's chased mercilessly by the débutantes, and equally enthusiastically by ladies of a different class,' she added as she recalled she'd once seen him at the theatre with several demi-reps in one evening. 'And he must have an enormous fortune, for Gavin jokes that he makes him feel like a pauper. But none of that excuses his rudeness to you.'

'Well, we must make allowances for such a popular fellow. It is not worth making a fuss.' Ruth shook her friend's arm gently to emphasise she meant what she'd said. 'I imagine Sir Clayton is now feeling awkward too. There's just this evening for us to get through, then tomorrow I shall go home and that will be an end to it. When we go back to the drawing room, shall we suggest a game of cards until bedtime?'

'I was going to ask you to play and sing for us, but after what you've told me he doesn't deserve to listen to your fine voice.'

Ruth clucked her tongue and raised her eyes heavenwards. 'You will have it I can hold a tune. I cannot, Sarah. Honestly, I cannot.'

'Of course you can!' Sarah contradicted. 'Compared to my musical efforts, you are talented enough to perform at Drury Lane.'

'That's true,' Ruth said, mock solemn. Sarah's description of her attempt to warble soprano sounding like a cat having its tail trodden on, was, alas, correct.

'Well, really! I was hoping you might fib and flatter me just a little bit,' Sarah reproved with a twinkling smile. 'Come, let's join the gentlemen. I won't say anything to Gavin about Clayton's behaviour, but I'm not sure I'll let him off too lightly either. If the rogue thinks me capable of meddling, I might feel inclined to prove him right.'

'Ah…we were just saying, my dear, that if horse riding is out of the question in the morning Clayton and I might take a different sort of constitutional and have a snowball fight.'

'What a good idea!' Sarah chirped gaily as she and Ruth, in a cloud of freshly sprayed French perfume, joined the gentlemen in the drawing room. 'Perhaps we might join you. I doubt Ruth would be averse to throwing missiles at Clayton.'

Ruth inwardly winced. Sarah had not after all been able to refrain from a little barbed remark about what had occurred between her guests.

'What is your answer, Mrs Hayden?' Clayton asked mildly, apparently unperturbed to discover that she'd told tales about him. 'Shall we draw battle lines and bombard each other?'

'I'm not sure it would be a fair fight,' Ruth responded lightly. 'You have an unfair advantage, sir, having been in the army.'

'Did I tell you that?' Clayton inquired in surprise.

'Um...yes,' Ruth answered quietly and quickly looked away. Why on earth had she mentioned the army? Obviously he'd forgotten that when they'd met in Willowdene last year he'd commented that he was acquainted with her father-in-law, Colonel Walter Hayden, from his army days. Now she'd idiotically paved the way for the conversation to once more turn to her marriage and perhaps her late husband, Captain Paul Hayden. And she certainly had no desire for that.

'We could make a snowman,' Sarah blurted, once more coming to her friend's rescue. She knew very well how loath Ruth was to talk about Paul, for invariably questions would be asked about his untimely demise. 'If there's no sign of a thaw tomorrow, I think we should do that. Of course, we wouldn't want to sculpt the fellow, then see him too soon melt away before our eyes.'

Ruth rewarded her friend with a subtle smile for valiantly attempting to divert the conversation away from a sensitive subject. 'But let's hope for a thaw,' she commented lightly. 'Then Sir Clayton can ride to his heart's content.'

'Towards London?' Clayton ventured in a drawl, with a steady look at Ruth.

'If you wish, sir,' she responded and held his eyes.

'And what do you wish, Mrs Hayden?'

'Shall we play cards?' Sarah interjected hastily and gave her husband a meaningful frown. Gavin seemed privately amused by the verbal battle between their guests. 'I know Ruth is good at piquet and so am I. We shall play together and beat you two gentlemen,' she declared. 'And the losers must…well, we'll decide that later,' she said, rather flustered by the sultry look her husband bestowed on her.

The following morning Ruth arose early, despite being reluctant to quit her bed as it was wonderfully warm and comfy. Her cold toes sought the satin slippers Sarah had lent her. Drawing about her the warm dressing gown that was also being loaned by her friend, she padded to the window.

She drew back the heavy velvet curtains and gazed out, rather blearily, at a stunning sight. Small clouds were scantily placed on a high azure sky. The sun was blindingly bright and beneath its rays the ground was a sheet of twinkling white. The trees, shrubs, hedges gracefully bore their sugar coating, only rarely shedding granules as the breeze stirred branches to life. Despite being disappointedly aware that the conditions were still too perilous for even a short journey through back lanes, Ruth marvelled at the natural beauty she gazed upon. It made her wish that she had an ability to paint or draw and capture the pristine scene.

Turning into the room, she approached the dresser and tested the water in the pitcher. It was cold, but not unbearably so. Logs had burned in the grate all night and were only now disintegrating into flaky grey ash. Quickly she filled the bowl and used the scented washing things Sarah had thoughtfully provided for her.

Having freshened up, she quickly donned her clothes without waiting for a maid to appear. She knew that Sarah would send someone to attend on her, but not yet, it was far too early. She would not be expected to rise till after ten at the earliest. Now she looked down at her silver silk dress with a frown. It was not suitable daywear, but would have to suffice for just this morning. This afternoon she hoped to be in her own home.

Now ready to face the day, she none the less lingered in her chamber. She sat upon the bed and wondered if it was too early to go downstairs. Not that she was expected to stand on ceremony when enjoying the Tremaynes' hospitality—she was treated as one of the family. But she'd guessed that Sarah and Gavin might enjoy a lie in while their other guest might be up and about as early as she was. She'd no intention of again finding herself alone with Clayton, desperately seeking to engage him in some innocuous conversation till their hosts appeared.

When she'd bid Clayton a goodnight yesterday evening at close to midnight, and had received a similar cordiality from him, they had seemed to part on fair terms. It would be wise to keep it that way for the short time they remained penned together in close proximity.

After they had played piquet together and each team had won a game, Gavin and Sarah had opted to play dominoes. Ruth and Clayton had persevered with the pack of cards.

Ruth had then won two hands of piquet, playing solo. She'd had a suspicion that Clayton had allowed her to do so and had been initially rather miffed in case he was attempting to patronise her. Then she'd mused that his intentions could be philanthropic. He might have been seeking to compensate for his boorish behaviour earlier and so she'd graciously accepted her victory. But it had been impossible not to bring to his notice their wager. She'd been correct in guessing they would dine on poultry with stuffing. She'd also beaten him at cards, yet he'd cheated her of her prize in bringing a musical evening to Sarah's notice. He'd affected to look chastened and had offered to make amends by fetching for her another small sherry. But when he'd handed it over he'd again raised her hackles by giving the softly scornful advice that it might be advisable to sip at this one slowly.

Thus had the evening progressed in an atmosphere of gentle joviality till bedtime. Yet she knew that, for all his sophisticated charm and easy smiles when their eyes had held for a second more than necessary or their fingers had inadvertently brushed together, an undeniable tension had strained between them.

With that thought in her mind, Ruth lingered by the dressing table and again picked up the hairbrush. She drew it slowly through her thick dusky hair and, raising her eyes to the mirror, gave her reflection a wistful smile. At least her unexpected meeting with Clayton had helped her forget the other gentleman unsettling her. She'd given Ian Bryant very little thought since she'd again made Clayton's acquaintance. Nevertheless, she must soon return to Fernlea and the gossip that would spread about her rejecting the doctor's proposal.

A noise from outside her window was slowly penetrating Ruth's introspection. She approached the glass to peer out. A groom was by the stables and she craned her neck to see more of what was going on. It was a bright sunny day, but surely the conditions were still too perilous for the gentlemen to ride? The stable lad had a black horse by the bridle and it skittered in his grasp, prancing and pulling as though to gain its freedom. The boy seemed to gratefully relinquish the steam-snorting beast to someone just emerging from the stalls. With lithe ease Clayton swung himself into the saddle and gave the boy a nod of thanks.

He cut a dashing figure in his long leather riding coat and with the sun burnishing his pale hair. He appeared to be an impressive horseman, too—the stallion seemed calmer beneath his mastery despite Ruth not seeing him do much to bring it about. But then she knew very little about equestrian matters, having only ridden infrequently. But she could drive a pony and trap very well, she reminded herself with a little smile. Her humour faded as she became aware that he was looking up at her window and it was too late to duck from sight. She stood quite still, solemnly returning his gaze although every fibre of her being urged her to slip aside. With acute embarrassment she saw him smile slowly as though he guessed her predicament. With exaggerated politeness he tipped his hat before he turned the horse's head and was galloping away over virgin snow.

For a moment longer Ruth stood where she was, her cheeks flaming. She put a cool hand to her hot cheek to ease the burn. Little wonder the man thought she had an interest in him! That was the second time he'd caught her gawping at him like an infatuated schoolgirl.

Annoyed with herself, she flung the silver-backed brush on to the bed and made for the door. At least he'd taken himself off and left the coast clear for her to venture downstairs and find some breakfast. Then, if the weather stayed fine and the sun continued to shine and melt the snow, she hoped she might escape to her own home before the infernal man reappeared.

And come back he would, she was sure of it. He hadn't looked set for a long journey. No doubt when he set off back to London he would take a carriage and luggage with him.

'Did you sleep well?'

'Indeed I did, thank you. I slept like a log in that comfy bed.' Ruth smiled at Sarah as she swept into the small salon with baby James cradled in her arms.

'Good, I hoped you would be cosy. I told the servants to warm the bed with a pan and build you up a good fire. Did it last the night through?'

'It did,' Ruth reassured her. 'I was warm as toast. I think the sherry helped, too,' she said with a little laugh. She rarely drank alcohol and had indeed felt quite flushed and tipsy by the end of the evening. The glasses of sherry that Clayton had brought to her, added to the wine that had been taken with dinner, had been rather too much for a novice imbiber.

Without ceremony or permission Sarah took her son to Ruth and handed him over. 'I'm quite famished,' she announced and went to the sideboard laden with silver dishes that contained a breakfast selection. Sarah removed the covers and peered within. Taking a plate, she began to ladle food on to it.

Ruth had already breakfasted abstemiously, being still rather full from the delicious dinner she'd eaten the previous evening. Now she looked on in amazement as Sarah sat down at the table and tucked heartily in to scrambled eggs, bacon, kidneys and toast.

'You *are* hungry.' Ruth choked a laugh. 'I shall refrain from inquiring how you got such an appetite.'

Sarah slid her friend a wicked smile and continued to eat. 'I miss him so when we're apart.'

'And I can tell he misses you, too,' Ruth said. 'I'm surprised you're yet out of bed. Are you not exhausted? It was past midnight when we all retired.'

'I shall have a nap this afternoon by the fire in the library. Gavin's gone to check outside. He wants to see if the ground is too slippery to take a horse or carriage out. He intends going in to Willowdene on business, weather permitting.'

'Thankfully, it looks like a thaw might set in,' Ruth said. 'It is a glorious day.' With the baby in her arms, she rose from the chair and went to the window. She gazed again with rapt wonderment at the quiet white landscape. 'If the sun continues to shine, I expect the snow will quickly disappear.'

Sarah sighed. 'So I suppose you will then go home.'

'I will,' Ruth said. 'I must,' she said with smiling emphasis for her downcast friend. 'I haven't told Cissie that I will be staying away. She will come as usual to do her chores if the track is passable and worry herself half to death on finding me not at home.'

'You could send her a message.'

'No. I must go home,' Ruth insisted and handed over James as Sarah came to take him.

'If Clayton were not a guest, too, you would stay, wouldn't you?'

Ruth made a dismissive gesture. 'It's not just that the two of us don't get on…I've much on my mind.'

'Another vexing gentleman, you mean?' Sarah guessed that Dr Bryant's proposal was still preying on Ruth's mind. Her friend's immediate nod proved her right. 'At least the doctor won't venture out to Fernlea in this weather to see you. You have a while to plan your response in case he comes to propose again.'

'I hadn't thought of that.' A rueful smile from Ruth rewarded Sarah's wisdom. 'Now I don't know if I want the wretched weather to improve or worsen.'

'Well, I would have it worsen, simply so you must stay here with me.'

'I'm not sure your other guest would agree with

you on that. During our spat I said I'd definitely go home today. I expect Sir Clayton will return later hoping to find me gone.'

'Have you seen him this morning?' Sarah inquired while cooing against her son's soft pink cheek to make him give her a gummy smile.

'I saw him from my window. He went out riding on a lively black horse quite early.'

'He took Storm out?' Sarah raised her eyebrows, her tawny eyes widening. 'That stallion has a wild temperament. He's not the sort of animal to ride for the first time in hazardous conditions. I hope he knows what he's doing.' Sarah frowned in concern. 'Gavin's an excellent rider, yet sometimes he opts to leave Storm in his stall if he seems agitated.'

'Sir Clayton looked quite competent in the saddle,' Ruth reassured Sarah. And indeed he had, casually giving her that mocking salute. Yet what Sarah had said about the beast was undoubtedly valid. The horse had seemed highly strung. Oddly, she felt a quiver of anxiety pass through her. She might not like the man, she might think him arrogant and conceited, yet she hoped no harm came to him. Had he gone off specifically to avoid her and give her time to return home as she'd said she would? That thought made her feel guilty and even more concerned that he should return safely from his ride.

Chapter Six

'The snow on the eaves and gutters is melting so fast that puddles have formed everywhere.'

Gavin strode in, brushing water droplets from his elegant dark riding jacket. 'If the temperature drops later, the ground will be fit to skate on.' Having given his weather forecast, he gave Ruth a welcoming smile and pecked his wife modestly on the cheek. Rubbing his palms together to warm them, he went to the breakfast selection and, obviously as in need of energy as his wife, doled a good amount of food on to a plate.

'We were just saying,' Sarah began, 'is it wise for Clayton to ride Storm when the conditions are so unpredictable?'

'Is he?' Gavin asked, mildly surprised. He waved a fork dismissively. 'Clayton can ride practically anything you sit him on,' he praised his friend's skill. 'An ass…an Arabian…he'll bring them all soon under control.' Gavin seemed unperturbed to know his friend was even now negotiating snow-covered ditches on the most tempestuous beast in his stables.

'Yet he spends little time at his estate in Devon,' Sarah commented. 'One would think that a man who loves to ride would be there often. It's a good hunting estate, is it not?'

'It is,' Gavin confirmed. 'I expect it's overrun with game, too, as he hunts there so infrequently. I must persuade him to hold a rout.'

'That would be excellent!' Sarah exclaimed. 'The estate is close to the sea, isn't it? I should like to see the coast again. I was a child on a visit with my parents the last time I visited Lyme Regis.'

'Have you been to the coast, Ruth?' Gavin asked pleasantly while enthusiastically tucking in to his breakfast.

'No…I have not,' she admitted rather wistfully. 'I've spent all my life in town and country.'

'It's high time you went there, then,' Gavin said from behind a linen napkin.

A neutral smile met that declaration before Ruth blurted, 'If the thaw continues, I should be home by mid-afternoon.' For a moment she had feared Gavin might suggest speaking to Clayton, on his return, about planning a visit to his country estate, specifically so she might have her first sight of the sea. Gavin might see no harm in it, but his friend was sure to think the reason she was wangling for an invitation was inspired by her hankering to peer at him rather than at the beach. The very thought that Sir Clayton Powell might look at her again with hard mockery in his eyes because he believed she'd taken a fancy to him made her determined to be on her way today. 'Might I have use of one of your carriages to take me home? I think perhaps by three o'clock the sun will have done its work.'

'Of course,' Gavin said, pushing away his empty plate. 'If you want to go, and the roads are passable, you are welcome to a ride. But I'm not so sure the bad weather is yet over.'

A short while later Gavin's prediction that the weather might take a turn for the worse was proved correct. The sun was eclipsed by woolly cloud and darkness hung over the horizon. The air felt colder, too, and the servants started to scurry to and fro, making sure that all the fires were heartily ablaze and that apple-scented logs were stacked high on the hearths.

Ruth knew that it was unlikely she would now journey the few miles to Fernlea today. In truth, if she'd not clashed with Clayton, she'd have happily spent more time with the Tremaynes in the cosy confines of Willowdene Manor. It was a rare treat for her to be a houseguest in such splendid surroundings. When she went home she would enter a stone-cold cottage housing larders ready for replenishment.

With a sigh Ruth turned from the dispiriting sight outside the library window and again sought the warmth of the fire. She sat down and gazed across at her friend with an indulgent smile curving her lips.

Shortly after his papa went to his study to deal with his papers, baby James, protesting loudly, had been carried off by his nursemaid to be put to bed for a nap. The little chap had become fractious and Sarah's attempts to soothe him had come to nought. It was his teeth troubling him, she'd said, and had summoned Mrs Plover to find something soothing for his inflamed gums. After that little drama had passed, the boy's mama had gratefully nestled in to a fireside chair in the library. Before Sarah had finally succumbed to the soporific warmth cocooning her, she'd urged Ruth to take a snooze too.

Now as Ruth listened to Sarah's gentle snuffles and sighs she wished she could catnap for a while. But she didn't feel tired; she'd slept soundly last night, no doubt helped into slumber by the sherry she'd drunk. But primarily her mind was too alert to allow her to relax.

Spending time with her friends was a wonderful interlude in her humdrum life and she wished to squeeze from it every drop of enjoyment. But she must go home and face reality.

Would Ian Bryant come to see her again? And if he did, what would be her answer now she'd had time to reflect on what he'd offered? He'd been civil to her, if unable to conceal his disappointment at her rejection. She felt rather ashamed that she'd so gracelessly sent him packing.

Still, she baulked at the idea of spending all her days…and nights…with him, providing him with all the comforts a good wife should ungrudgingly supply. Mentally she chided herself for desiring romance when harmony would do. Yearning for handsome heroes to love was all very well for dreams at bedtime. What she needed was a husband to help her get through the day. The little pot of investments her papa had left to her was dwindling too fast.

Quietly she got up and took a slow promenade of the room's perimeter simply to stretch her legs. She wandered to the door and on impulse went out into the corridor. Finding it quite draughty out there, she decided it was a too rigorous constitutional and turned back towards the library. As she passed the window she peered up at the murky heavens. It was snowing again.

An icy draught stirring her skirts first alerted Ruth to the fact that the huge double doors, situated many yards away, had been opened. She'd moved into the window embrasure and now peeked around stone to see the butler helping Clayton remove his coat. A hum of male voices reached Ruth's ears as the servant busily shook snow from the coat's capes, then took Clayton's hat and gloves. His duties done, the elderly servant ambled away towards the cloakroom with the garments. Suddenly conscious that she was still craning her neck to spy on the scene in a most unladylike fashion, Ruth stepped back briskly into the deep recess, her heart pounding.

She didn't want Clayton to see her loitering about in the hallway. He'd already made it clear he believed she was attracted to him…or perhaps he thought his fortune was tempting to her. A man of his conceit might readily jump to the conclusion that she'd been patrolling the vestibule to intercept his return. If she attempted to dart back to the library door and disappear within, she was sure to be spotted. Beneath her breath she cursed that she had, for no good reason, left that warm sanctuary. She decided to stay where she was while hoping he would head straight to his chamber. If he went to the stairs, there would be no need for him to pass this spot, thus he would remain oblivious to her presence.

Huddled against the stone window ledge, she listened as rapid footsteps cracked smartly over marble. She pivoted about to look through glass just in case he came her way…

'Are you hiding from someone?'

Ruth spun about, her complexion turning a violent

pink. 'Oh…Sir Clayton…no, of course I am not hiding,' she fibbed while feigning surprise at seeing him. There was no need for him to utter a word for Ruth to inwardly wince at his reaction. The expression in his eyes was concealed with long dark lashes, but his mouth formed a half-smile. She had the impression he'd known of her whereabouts all along. An awful thought assailed her that he might have glimpsed her peeping around the corner at him.

'I'm surprised to find you still here,' Clayton said. 'I imagined you would make use of the thaw and go home.'

'I intended to, sir,' Ruth returned sharply. 'Unfortunately, the sunshine didn't last quite long enough for me to take advantage of it.'

Clayton came a little closer to her and looked out of the window. 'The road to Willowdene was just about passable earlier and will remain so if this fresh fall doesn't settle.'

Ruth felt more disturbed by his closeness than by his inference that she could have gone home had she really wanted to do so.

'I don't travel on that road, sir,' she replied tartly while stepping back from him. She dismissed the *frisson* that raced through her as being caused by the crisp winter air that clung to his clothes. Close to, she could see that his lean complexion looked taut and chilled. 'My home is in the village of Fernlea and the track to it isn't nearly so wide or even as the road to Willowdene.'

'Do you still want to go home?'

'Of course,' Ruth confirmed after a small pause. 'But I have no intention of putting at risk a coach and driver to take me there.'

'If you want to go, I'll take you home,' Clayton said. 'It's the least I can do as it's my presence here that is making you uneasy.'

Ruth gazed at him, her soft lips slightly parted in surprise. Sir Clayton Powell had no qualms over being blunt, that much was obvious. It was also obvious that his arrogance had in no way diminished. 'You overestimate your importance in the matter, sir.' Her flashing dark eyes clashed on his. 'I have pressing affairs to attend to at home. Nevertheless, I think the Manor is roomy enough to accommodate us both. It should be possible for us to avoid one another for a short while longer.'

'And if the weather tomorrow is no better… perhaps worse?'

'Then I shall go home regardless,' she said, vexed by his persistence in pursuing the matter. 'Unless you withdraw your offer to risk the journey, I shall spare the Manor's coachman and allow you to take me there.'

'And I shall be very happy to oblige you on that,' Clayton drawled with a glimmer of a sultry smile. He raised a hand to brace it on the stone, casually, as though he was unaware he'd trapped her between his body and the window, or that he'd brought a heightened bloom to her cheeks with his suggestive tone. 'So what were you doing out here in this draughty hallway when you might have instead been curled up by the fire? Cursing to the devil the weather? Or were you anxious that some harm might have befallen me while gallantly I removed my odious person from your vicinity for the best part of the day?'

'Perhaps if I believed that to be true, I might have given a thought to your safety,' Ruth retorted sourly.

'It's the truth,' he said mildly. His storm-grey eyes slid immediately to watch the movement of her tongue tip as it circled moisture to her soft red lips.

'In that case, sir, you overestimate *my* importance in the matter. There's no need for you to risk life and limb on my account.'

Clayton continued to study the bristling beauty beside him. Her eyes were lustrous and dark as bitter chocolate, her cheekbones flushed with a mix of embarrassment and annoyance.

'I've risked my health for less worthy individuals.'

'I'm sure...' Ruth purred and made a move to pass him. But he seemed unwilling to budge and she was reluctant to attempt to push at the muscular arm that imprisoned her. She wouldn't risk an undignified tussle with him.

As though he had read her thoughts, Clayton

dropped his arm and gave her a lopsided smile when she didn't immediately rush off. He wanted her to stay and talk to him, but he wasn't sure why. She'd made it clear that she thought him rude and arrogant. Considering his behaviour yesterday, it wasn't surprising she'd drawn that conclusion about him. But he'd apologised at length at the time and to do so again now would be pointless.

He sensed she remained where she was because she found him as intriguing as he found her. But she didn't like him. Unfortunately, he knew he liked her rather too much. Just being this close to her put a throb in his loins. He had a nagging urge to trap her against the wall and kiss her despite knowing she was, or was soon to be, betrothed to a fellow described as a pillar of Willowdene society. The thought of another man having her annoyed Clayton and that made him ashamed of his selfishness.

Despite Gavin's suggestions that a wife would protect him from the likes of Loretta, he had no intention of ever again offering marriage to a woman. Yet he envied the rustic dignitary who had Ruth Hayden as his future bride. In no small part his resentment sprang from knowing that he'd arrived here in Willowdene only fractionally too late to proposition her. And he would have generously offered her *carte blanche* as his mistress despite Gavin's caution that she wasn't that sort of woman. In Clayton's vast and varied experience, every woman had her price.

'I know we both want to enjoy the unexpected extra time we have to spend with our friends,' Ruth blurted, making an emphatic little hand movement. She felt flustered by his brooding silence, and his broad, muscular body just inches from hers...warming her. 'It's surely not too difficult for us to tolerate one another's company for a further day?'

A dry chuckle rolled in Clayton's throat. 'It's no hardship at all on my part, Mrs Hayden.'

For a moment longer Ruth hesitated, then, with a slight nod, she slipped swiftly past him. She hastened to the library door, well aware that his eyes were following her.

As the door to the library closed Clayton turned towards the stairs, his expression a study of ironic amusement. Could he tolerate her company? she'd pleaded to know in that calm yet appealingly breathy way she had. A corner of his mouth pulled upwards. Given the opportunity, he'd slowly savour her company. He greatly desired seeing much more of her and in the early hours of the morning had almost succumbed to that wild need.

At half past midnight he'd been sitting by the fire in his bedchamber still fully clothed and tapping his booted feet restlessly. At one o'clock he'd sprung up and quit his room with purposeful speed. In a moment of delirium—brought about by lustful images of Ruth sprawled, naked, beneath crumpled sheets—he'd set off towards her chamber specifically to seduce her. Thankfully a long walk through cool corridors had brought him to his senses and he'd continued, without faltering, past her door.

Downstairs in the drawing room he'd swirled to warmth by the fire, then downed, several cognacs. By three o'clock he'd been sufficiently relaxed by alcohol and tobacco to meander back to his bed and sleep fitfully till dawn. He'd risen early and put distance between them for his own benefit as much as for hers. He was awkwardly aware that he'd been acting like a horny youth stalking his first conquest, and, worse, Gavin had noticed him doing it.

Clayton accelerated his pace up the stairs, taking the final treads two at a time. Still he couldn't shake thoughts of Ruth from his mind. The memory of her peeking at him from behind stone brought a smile to hover on his lips. She'd tried to hide from him in the hall because she'd feared he'd suspect her of loitering with intent. With any other single female that cynical conclusion might have been valid. He'd lost count of the number of times he'd been ambushed by determined women concealing themselves behind pillars or in alcoves.

But it hadn't been the case on this occasion. Ruth had probably been pacing restlessly to while away the time. She had domestic affairs to see to, she'd said. So had he. They both had been prevented from leaving the Manor and going about their usual business by the heavy snowfall. But it gnawed at his consciousness that she might be pining to go home to see her lover whereas he had no desire to see Loretta...yet see her he must, if only to make sure she understood she was now out of his life for good.

Chapter Seven

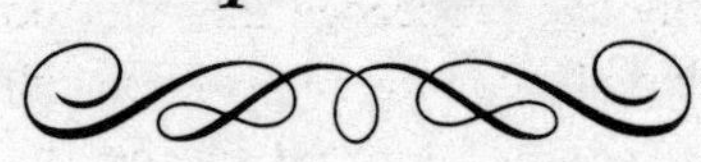

'Good evening, sir.'

'Good evening to you, Mrs Hayden.'

Ruth's sepia gaze swept the dining room she had just entered but the only person within its quiet confines was Sir Clayton. It appeared that their hosts were late down to dine this evening just as they had been yesterday. But Ruth doubted they had this time been delayed for delightfully amorous reasons. As she had descended the stairs she had heard little James wailing. The poor mite was no doubt still suffering with teething pains. Ruth had guessed that Sarah might arrive late, choosing to stay in the nursery until the baby settled down to sleep. Gavin's absence indicated he too might be attempting to soothe his son, or his anxious wife.

It had been a full ten minutes after the gong had

sounded that Ruth had left her room. She had loitered upstairs in the hope of avoiding again being stranded alone with this unsettling aristocrat. Inwardly she sighed; it seemed she must once more strive to calm the friction between them and ferret in her mind for something to talk about while they waited for their friends to join them.

Gracefully she proceeded into the room while a subtle sliding glance took in his immaculate appearance. He'd stationed himself by the chimneypiece with a hand resting negligently on the marble mantel and the other thrust into a pocket. This evening he was dressed in a charcoal grey suit of clothes that looked to be of excellent cut and quality. An intricate knot had been formed in his cravat and in its centre winked a sapphire stone of considerable size.

Ruth's awkwardness was momentarily overcome by an unexpected burst of exuberance at having all to herself such a handsome and distinguished gentleman. Mercilessly she quashed it. She'd been made aware of an unpleasant side to his character yesterday evening, she reminded herself, and no amount of suave good looks or polished charm could alter it.

Unconsciously Ruth smoothed a hand over her grey dress, feeling rather shabby in the presence of such sartorial elegance. Earlier in the day she'd turned down Sarah's offer to choose something from her wardrobe to wear to dinner. Normally she might have enjoyed dressing up in one of her friend's glamorous gowns. They were about the same size, although Ruth's bust was a little fuller.

In the past she'd worn Sarah's cast-offs. Accepting charity was abhorrent to her, but it was different with her friend's gifts. Sarah had known what it was to be strapped for cash and donated useful clothes in a manner far removed from condescension. Ruth knew Sarah would never patronise her. But today she had declined her friend's kindness and now she knew her reason for doing so. She'd not wanted this man to suspect she might be primping in his honour.

'You rode quite a spirited mount earlier…'

'Will a servant tend to your pony?'

They both had started a conversation at the same time, as they had yesterday on meeting by the stairs and after suffering a protracted silence.

Ruth received an apologetic smile and returned him one of her own. A speaking gesture invited him to continue.

'I was inquiring after your pony. You were driving a pony and trap the first time I saw you in Willowdene. Will he be fed and watered while you are here?'

'I no longer have that little mare,' Ruth told him with a wistful smile. 'I let her go to a friend. But he's good enough to allow me to borrow her and the cart, too, when I need to go to town.'

'A friend?' Clayton echoed casually while strolling

to the decanters on the sideboard. 'Would you like a sherry?' he asked while waiting to discover who her generous gentleman friend might be.

'I will not, thank you. I think I overindulged yesterday. I had quite a headache this morning,' she told him ruefully.

That admission drew a slow grin from Clayton, although he continued watching cognac flow into a glass. 'I imagine you're quite a stranger to overindulgence.'

Ruth bristled slightly. Was he inferring that she was a prude of some sort? 'It's true I rarely drink alcohol,' she confirmed, managing to keep her tone light.

'Or have many vices at all, I shouldn't wonder,' he said as he turned back to her and took a hefty swig from his glass.

He *was* inferring she was a prude. No ready retort sprang to mind to close the conversation, so Ruth sent him a tight smile and said nothing at all. As he'd left the cosy fireside vacant, she took up position there and warmed her palms by the glow.

'So...you were about to tell me which of your friends now has your pony and trap.'

A sharp dark look met that comment. She'd been about to do no such thing. And he knew it. But she wouldn't dispute the point. It seemed he had a love of trying to ruffle her and allowing him his mischievous way wasn't at all what she wanted. Besides, what did it matter if he knew to whom she'd sold her transport?

'Parson Greene bought them from me. He lives quite close by in the village.'

Clayton lifted his glass and gave her a thoughtful glance over its rim. Was Parson Greene her suitor? Her lover? It would explain why the fellow put his property at her disposal. It was hardly an extravagant gesture compared to what a mistress of his might expect him to provide to take her about town. Loretta had had the use of one of his new carriages and two pair of matching greys while his mistress. But then Ruth Hayden was not a woman much impressed by a gentleman's rank. She'd let him know that, in no uncertain terms, yesterday. And the parson might not be a man of wealth or position just because he was classed as a pillar of the community. The man's worth and importance hereabouts might be linked to what he did rather than what he had.

Clayton acknowledged that he knew nothing of Willowdene or its social hierarchies. He mused, too, that it might be time to rectify his ignorance. 'I expect you're friendly with the parson's wife as well,' he ventured innocently.

'Why do you think that?' Ruth returned.

'In London ladies usually have friends with whom they shop or take afternoon tea,' he smoothly explained. 'I imagine the women in rural communities socialise in much the same way.'

'The parson is a widower,' Ruth said and suspiciously narrowed her eyes on him. She sensed he was probing for information about the elderly parson for reasons unknown to her. Or perhaps he was just trying to spin out their dialogue in the hope their friends would soon arrive to rescue them. She decided to be charitable and settle on that theory. 'Parson Greene lost his wife several years ago. He has a daughter of about my age who lives with him.'

'Ah…so she is your friend.'

'An acquaintance,' Ruth supplied, turning away and briskly rubbing together her palms. She wasn't about to disclose to him that Verity Greene, along with the majority of the villagers, snubbed her because of the manner of her husband's death.

It was a long while since Paul had been court-martialled, then shot for desertion from the army, but, in her experience, small-minded people, with nothing better to do, liked to keep alive their prejudices. And tales of Captain Paul Hayden's cowardice—oh, how wrong they were about him!—were still resurrected and gossiped over in the absence of any fresh grist for the mill.

She was thankful that Parson Greene was more neighbourly towards her than was his daughter and the other local ladies. No sisterhood existed in these parts, as Sarah also had learned to her cost when she'd been a notorious, ostracised spinster. Attention and assistance were more likely to be forthcoming from those ladies' husbands and Ruth knew therein lay the crux of the problem.

She was a young widow of fine looks—such praise having been bestowed by her doting parents and her late beloved husband—therefore she was deemed a threat, despite never having harboured a romantic interest in any local fellow, even the extremely eligible Dr Ian Bryant. And perhaps, she reflected, she might soon rue that fact…

Swiftly she gathered her wayward thoughts and decided to make an effort to be pleasant to her extremely eligible companion.

'I was talking to Gavin and Sarah earlier about the black stallion…Storm, I believe is his name.' Ruth had spoken rapidly, hoping to prevent Clayton interrogating her further over her neighbours. 'That horse is, by all accounts, a very spirited beast. Did you know he was a difficult ride before you decided to take him out?'

'Were you concerned for my safety?'

'No more than I would have been for any person who unwisely decided to mount such an animal in perilous conditions,' Ruth said. His smile deepened, infuriatingly, prompting her to continue briskly, 'Such a foolhardy action might make the perpetrator appear cocksure about his prowess, don't you think?'

Clayton came closer, stood by her side by the fire and let out a regretful sigh. 'And I know you deem it possible I might possess that deplorable character trait.'

Ruth tipped up her dark head, gave him a bold speaking look, her lips pressed together to contain a glimmer of a smile. At times he had quite an appealing way about him, even if his self-deprecation was, in itself, an irony. She imagined he could be very amusing company if he wished to be. 'And do *you* deem it possible you might possess that deplorable character trait?' she audaciously inquired with a tremor of suppressed laughter.

'At present I'm deeming it possible to curb every bad habit I possess in order to win your approval.' It was stated with a mock-solemn frown at the shadows cast upon the ceiling.

'And why would you seek my approval?' Ruth asked lightly. 'You need not strive to improve your character for my benefit. We inhabit different worlds, you and I, and will probably meet but rarely through our mutual friends.' She tilted him a mischievous smile. 'You may continue to be as bumptious as you please, sir. I shall never know.'

'Ah, but you will, and soon, so I have little time to make the required changes. James is to be christened in a few months' time. I hear from Gavin that you have agreed to be his godmother.'

'I have,' Ruth said, her eyes softening as she reflected on that honour. 'And very gladly do I undertake the role.' She had momentarily forgotten that she was to share the responsibility of godparent with this gentleman.

'Then, as I have agreed to be the boy's godfather, we have at least one future meeting already planned,' Clayton said with a steady look that made an odd sensation accelerate through Ruth's veins. 'And I'd very much like to secure your good opinion before then.' His tone became velvety. 'In truth, I'd like a little kindness from you far sooner.'

Swiftly Ruth tore her eyes from the overpowering pull of his smouldering grey gaze. The gentle banter between them had transformed into something far more deadly serious. She turned her head, frowned in confusion. He was flirting outrageously with her, making her think unsuitable thoughts, making her feel emotions she didn't want to feel…hadn't indulged since she'd revelled in Paul's loving words and intimate touches.

Foolishly she'd encouraged the attention of a notorious rake in the belief she could match his sophisticated skill in a trifling game. But she was at a loss to know what to say next to ease the heady atmosphere. The small space between them seemed to throb with tension. She sensed he was about to stretch a hand towards her, and she shot back a pace as speedily as she would have had a spark been spat out by the fire.

For an interminable moment she refused to meet his eyes while a riot of thoughts whirled in her head. She must cede him his victory in their verbal duel, but not let him know how greatly he'd unsettled her. She might be unworldly and wearing a tired-looking dress, but she'd not crumple beneath the sensual challenge he'd thrown down. She raised deep brown eyes to find he was watching her closely and with a lot less amusement in his eyes than she'd feared to see.

'Were you concerned for my safety, today?' he demanded to know in a gruff tone.

Ruth simply nodded, unable to lie or prevaricate or say anything at all.

'I chose that mount because I hoped riding him would focus my mind purely on the sport in hand and stop me thinking about a more dangerous distraction.'

'And did it work?' she whispered. His cryptic answer seemed to have some hidden significance that she instinctively knew applied to her.

Seductive grey eyes coupled with her shy earthy gaze, but the door opened and Clayton was prevented from telling her that despite the ice all around he'd burned hot as hell for her.

Gavin entered the dining room with a falsely cheerful smile that immediately dispersed the sultry atmosphere. It was obvious to both Ruth and Clayton that something was very wrong.

'Sarah shouldn't be too long. James is still coughing and spluttering, poor little lad, but once he's settled down we can dine.' Gavin had left the door ajar and the infant's loud wails could again be heard, causing him to turn and frown. But, ever the perfect host, he said, 'Of course, you both may dine now if you wish to. Dinner is ready to be served and there's no need to wait for us…'

His further offers and assurances were cut off as Clayton and Ruth simultaneously demurred at taking any such action.

'It is probably just the pain of cutting his teeth bothering him,' Gavin continued with a constrained smile. 'But Sarah wants to see James sleeping peacefully before she leaves the nursery.'

'Might I help in any way? Or keep Sarah company?' Ruth asked, a tremor of concern in her voice.

'I expect she might like that,' Gavin replied.

The immediate gratitude in Gavin's tone made anxiety roll in the pit of Ruth's stomach. For all Gavin's composure, she feared the situation was worse than he was prepared to admit. She quickly went from the room.

'Why do I not know what to do?' Sarah put a frantic hand to worry her pale brow. 'He is my flesh and blood, my darling son, yet I can't comfort him and it's breaking my heart.'

Ruth enclosed her tearful friend in her arms and watched the nursemaid pacing to and fro, trying to calm the howling baby with little coos and clucks. James's tiny face was scarlet and scrunched up tight as he filled his lungs to recommence protesting against his discomfort.

'He is clean and dry, so that's not the trouble,' Sarah said. 'He cannot be hungry, for it's not yet the hour for his feed. Besides, I've tried to comfort him that way, but he won't suck,' she added with a frown. 'Cutting teeth surely can't be such an ordeal.'

Ruth murmured consoling words to her friend as she went to take a closer look at the baby. His distress was mounting and his cries had hoarsened as he wriggled this way and that in Rosie's arms.

'I was so foolish in not employing a nursemaid of experience and maturity. But I wanted to be a proper mother and do most for James myself. It was idiotic to take on a girl of such limited experience.'

If Rosie heard her mistress's comments and was offended she gave no sign and continued rocking the baby and crooning a lullaby.

'Perhaps he's taken a slight chill,' Ruth ventured on hearing the little mite start to cough with such force he shook in Rosie's arms.

'I fear his temperature is higher than it was this afternoon.' Sarah gave Ruth a look that appealed for reassurance. 'Is he ill, do you think? Or is it simply the teeth breaking through? Oh, why am I so ignorant of all this? Mothers should have an instinct about their infant's health, surely?'

Again Ruth drew her friend to her. 'I'm afraid that I don't know either what's wrong,' she admitted gently. 'You mustn't blame yourself for your lack of experience. James is your first-born. Rearing babies is, I imagine, something only learned through practice.'

'I don't know if I am being too silly over it all…but it is better to be safe than sorry. I want Gavin to fetch the doctor; it's the only way to ease my mind. Would it be awkward for you to see Dr Bryant so soon after having rejected his proposal?'

'Of course you must send for him!' Ruth said emphatically. 'If you think he might help James in any small way, he must be fetched directly.'

'I shall go and tell Gavin to ride to Willowdene at once,' Sarah blurted on a sob of determination and was immediately hurrying towards the door.

After listening for a few moments to the baby's plaintive cries, Ruth relieved Rosie of her squirming burden. The poor little lad might be suffering, but he certainly had energy and strength left. Ruth rocked him in her arms to no avail—his clenched fists continued to wave at her. She then attempted to settle him against her shoulder. But he seemed all elbows and knees and refused to be comforted or calmed by strokes and pats or whispered words.

She laid a cool hand against his hot little brow, curved it over his downy pate. He certainly did feel very feverish.

'Is there some water to cool him?' she asked Rosie.

Immediately the girl sped to the water pitcher and

returned with a cold damp cloth. 'The mistress tried bathing him earlier, but it made no difference,' she told Ruth with a worried frown. 'He's been crying too long; he needs something to drink is what I reckon. He must be thirsty for sure, but he's too exhausted to suckle.'

'Ask cook to have some water set to boil. When it's cool enough he might take a little of it from a spoon.' Ruth thought Rosie's advice sensible.

As Rosie went out on her errand Ruth patted very gently at James's blotchy complexion with the cool cloth and was greatly relieved when, for a moment, it seemed to soothe him. Gently she wiped the damp compress against his scarlet cheeks. But soon he again began to cough and rattle and then high-pitched hear-trending cries broke from him. Ruth felt panic needle her skin at the force of his distress. At that moment she was far from wishing Ian Bryant away from her. Indeed, she longed to see him very, very soon.

Chapter Eight

It was close to ten o'clock when Clayton arrived back at the Manor with Ian Bryant. He'd insisted on taking the mission, sensing that Gavin would sooner stay with his distraught wife than travel to Willowdene to fetch the doctor. Gavin knew his friend was as competent tooling the ribbons as he was in the saddle and had gratefully succumbed to Clayton's arguments. If anyone could get the doctor to the Manor in good time, over bad ground, Clayton could. Just an hour after quitting the Manor he was back with Ian, proving Gavin's trust in him to be well placed.

Following concise words in the vestibule as to the infant's symptoms, Ian was soon swiftly taking the stairs with the worried father. Seconds later the gentlemen entered an ominously hushed nursery.

Ruth and Sarah were still within the warm room,

both stationed close to the crib where the little boy silently lay. James now appeared lethargic rather than restful. He'd taken a few spoonfuls of warm water, but it hadn't seemed to either worsen or improve his condition. Neither had he wanted his mama's milk when she cuddled him close to her breast and tried again to feed him.

Only very briefly did the doctor's professional manner slip when he spied Ruth. His eyes fixed on her for several long moments, his surprise, and something else—pleasure, perhaps, at seeing her—apparent in his intense gaze. Then once more he was briskly attending to James. He began to unclothe the boy to examine him.

Feeling now superfluous and, in any case, keen to be gone lest her presence again distract Ian from his vital work, Ruth murmured a few words to Sarah, then withdrew.

Clayton was pacing the vestibule as Ruth descended the stairs. When he saw her, he strode to the banisters and waited for her to come closer before issuing an inevitable question. 'How is he?' he urgently demanded to know as she reached the bottom step.

'A little calmer, but I'm not sure that's a good thing.' An anxious frown accompanied her shake of the head. 'The poor mite was coughing fit to burst his lungs.' Tears needled her eyes at the memory of it. 'I can understand why Sarah is so distraught. He looks and sounds a very sorry little chap.'

Instinctively Clayton took one of her pale trembling hands into his to comfort her, for he'd noted the distress in her voice. 'The doctor is here now.' His fingers stroked quite naturally to soothe her. 'All that can be done will be done. He seems a good enough fellow and needed no persuading to come out on such a treacherous night.'

Clayton drew Ruth down from the step she stood upon and linked her arm in his. Immediately Ruth turned to gaze at whence she'd just come, reluctant to move away in case she might again be of some small assistance upstairs.

'You're cold and there's nothing for us to do to help,' Clayton urged, moving her again about. 'Come into the library and warm yourself by the fire. We shall know soon enough how James fares.'

Ruth nodded absently and went with him. She sat in the chair to which he led her and accepted, without demur, the glass of warming sherry he pressed firmly into her chilly hand.

'When one has no children of one's own, it's hard to imagine the heartache a parent must endure watching a child suffering,' Clayton quietly mused, his solemn gaze contemplating flames leaping from the grate. 'The threat of illness and loss must be a constant torment.' He slanted a grave look at Ruth, probably anticipating her murmur of agreement.

But she simply gazed back at him, her eyes slowly filling with brine until some spilled on to her cheeks.

Clayton frowned, then a dawning realisation tautened his features. With a silent oath he closed his eyes, passed a hand over his jaw. He made a small gesture, croaked a gruff apology, although she'd said not one word to confirm his awful suspicions.

Without understanding why she did so, Ruth confided quietly to a man she barely knew the bare bones of her greatest heartache. 'A daughter...still-born...she would now have been eight years old.'

Clayton cast again a long sideways look at her, watching her lower her beautiful soulful eyes beneath his steady, sorry scrutiny. By the time he'd thought of something that he prayed might be right to say, the door had opened and the doctor and the boy's parents entered the room.

Ruth jumped to her feet as Sarah sped across the room to her.

'He seems a little better,' Sarah breathlessly told Ruth. 'Doctor Bryant has given James a draught to help him sleep. He seems cooler and able to breathe more easily.'

Having listened to the good news intently, then asked for it to be repeated, so welcome was it, Ruth hugged her friend happily to her. Over Sarah's shoulder she saw that Ian was watching the scene. She sent him a small smile that she hoped conveyed her very great gratitude for his prompt arrival. For a moment she thought he might remain impassive, but eventually he returned her a similar salute. She was glad he appeared to harbour no resentment towards her. She didn't want them to be enemies, she knew that for definite, even if all else regarding the outcome of their relationship was uncertain.

'Please stay and take a drink before you venture back into this awful night,' Gavin urged the doctor. He proffered a glass and, at a murmur of acceptance from Ian, poured a generous measure of cognac into it.

Ruth and Sarah joined the group of gentlemen and contributed a few words to the general dialogue about the severe weather. Inevitably the talk turned to the evening's horrible drama.

'That was an experience I hope never will be repeated,' Gavin declared vehemently as he drew his wife close to his side and comforted her with a subtle little caress. Sarah was still trembling despite her relieved smiles and constant burbling chatter.

'I'm afraid I anticipate it will be repeated,' Ian disabused them bluntly. 'These early maladies are quite common, but you must take heart from the fact that even very young children are surprising in their resilience.' His eyes again strayed to Ruth, lingered just a little too long before moving on to the boy's mother. 'He is obviously a well-nourished and healthy little chap. You are caring very well for him and will find in the morning that James is much better after a good night's rest.'

'And the mixture for his gums and tummy ache?' Sarah asked anxiously. 'Are we wrong to try and ease his discomfort with it?'

'It's a mild herbal remedy and quite frequently used. I've not known it to cause any problems. But at present it's best to give him nothing other than a little boiled water if he seems thirsty or colicky between feeds. His digestion might be delicate and the mixture not efficacious.'

Sarah nodded, then turned to Clayton, who had been standing a little aside from the group, observing the proceedings and the two couples from beneath closely drawn brows.

'You, sir, have proved to be an invaluable friend tonight, fetching Dr Bryant so quickly to us through the snow.'

Sarah's praise drew a quiet simple response from Clayton. 'I would have undertaken far more than I did to ensure James's health and comfort.'

'You haven't seen your future godson today,' Sarah said in a choked little voice. 'Would you like to see how peacefully he is now sleeping?'

'Indeed I would,' Clayton said gently and, at Sarah's beckoning, he accompanied her to the door.

Shortly after his wife and friend departed the room, Gavin swung a discreet glance between the doctor and Ruth. Having drawn the conclusion that the atmosphere was thick enough to slice, and thus supposing they might appreciate a little time alone, he excused himself with the perfectly credible comment that the kitchen staff must be eager to know whether to continue to keep warm their dinner. At the door Gavin turned and frowned an apology at his lack of manners in not issuing the invitation sooner. 'Will you stay and dine with us, Dr Bryant?'

Ruth's startled gaze flew to Ian's face, causing his top lip to lightly curl. He understood her silent demand as to what response he must give. 'I thank you, but no,' he politely declined. 'I have a young son of my own asleep in his bed and would like to return directly to him.'

'How old is he?' Gavin asked.

'Joseph has just had his first birthday.'

Gavin nodded and smiled wryly. But he said nothing more as he opened the door.

Once Gavin had quit the room, Ruth attempted to set a neutral tone between them. 'The poor cook must be praying that her hard work is not in vain, and the food is still presentable. But I'm sure all the servants will be greatly relieved to know how James is improved. They dote on him—'

'I didn't realise you were so well acquainted with the Tremaynes.' If Ian had perceived her desire to avoid personal questions, he'd blatantly ignored it.

A little frown from Ruth met that blunt interruption,

but she gave thanks that at least he'd not referred to their last meeting. 'Sarah...Lady Tremayne...and I are good friends,' she mildly replied. 'We became close when Sarah lived in Willowdene, before her marriage to the Viscount.'

'I recall she lived alone at Elm Lodge.' A significant pause preceded Ian adding acidly, 'A great triumph it was, too, for Miss Sarah Marchant to catch an aristocrat and move from an estate cottage to the manor house, especially when one considers her previous...*unfortunate*...circumstances.'

Ruth's eyes flared in astonishment at his quite obvious disdain for her friend. Of course, everybody hereabouts knew that Sarah once had been a scandal-wrecked woman, but most accepted that her reputation had been repaired when she married. 'I know the Viscount deems himself to be the lucky one to have secured such a wonderful woman for his wife.' Ruth's voice remained calm, but a steely inflection stressed her great disapproval for what he'd said. She moved away from Ian in a way that displayed her disgust at his attitude more clearly than any words might have done.

'So...you believe that baby James is not afflicted with any dreadful complaint,' she said before he could add to his impertinent opinions about her friends. 'Is it often the case that babies cut their teeth with such worrying symptoms?'

Just for a moment Ian continued gazing at her as

though deciding whether to this time bow to her unspoken demand that their conversation be limited to the circumstances requiring his presence here this evening. Abruptly he swallowed what was left of his cognac and carelessly replenished his glass from the Viscount's decanter. 'The pain of teething causes great discomfort,' he shortly explained. 'Distress is a self-perpetuating malady and can result in such symptoms as exhaustion and thirst. Once assuaged, the patient usually recuperates and gains strength enough to once more display distress at whatever ails them. And so the cycle continues until the pain abates or is controlled.'

'Well, we are greatly relieved and thankful that you came here this evening, put an end to James's suffering and allowed him some restful sleep. We must hope that tomorrow the tooth appears.'

A curt nod was all the agreement she received to her heartfelt wish. A silence developed and Ruth prayed that someone…anyone…would soon return to disperse the stifling atmosphere. She knew that Ian's taciturnity indicated he was brooding on presenting her with another awkward question. It wasn't long in coming.

'And are you also friendly with Sir Clayton Powell?'

'Why…no…I hardly know him at all,' Ruth returned truthfully. Briskly she approached the window to peer at the night. 'I hope your journey home will be as safe and speedy as the one that brought you here,' she said over a shoulder. 'It's atrocious weather for this time of the year.'

'If I return with Sir Clayton driving me, no doubt I'll be within doors in no time at all.' The inference that she hoped him soon gone from the Manor had not been lost on Ian.

'He is a very good horseman, so I've been told.'

'He is a very great scoundrel, so I've been told,' Ian returned scathingly.

'Perhaps he is, but tonight we must cast him very credibly in the role of hero,' Ruth shot back. 'Sir Clayton insisted on being the one to brave the elements and fetch you despite the Viscount's protests that the duty was his.'

'Ah…I think I can guess the reason why you praise him so prettily.' Ian barked a low laugh. 'Is the notorious Lothario close to making another conquest? You would be well advised, madam, to give him a wide berth. I have a town residence and know a little of London society and the debauchery that goes on in his vicinity.'

'But you can know very little of me, sir,' Ruth smartly cut him off, 'or you wouldn't hint at my behaving so ridiculously. And I hope you aren't about to be very indiscreet, and repeat vulgar town tattle that might have reached your ears.'

That fluent rebuke caused Ian's cheeks to mottle,

but he forced a smile to twist his lips. 'I take it you already know of his rakish reputation and yet have no objection to remaining in his company. I think that ridiculous, madam.'

Ruth's eyes flashed a warning at him and she took a pace or two closer. If he added just a little more to his insolent opinions, she'd give him a piece of her mind. How dare Ian Bryant sermonise about philandering gentlemen when he had propositioned her to be his mistress while his wife was alive and well! How dare he imagine she'd act the simpering flirt with any gentleman! He certainly couldn't be drawing on his own experience of her character. She'd smartly rebuffed his wooing on both the occasions it had been forthcoming. She was just in the right frame of mind to remind him of it.

It was at that moment that Clayton entered the room and, seeing Ian Bryant and Ruth Hayden so close, their eyes locked together, the atmosphere solid with tension, confirmed the suspicions he'd had earlier. He'd now met the gentleman who'd proposed to Ruth Hayden. They were lovers…or soon to be…

A corner of Clayton's mouth moved, but scant humour warmed his eyes. On realising they were no longer alone, Ruth had guiltily skittered back and put a decent distance between her and the doctor. Clayton sauntered to the sideboard and snatched the decanter, allowing the startled couple time to compose themselves.

He also needed to compose himself, he realised as the fist that held the fragile neck of the bottle began tightening perilously on the glass. A rush of ferocious jealousy had stormed his veins at having his suspicions about the pair confirmed and it was a novel and unpleasant experience. He felt a fool, too, for having just hours ago considered that this beautiful, principled woman might be involved romantically with an elderly man of the cloth who loaned her a horse and cart. She deserved far better. Grudgingly he accepted that if Dr Ian Bryant was about to become her husband, he looked to be a fitting partner for her.

He guessed the doctor to be about his own age, in his middle thirties. He was of good height, well built and seemed personable enough in character. Having visited his Willowdene residence, Clayton knew he possessed a very presentable house staffed by neatly attired servants. Clayton uncharitably wished to see the damnable fellow return there without delay.

With a tumbler in his hand and a smile on his lips, Clayton pivoted about to face the couple. 'James looks very peaceful now. I think he'll sleep the night through.' It was pleasantly observed; not a trace of his mood showed in his face or speech.

'Good…that's good,' Ruth blurted. 'Is Sarah staying with him in the nursery for a while longer?' She wished that her friend would arrive and take the focus of attention. For all Clayton's easy words and smiles, she sensed he too was brooding on something other than the drama surrounding the little boy upstairs. She noted his piercing grey gaze was on Ian, and little welcome was in his eyes. Ruth felt her stomach lurch as it occurred to her that Clayton might have overheard the slanderous remarks that Ian had made about his character and reputation. She didn't believe Clayton would intentionally eavesdrop, but he might have also overheard Ian disparage Sarah. By association he'd criticised Clayton's best friend on his choice of wife.

'I believe Lady Tremayne went to speak to the servants about dinner.' Clayton gave Ruth a charming smile that served only to unsettle her further.

'Gavin has gone to do so, too,' Ruth replied to fill the ensuing quiet. 'Why is it that disasters always strike when one is least able to promptly deal with them?' she continued, chattering aimlessly. 'It would be a miracle indeed if just once such an emergency were to occur during daylight in fine weather.'

Her eyes flitted between the two gentlemen, imploring for a contribution of bland dialogue from one of them.

Clayton removed his pitiless gaze from the doctor, who had become a mite uneasy beneath it. He looked at Ruth and immediately his eyes warmed as he noted her strained features. She looked anxious that he might say or do something to upset her lover. And much as he wanted to—for purely selfish reasons—he decided not to invite the fellow to drink up so he could get him back to his own home. 'I imagine Dr Bryant would know about fate's contrariness, Mrs Hayden. I expect he has such a tale to quote.'

If either Clayton or Ruth expected the fellow might regale them with a few interesting anecdotes, while they waited for the Tremaynes to appear, they were to be disappointed.

Ian continued moodily brooding and simply muttered an agreement to the hypothesis that this wasn't the first time he'd been called out at dead of night in foul weather to attend the sick or needy. He abruptly took a gulp of brandy.

'Another?' Clayton held out the decanter indicatively towards Ian, a ghost of a smile acknowledging that he was rather contented to know that the worthy pillar of Willowdene Society could act unpleasantly sullen.

Clayton's glimmer of private amusement was not lost on Ruth. She'd recently been subjected to that sardonic look and knew what lay behind it. And indeed Ian was acting in a most idiotic way. 'I hope the road has not worsened,' she said in a desperately small voice.

'Indeed, so do I,' Ian gritted drily. 'Or I might be forced to remain here the night.'

'Oh, you won't,' Clayton promised silkily. 'Whatever the weather, I'll get you home. You've no fears on that score.'

The two men exchanged a combatant stare before Ian turned away.

Ruth glowered at Ian. The doctor seemed determined to make a show of his bad humour rather than act courteously until the viscount and viscountess returned and he might properly take his leave. In answer to Ruth's prayers, Gavin and Sarah appeared, arm in arm.

'Um…dinner is still quite presentable,' Gavin announced, having sensed at once that the crackle in the atmosphere hadn't dispersed in his absence. When the doctor made no move to take his leave at that hint and remained looking dour, Gavin added, 'Are you sure you won't stay and dine with us, Dr Bryant?'

'I thank you, but no,' Ian retorted. His eyes quit Ruth and returned to the glass that rocked in his palm. He swiftly despatched what remained in it and put down the empty vessel.

Clayton mirrored the movement, returning his own glass to the sideboard. 'I'll have the carriage brought round,' he said.

Having firmly quashed Gavin's protests that it was his turn to go out, Clayton opened the door, allowing the doctor to go before him into the hallway. 'Don't wait longer for dinner on my account. I can get something to eat at the Red Lion tonight, and a bed too,' he said. 'I insist, Sarah,' he stated softly to his hostess, for she looked appalled at the very idea of him taking bed and board in a tavern. 'The roads might be yet worse to travel on. In any case, it will be well past midnight by the time I reach Willowdene and into the wee small hours before I again reached the Manor.'

Sarah nodded a reluctant acceptance of his logic. She prayed that they would safely reach town; it was silly to expect Clayton to turn about and return in the dark over treacherous terrain.

Clayton's eyes slid to Ruth, tangled with her solemn sepia gaze. 'I bid you a goodnight, Mrs Hayden.'

Ruth moistened her lips. She knew very well she wouldn't see him in the morning. He wanted it that way. 'Goodbye, sir,' she replied quietly.

Chapter Nine

'I suppose you will go home, then.'

'You know I must,' Ruth told Sarah with a husky chuckle as she tied her bonnet strings beneath her chin. Her disappointed friend was given a hug as her mouth drooped. 'As soon as the puddles have gone you must come and visit me again.'

They were stationed just outside the great double doors of the Manor, on the top step of a wide flight that flowed gracefully to the gravel drive. Golden warmth played over Ruth's complexion, urging her to turn and squint at the waterlogged landscape. 'I hope there is no bad flooding.' Her earthy eyes soared to the azure heavens. 'But it is a glorious day and I'm sure there will be more fine weather on the way to dry the fields.'

'I thought Clayton might have returned by now,' Sarah said, peering into the distance. 'He knew you would leave today if the conditions improved. I'm surprised he is not here to bid you farewell. I hope he is not planning to abandon us and return home too.'

'I'm sure you and Gavin will find some occupation,' Ruth blurted, unaware of the *double entendre* in her comment. She was simply keen to change the subject, for just a mention of Clayton's name was enough to make her stomach lurch and a wistfulness assail her.

'I suppose we might.' Sarah's saucy smile brightened her countenance. 'Do you think Dr Bryant will visit you soon? Did he hint he might propose again?' she probed earnestly. 'I didn't have a chance to speak to you about it yesterday evening. Despite the crisis with James, I recall thinking I'd never seen a man look so smouldering and smitten. He hardly took his eyes from you and seemed marvellously Byronic in your company.'

'I know,' Ruth said flatly. 'Although I'm not sure I was impressed by his sulking.'

'I can't find fault with him,' Sarah said simply. 'However odd his attitude, he gave James expert treatment. The little love is greatly improved this morning.'

Ruth smiled her agreement. She couldn't deny that Ian was a conscientious doctor. He'd done his professional duty before he allowed his personal feelings to spoil his humour. 'I hope he will *not* arrive today,' she said with quiet vehemence, 'for I am still at a loss as to what to say if he proposes to me again. It's no love match on either side, but I suppose he has proved his worth despite his scowls.' A small sigh escaped Ruth before she continued to voice her uncertainties. 'Of course, he needs a mother for his infant son and perhaps wants one quite soon, before the boy gets much older…'

Sarah took Ruth's hands and gave them a comforting squeeze. Her friend's predicament was an unenviable one, but the conclusion she drew to it must be hers alone. 'I can't help you make up your mind,' she said gently. 'Yet I wish I could, for you were a very great help and a dear friend to me last night.'

Sarah's oblique reference to her baby prompted Ruth to smile. 'And you must give that darling boy a cuddle for me when he wakes.'

'I shall,' Sarah said, then looked past Ruth's shoulder and waved. 'Here is Gavin. He said he'd return from his ride in time to bid you farewell.'

Once the viscount and viscountess were lost to sight and she could no longer wave at them through the carriage window, Ruth settled in to the comfy vehicle and closed her eyes. In her mind reeled unwanted thoughts, the most persistent of which was that she'd wished, since she'd risen that morning and seen the snow had gone and the sun was shining, that the dawn had been kinder and brought with it just one more icy blast to strand her at the Manor.

Clayton wouldn't have reneged on his promise to take her home whatever the weather. He would have come back to carry out the duty. But in the event he'd not needed to return. The day was fine, the roads passable. The viscount's coachmen risked no more personal injury than splashes of mud to their smart uniforms in returning her to Fernlea this afternoon.

Clayton had purposely stayed where he was, in Willowdene's Red Lion tavern, avoiding her...removing his presence from her vicinity...she imagined he might say.

It was a test for her and her pride would not allow her to fail it. He knew, as did she, that if she chose to stay on, she did so because of him, because she wanted to see him again. On almost every occasion that they'd been alone he'd told her he found her attractive, then watched for her reaction and ultimately been amused by her blushes or protests. Yesterday evening, before the drama unfolded, she'd been sure he was about to reach for her to kiss her. At the time she'd felt agitated by his cool audacity; now she felt cheated that they hadn't gained just a few more private minutes together.

There was no longer an available barrier behind which she might conceal and indulge her fascination for him. The way was clear for her to go home, and if she did not, he would think he'd been right about her all along. He'd think she was finally ceding the game, signalling her interest in him and that she was his for the taking.

Ruth lowered her eyes, clasping tight her hands to steel against a tremor of warring emotions that burned her to the core. Despite knowing all of it, and feeling the greatest hussy alive, she was sorely tempted to tell the driver to turn about and take her back.

'Are you to dine with us tonight?'

Having just spent a tedious yet necessary hour with his lawyer in Willowdene, Gavin gratefully slouched in to the battered old armchair in the Red Lion's private parlour. Opposite him sat Clayton, idly flicking over the pages of a newspaper while occasionally prodding the smouldering logs with the toe of a boot.

Clayton folded the paper and let it drop to the rug in the space between them. Gavin picked it up and perused the headlines. Finding nothing worth commenting upon, he discarded it and gazed idly about. Realising his question remained unanswered, he looked at his vacant-eyed friend. Clayton's hands were clasped at the back of his flaxen head and he was gazing into space.

'Did you hear what I said?' Gavin asked, rather miffed that his hospitality was being ignored.

'Sorry…'Clayton murmured and frowned an apology. 'What did you say?'

'You're not still fretting over that silly jade Loretta and her mischief making, are you?' Gavin said derisively.

Clayton grunted a mirthless laugh and, folding forwards, plunged his elbows on his knees and examined his knuckles. He'd forgotten about Loretta and her scheming until Gavin just again brought it to mind. 'No, I'm not thinking about any of that. But I should return to London.'

'Whatever for?' Gavin said. 'There's nothing there that won't wait a few more days. Why not stay in Willowdene a while longer? It's obvious to me you enjoy Ruth's company…'

'And it's obvious to me Mrs Hayden would sooner be in Bryant's company,' Clayton gritted out as he surged to his feet. 'Had you not already told me she'd received a proposal of marriage, I'd have seen the evidence for myself last night when I watched the two of them together. She's not wearing a ring. Is she engaged to him yet?'

That fluent and forthright piece of dialogue brought a surprised smile to Gavin's lips. So…indeed, his friend had not been fretting on Loretta. A different woman entirely was occupying his thoughts.

'I wonder that you didn't ask the doctor outright when you drove him home. You're not usually shy and you've obviously been brooding on it.' At Clayton's scowl, Gavin continued, 'Did Ruth say she was soon to be married?'

'No...but then she wouldn't confide in me anything so private. I'm not sure she trusts me.' It was a spontaneous response and it was a moment or two before Clayton realised it might be untrue. She'd confided something terribly private: that she'd lost a daughter in childbirth. It was hardly something you'd say to a person you didn't trust. But perhaps it had been an aberration due to the drama and emotion of the moment when they were united in acute anxiety over James. No doubt she now considered having mentioned the tragedy at all an embarrassing and regrettable weakness.

'What sort of fellow is he?' Clayton abruptly asked.

'I hardly know him,' Gavin answered truthfully. 'I've spent little time in these parts. Sarah knows Ian Bryant better than I do, for she lived here for several years. I've heard nothing bad, and, if I were to judge him on the way he treated James I'd have to say the doctor's a top fellow.'

Clayton grasped the mantelpiece with long fingers and averted his face from his friend's astute gaze. 'Good...glad to hear it,' he said in a strange voice as he watched smoke curl from the logs. 'She deserves to have such a husband.'

'Indeed she does. But she won't have him.'

'What?' Clayton's face whipped up, revealing eyes that were narrowed and stormy.

'She turned him down,' Gavin explained. 'If you were watching them together I'm surprised you hadn't deduced that for yourself. The atmosphere between them was thick enough to carve up.' Gavin picked up the newspaper again and flicked it open. 'Let's pretend that you did guess about that. I've already told you that I very much like Ruth and I'd hate her to think I've spoken out of turn.' Gavin shot his friend a penetrating look. 'The rest is up to you. It's as much as I'm going to tell you.'

Clayton's face swung back to the fire. 'Thanks…I appreciate knowing it,' he muttered hoarsely.

'But I meant what I said when you first arrived: she's no man's mistress.'

'I thought you weren't going to say anything else on the subject,' Clayton reminded him sarcastically.

'Wouldn't like to see you wasting your time…or your money. Don't bother trying to blind her with expensive trinkets before you leave,' Gavin said smoothly and shook the paper to remove a crease from an amusing article. He drew the paper closer to his face. 'A plain gold band might do it…'

'God's teeth!' Clayton exploded. 'How many times do I have to tell you that I'm not marrying anyone ever again!'

'Why not?' Gavin asked from behind the newsprint.

'Have you forgotten that I once had a wife who made my life hell?' Clayton thundered.

'No, I haven't forgotten,' Gavin returned quietly, 'and unfortunately neither have you.' He returned the paper to the floor and looked Clayton directly in the eye. 'Marrying Priscilla was a grave mistake, I'll grant you. But it's the sort of mistake any man in love might have made. She had the face of an angel, the body of a goddess and aristocratic breeding. How were you to know she had the nature of a harlot?'

'I should've known,' Clayton sneered with savage self-mockery. 'God knows I've had enough dealings with them.'

'And plenty more to come, I suppose,' Gavin suggested. 'As you're so determined not to settle down with a decent woman.'

'I've never said I don't want a decent woman,' Clayton protested.

'I know, but there we have the problem as I see it—if you want a proper lady to act indecently for you, you'll have to marry her.'

'Not necessarily,' Clayton returned mordantly. 'I can think of plenty of reputable ladies who've very much enjoyed my company.'

'And your money,' Gavin reminded him acidly.

'That's perfectly acceptable,' Clayton said with a grin. 'I'm glad when we understand each other too.'

Gavin stared lengthily at him before saying, 'Believe me, you're wasting your time with Ruth. She would never understand you in a million years.'

'All women understand the offer of unlimited luxury and security.'

'I never thought I'd say this, but…at times you can be a callous bastard, my friend.'

'And I never thought I'd say this,' Clayton returned through his teeth, 'but you've turned in to a pious prick since you got married.'

'I'll take it as a compliment,' Gavin replied coolly. 'For God knows if I hadn't married I might have ended up like you—a bitter man who's allowed a disastrous alliance that lasted not even one year to ruin his prospect of having a happy family life.'

'Well, what are you waiting for?' Clayton asked in a deadly soft sneer. 'Why don't you quit my loathsome company and return to your happy family life?'

Gavin pushed himself out of the armchair and stood for a moment facing Clayton. The space between them crackled dangerously with belligerence. 'And what are you going to do?' Gavin jeered. 'Return to London and Loretta?'

'Not yet,' Clayton bit out grimly. 'I'm going to test your theory that not every woman's a harlot at heart.' With that he turned on his heel and, on quitting the room, crashed the door shut behind him.

'What is it, Cissie?' Ruth asked, looking up from the linen she'd been hemming. She'd been home some hours and, while Cissie had flown to and fro from hearth to hearth trying to bring some warmth to the cottage's stone-cold rooms, Ruth had taken on the mending basket that was her servant's usual mid-week task.

Cissie wiped coal dust from her palms on to her crumpled pinafore. 'A gentleman caller, ma'am, and he says not to announce him.' Cissie's voice was low and her eyes slid sideways, indicating that the gentleman was probably within earshot in the hallway.

Ruth looked startled and the colour in her cheeks ebbed away. The conversation she'd had with Sarah earlier came back to haunt her. She'd not heard a knock at the door and she had been primed to listen for it. But surely Ian had not come so soon! It was bad manners indeed not to have allowed her even one day to settle back home before he visited. Yet she had sensed as soon as they met at the Tremaynes' that he wanted to approach her again and would quite quickly do so.

Reading her mistress's confusion in her puckered features, Cissie hissed, 'You wouldn't have heard him arrive, ma'am. He didn't have to knock 'cos the door was open where I was lugging in the scuttle to the front sitting room.'

Ruth nodded her understanding of the situation and stuffed the needles and cottons quickly back in to the workbox on the table. She stood and brushed down her dress, for small, snipped threads littered her plain dark skirt.

So engaged, and conscious of the proximity of her

visitor, she instructed in an underbreath, 'Show him in, please, Cissie. And you may go. Thank you for staying on. I know it is well past the hour you usually return home.'

'I don't mind staying on a bit longer, ma'am...' Cissie began.

Ruth was ruefully sure Cissie meant what she'd said. Cissie was a good girl, but no doubt as eager as the other villagers to discover the likely outcome of the negotiations between the widow and the doctor.

When she'd arrived home earlier that day she'd barely stepped a foot outside the Tremaynes' carriage before having proof that the rumour mill had been grinding in her absence. Two of the village matrons had materialised from nowhere, huddled into their warm woolly shawls. Already aware of Mrs Hayden's acquaintance with the local gentry, they'd given short shrift to the splendid carriage. What had brought Mrs Stern and Mrs Brewer out in the cold was a great desire to know, as they'd not seen her for a while, whether Mrs Hayden had lately been keeping well. Or had she been in need of the doctor...? they'd slyly enquired.

'Are the fires lit? And the cooking range?' Ruth asked in a hushed tone.

Cissie nodded. 'All of 'em got going,' she confirmed. 'I'll fetch him in and be off, then.'

Ruth nodded. As her servant disappeared, she

closed her eyes and drew in a deep calming breath. No amount of stitching and thinking this afternoon had brought her to any definite conclusion on what she must now say. Advantages and disadvantages had refused to stay still for her to weigh them. Her concentration had been hijacked at every turn by memories of another gentleman. Drat the charming rogue!

As she heard the door click shut, she twisted about and what little blood remained in her cheeks fled before returning with a vengeance. The charming rogue she'd been silently cursing was before her in all his sartorial elegance and with a very disturbing glint in his eye.

'Sir Clayton…I…I was not expecting to see *you*…' She lapsed into silence and her small white teeth attacked her lower lip. Her rattled comment had sounded very unwelcoming, the more so because it had been ejected so spontaneously.

'But you were expecting another gentleman to visit?' Clayton suggested in that dry tone of his.

It was obvious he'd guessed the identity of the person to whom he alluded, but Ruth had no intention of confirming his suspicions. 'My maid didn't give the caller's name. She said he wanted it that way.' Inwardly Ruth chided herself for not having prised such a vital fact from Cissie. She'd not done so because she'd immediately jumped to a wrong conclusion—that the caller was Ian Bryant and he'd wanted to remain incognito because he feared being turned away after their run- in yesterday.

'I didn't give her my name,' Clayton said simply as he proceeded further into the room. 'Don't tell her off; she did ask for it.'

'Did you want me to think you were someone else?' Ruth asked, confused.

'No; I thought if you knew it was me you might decide to feel indisposed,' Clayton answered with a quiet truthfulness.

Having digested that, Ruth said, 'I know we've had our differences, sir, but I thought we parted on reasonable terms.' She clasped her hands behind her back, out of sight, for they were visibly quivering. 'Am I to deduce that you've come to say something you believe might give offence?'

'As you say, we parted harmoniously yesterday,' he replied, smoothly sidestepping her question. 'Nevertheless, I'm not certain that you've forgiven me for my brutish behaviour at the Manor.'

'And have you come to repeat such behaviour?' Ruth asked quietly, determined to have her answer. Her earthy brown eyes clung to his in mute appeal as she awaited his response. It was a long time in coming.

A silence had developed between them that seemed heavy with sensual tension. He'd not come closer to touch her; the aura of cold air and cologne that clung to his clothes was only faintly scenting the room. Yet Ruth felt so acutely conscious of his presence that her limbs had weakened and her lips lightly parted in anticipation of him soon plunging his mouth on to hers. As the seconds passed, Ruth finally tore her gaze from his and grew pale.

'I've said before that I want your good opinion. Why would I want to hurt you?' Clayton said gently. Even as he uttered the words he felt the callous bastard that Gavin had named him.

She knew what he wanted. Ruth Hayden was bright as well as beautiful. She was aware that he was here to proposition her and he'd read her reaction to it in her face. Yet she'd allowed him to stay. Not that he'd imagined for one moment that he wouldn't eventually get his way. She'd turn him down, perhaps once or twice. But she'd succumb in the end.

She'd changed out of her silk dress and now was garbed in a plain and serviceable day dress. The room was spartan and cold. She had one servant—a young maid who had hurried off home, leaving her quite alone. She was shabby genteel, eking out a small inheritance that barely covered necessities, and too proud to accept financial aid from her friends. And he knew Gavin, or perhaps Sarah, would have offered it.

He'd had dealings with a lot of widows in just such frugal circumstances…not one of them had blenched and avoided his eye on guessing his purpose in visiting them. Some had turned him down to test his generosity. Ruth would turn him down to test his leniency, and when she found it lacking she'd turn him down again. And then when the enormity of what he was offering her was too great a temptation to resist, she'd acquiesce…unless she decided to settle for Bryant instead. But for some reason Clayton no longer considered the doctor a serious rival.

Once he'd learned that Ruth had rejected the doctor's proposal, the reason for the fellow's sullen disposition had become clearer. Clayton had imagined that a lovers' tiff had been the cause of the tension between them last night. Now he knew that the fellow was unhappy because the attraction between them was one-sided.

Whereas Clayton knew that, wary and disapproving of him as she was, Ruth Hayden found him as fascinating as he found her, and it would take no more than a kiss to know for sure…

Chapter Ten

'Would you like a drink, sir?' Ruth's offer of hospitality sounded stilted to her own ears, thus she strove to be more affable, adding, 'There is a bottle of port in the front sitting room.'

'Do you prefer port to sherry?'

A corner of Ruth's lips twitched and a cluck of her tongue denied any such thing. 'I keep it for visitors, sir.'

'Doctor Bryant?'

'Have you something you wish to ask me about Dr Bryant?' she demanded, faintly annoyed by his indolent hints.

'I've no need to ask about him. I think he proposed and you rejected him. Am I right?'

So…indeed he did not need to ask about her dealings with the doctor. Ruth felt indignation grip her chest. 'Did he tell you that when you took him home yesterday?' she choked out, appalled to think they might have discussed her.

'We shared little conversation on that return trip. Bryant said nothing about you. And neither did I.'

'I don't believe that Sarah would have mentioned I'd received a marriage proposal from him.'

Despite his clash with his friend, Clayton's loyalty to Gavin remained resolute. Besides, Gavin had not betrayed the identity of Ruth's suitor. He'd easily deduced that for himself.

'It wasn't difficult to guess the nature of your relationship. I needed only to watch the two of you together yesterday to form an opinion on it.'

It wasn't the first time this man had rendered Ruth at a loss for a reply. 'How perceptive you are,' she resorted to murmuring.

'And am I right in thinking that you expect Bryant to return to try again?'

'I can't fault your perception, sir, but I think your manners are still lacking,' Ruth breathed. 'What business is it of yours, pray?'

'None, of course,' Clayton said quite impenitently as their eyes held in the muted light. 'Will you accept him next time?'

Ruth made an exasperated little movement. But eventually his silent persistence beat her defences and she gave him a stuttered answer. 'I…I don't know…'

'Why not?'

'Please, sir…' Ruth begged through an ache in her throat.

'Why not?' Clayton persisted in a treacherously appealing way. 'Are you unsure because you know you don't love him?'

'I doubt he loves me either,' Ruth spontaneously returned. Now the admission was out, it seemed she was obliged to say more. 'There is more to it than that,' she carefully explained as her brunette brows drew together in concentration. 'Doctor Bryant is a widower. He has an infant son and wants a mother for his child. But he might choose a woman to fill the role too soon and deprive the boy of parents who feel affection for one another. Ian might yet find someone to love, who loves him. And that would be best,' she ended gruffly. To indicate the matter was most definitely closed she said, 'I shall fetch the port.'

She started for the door, her step faltering when she realised that her rash decision to gain a little respite from his overpowering presence would bring her very close to him. Every fateful pace was taken with her eyes screened behind long dark lashes and as she came within his reach they softly…naturally…fell closed.

One of his hands curved on her arm, turning her so the other might also assist in bringing her against him. Ruth felt honeyed warmth steal into her veins in response to his hard masculine body pressed to the softness of her curves. She was not expecting words from him and he gave none. His face lowered as hers angled up, their mouths meeting in a perfect blend of size and shape.

Clayton felt the pressure of small fingers on his forearms vary in strength as though inwardly she battled between pulling him closer or pushing him away. To help her decide, he kept the kiss sweet and courteous.

In rogue daydreams—that previously had been impatiently ejected from her mind—Ruth had imagined that an infamous womaniser would quite selfishly and swiftly seduce. Sir Clayton Powell was such a man, nobody denied that…not even him. But he was kissing her as though he had endless time to mould her mouth to his and give her innocent pleasure. Ruth had not expected brutality from him, but neither had she anticipated a touch so exquisitely tender that it began to melt her bones. Gently he coaxed her lips apart so his tongue could caress their silky inner plumpness while long fingers splayed beneath the soft curls at her nape to stroke and support.

Ruth's hands crept to his shoulders and anchored there, curving over solid muscles that almost defeated the span of her delicate grip.

With that tacit permission Clayton deepened the kiss, tantalising her tongue with his. He heard her little moan and sensed her opening explicitly for him.

His tongue plunged and retreated in slow erotic rhythm and a hand stroked from her back to her front to enclose a voluptuous breast and graze a nipple into rigidity.

Linking her fingers behind Clayton's neck, Ruth dragged his mouth to bruise hers while her back sensually bowed. The words might have refused to quit her throat, but Clayton understood her desire to have more of his touch.

It wasn't an invitation Clayton was able to resist. With his mouth fused to hers, swiftly, expertly, his fingers worked loose tiny buttons, then slipped inside her bodice. Above her camisole her lush breasts began rising to firmly fill his palms. As his thumbs circled skilfully, he felt her pelvis graze on his and, as he shifted position, her thighs instinctively parted, sweetly accommodating him. Having exposed milky silken skin on a slender shoulder, he slid his mouth to pay homage to it. He felt her become tense with excitement as his lips sought sensitive places and she swayed her head to better enjoy the bliss. Momentarily Clayton stopped the seduction to observe the rapturous expression tautening her features. Her head was back a little, her eyes closed and her mouth visibly pulsing, swollen and scarlet from his assault and still parted in willingness for more.

Yet despite the tormenting thud in his groin and the ache to see naked the superb figure he could feel heating beneath the cambric, a small part of his mind was urging him to let her go.

His courtly strategy had worked better than he'd expected, but instead of being satisfied Clayton felt ashamed. Ruth wanted him as much as he wanted her, he'd proved that to them both. He could take foreplay to a natural conclusion now if he wanted, and there would be no quibbling over whether or not she might agree to be his mistress. The deed would be done and only the delicate issue of money to be broached.

The fact that his powers of calculated seduction hadn't deserted him out in the sticks didn't make Ruth any less fine a person. It made him more egotistical and cruel than he cared to know.

A boast, made in anger, that he could prove Ruth no better, no worse, than any other woman with whom he kept company was troubling him. He could bed her…right now if he chose…his throbbing loins furiously taunted his conscience. But it wouldn't validate his cynicism, remonstrated a niggling voice of reason.

Ruth was the antithesis of the vain, self-centred woman that Loretta and her ilk represented and deserved so much more than he wanted to give her. She deserved what the doctor had offered—a lifetime of respectability and support from a circle of relatives and friends. She'd lost several loved ones in her twenty-eight years, including her baby daughter. She'd known much heartache, yet seemed devoid of self-pity. She was more concerned that a motherless child should feel secure in his parents' love than grasp at security for herself. She was all a woman…a wife…should be. She deserved that happy family life that Gavin had taunted him over.

Through a daze of warm lassitude Ruth sensed he might be withdrawing from her. But she dismissed disappointment, for a vital part of him was irresistibly hot and hard against her yielding belly. A vague sigh escaped her as, far back in her mind, she subdued pride and conscience simply by wallowing in the promise of more wonderful loving from him. A lonely moment later her weighty lids lifted and their eyes merged in sultry passion.

Clayton's gaze roved her rosy face and, as he saw confusion steal to stifle the fire in her eyes, he managed a slight smile. 'I should go,' he said gruffly, while feeling a wretched fool. Women were supposed to tease men and withdraw at a crucial moment, not the other way around. Gently he drew together her bodice and did up a button. He got no further than the first one.

With a stumble in her step, Ruth jerked and spun away from him, her trembling fingers flying over fasteners. 'I shall not fetch the port, then, sir, as you are leaving,' she said in a voice that was shrill, yet cold as ice. 'I know you are able to show yourself out as easily as you found your way in.'

'Ruth...listen to me...' Clayton began, his tense visage pale with guilt and regret. He took a step towards her ramrod-straight back. 'Would you truly have wanted me to continue?'

Ruth swished to face him, then backed up when she saw how close he'd again come to her. 'You were correct, sir, in saying you should go,' she snapped in a voice that sounded suffocated. 'You were correct about something else too—I *am* expecting the doctor to soon call. I shouldn't want him to arrive and find you here. Please leave.'

An involuntary laugh escaped Clayton, but his eyes were as mirthless as the sound. His head tilted back and a grimace of indecision distorted his handsome features.

'It isn't over between us, Ruth.'

It was issued as a soft vibrant promise that sent a tremor to shimmy through Ruth. A tongue flick soothed her swollen lips. 'I must contradict you on that, sir. It is.' A gulp of air and she continued, 'My neighbours are very alert to strangers arriving in the village. Your visit to me will have been noticed. I live alone and should not want to be the butt of salacious gossip, so please don't come here again.'

A fierce defiant stare made Ruth turn her head, then her body away from him. A moment later he turned on his heel. By the door he halted, casting a sideways look at her stiff form. 'I wish you a happy birthday for next week.'

Jolted from her humiliation by the unexpected felicitation, she spun to look at him, but he had gone.

When Ruth heard the front door close, the power in her tight little muscles seemed to ebb away. She crumpled forwards while forcing her hips against the wall for support. Tiny silent sobs jerked her as she fumbled her way to the armchair and fell into its familiar old embrace.

What a fool she'd been! From the moment at Willowdene Manor when Sir Clayton Powell had arrogantly inferred she had an interest in him, she'd vowed never to be a victim to his philandering. Henceforth she'd known that a challenge simmered between them. She'd sensed, too, that he wasn't a man to take defeat well. Deep down she'd known he wouldn't return home before he'd attempted to soothe his masculine conceit and claim victory in their battle of wills. And what an easy triumph it had been! She had possessed no defences, showed no resistance to his subtle assault.

In the most calculated and callous way he had just impressed on her how weak she was. And how unscrupulous! She'd implied she might accept Ian's proposal. Yet the prospect of becoming another man's wife hadn't curbed her wantonness. Her small palms flew to soothe the burn in her cheeks, for she felt utterly ashamed of her behaviour, and of having made Dr Bryant seem ridiculous.

Ruth had guessed that Clayton hadn't warmed to the doctor. And Ian had made it quite apparent that he considered Sir Clayton Powell a reprobate. Had their animosity spurred Clayton to act the predator? Had he gained some perverse satisfaction in discovering that he was able to take what the doctor wanted?

He'd had his answer. She'd revelled in his mesmerising virility. For those few witless minutes that she'd clung slavishly to him, and he had lavished on her his artful lovemaking, she'd felt more vital and attractive than she had in very many years.

What had he felt? Aroused by her female body? Certainly. Bored by the ease with which he'd secured the conquest? The distressing possibility pierced her heart, trapped a little painful noise in her throat. Her small hands scrubbed anew over her scalding cheeks. Swine! she whispered through her teeth before the epithet was ejected too vociferously.

A loud knock at the door brought Ruth immediately to her feet. In an odd way she hoped it was him come back again, because she had much straight in her mind now and she was ready to give vent to it.

'Is anything amiss, Mrs Hayden?' Mrs Brewer asked while Mrs Stern attempted to peer over Ruth's shoulder into the interior of her house.

'All is well, thank you.' Ruth quickly had subdued her dismay at seeing the women and had uttered the reassurance levelly.

Mrs Brewer accepted that with a twitch of a smile. 'It's just that we…' she indicated her friend with a tip of her cap '…believed we heard you shout out and thought, as we'd seen Cissie go off, that somebody else was with you and upsetting you. We came to make sure that you are not in need of anything.'

'I need nothing. Thank you for your concern,' Ruth said and, with a nod, withdrew and shut the door. She leaned back against the wooden panels and stuffed a fist to her mouth, stifling a hysterical giggle from her vigilant neighbours' acute faculties. The women must have been loitering in the lane to pounce as soon as an opportunity presented itself to quiz her over her imposing visitor. The arrival of a gentleman such as Sir Clayton Powell, with his handsome looks and distinct air of affluence, was sure to stir avid curiosity in a backwater such as Fernlea.

Ruth gained no cheer from having had the proof that she'd used a valid excuse to make Clayton go. She'd certainly given the gossips something to tattle about.

She heard the gate click shut and straightened, stood quite still for a moment as the events of the afternoon ebbed and flowed in her mind. The one that rushed in and stayed to make her eyes prickle once more was that he'd remembered something that she had forgot: next week she had a birthday.

* * *

The following day Clayton was up and about early. He'd enjoyed little sleep overnight, having been plagued by various frustrating discomforts. His unfinished business with Ruth was undoubtedly the most potent of them. But the revelry that had gone on into the small hours, in the private parlour below his chamber, had also kept him restless the night through.

On his return to the Red Lion yesterday the landlady, Mrs Rolley, had immediately accosted him, with much bowing and scraping. Would m'lord be obliging enough to give up the back parlour for one evening so an impromptu wedding party might take place? she'd begged to know. How could he refuse when the young bridegroom had gazed at him with solemn appeal in his bright boy's eyes? That inducement, together with signs of a very distended belly beneath his child-like wife's pretty dress, had disposed Clayton to be charitable.

His weary generosity had extended to the handing over of a banknote to the scrawny youth to wish them both well. Now he had his private domain back, and as he looked about the spick-and-span surfaces, he realised that Mrs Rolley and her maids must have toiled hard and fast to clean it up for him this morning. He took out his watch. It was just after eight o'clock and he had no idea what had prompted him to get up so early, unrefreshed, when a little peace might finally be had in his bedchamber. Now he would have to kick his heels for at least a couple of hours before collecting his belongings from the Manor and setting off back to London. He wanted to be on his way immediately, but it was an ungodly hour to make his farewells. It was equally unthinkable to collect his things and head for London without first thanking Gavin and Sarah for their hospitality.

'Will you be wanting your usual…or somethin' different?'

Clayton turned from contemplation of the cloudless sky to see Molly. She was an impish girl, and this morning her sly saucy comment served only to further irritate him. But he gave the serving maid a half-smile that made her blush. 'Just coffee and toast.'

'What of eggs 'n' bacon 'n' beefsteak 'n' ale?' Molly protested. She knew this fine fellow had eaten his fill of all of that just yesterday breakfast time.

'I'm going out,' Clayton said and turned his head to indicate he was in no mood for banter. In fact, he had enough time to while away to eat a very hearty meal, but had no appetite to do so.

Once Molly had gone, Clayton stood up and strolled to the window. He braced an arm on the timber frame and rested his forehead on it as he watched the ostlers going busily about their work. A few of the wedding guests who had taken rooms were preparing to leave. One of the women turned and waved up at a window just as she was about to clamber aboard her ride. Clayton slanted an idle look in that direction and saw the young bride returning the salute until her husband drew her back from the window and the curtain dropped.

Clayton's mouth tilted wryly. The romantic little tableau reminded him there'd been another reason why he'd got no sleep. The newlyweds had taken the room next to his and the wretched bed squeaked.

Thrusting his hands into his pockets he turned, leaned the back of his head against glass. Finally he allowed his mind to dwell on the real reason for his irascibility. He'd acted the moral martyr yesterday and now regretted it.

He should have ignored his conscience and stayed with Ruth last night. She was a widow approaching her third decade, not a virginal miss just out of the schoolroom. What in damnation did he think he was doing trying to save her from herself…or from him?

She'd rebuffed Bryant's proposal before he'd quit London. He'd not turned up to seduce her and take away her chance of happiness with the doctor. There was nothing for him to feel guilty about on that score.

After his bizarre behaviour yesterday, what did she think of him now? Did she believe he was playing a careless game and had no proper interest in her? He'd never been more deadly serious about bringing a woman under his protection. He wanted to see her wearing velvets and jewels that complemented the rich cocoa colour of her hair and eyes. He wanted her by his side, partnering him at salons and parties. Wryly he acknowledged that, despite that being quite true, his greatest desire was to see her naked next to him in bed.

So what was he to do? Go back and visit her in Fernlea despite her edict that he must never again darken her door? They were the same people; if she allowed him to get close enough to touch her, he could again seduce her.

Clayton's brooding was abruptly curtailed as the door opened and Molly sashayed in with a tray that held a silver coffee pot and a cup and saucer. 'Toast is coming,' she chirruped, as she poured. As she was leaving the room, her exit was blocked by a gentleman about to enter the parlour. 'Shall I fetch another cup?' she asked cheerily on recognising Sir Clayton's friend. A nod from Viscount Tremayne sent the girl on her way.

''Struth! What are you doing here at this time of the morning?'

'Being a good friend…which is more than you deserve,' Gavin grumbled in response. It was his oblique way of clearing the air between them after their heated exchange yesterday.

A bashful grimace and a gruff mutter from Clayton was his acknowledgement that he'd behaved badly. He also gave up the first cup of coffee from the pot.

Gavin fumbled in a pocket of his coat and drew out a letter. 'This arrived for you early this morning. It came express so I guessed it must be urgent and came to find you.'

Clayton took the proffered parchment and looked at it. His name and direction had been written in an unknown hand. Certainly it was not from Loretta. But somebody had taken the trouble to find out from his staff in Belgravia Place where he'd gone when he quit London. He broke the seal and quickly scanned the two paragraphs.

Gavin noticed his friend's expression altering from mild curiosity to contained wrath.

'Bad news?' Gavin ventured quietly.

Clayton wordlessly handed him the letter to read.

'The man's a fool. He can't hit a barn door at five paces.' Gavin gave back the letter and watched Clayton once more frown fiercely at the note from Ralph Pomfrey challenging him to a duel.

'He's an enthusiastic amateur out for my blood and that makes him dangerous,' Clayton said grimly.

Chapter Eleven

'You are off *where*?'

'To town, sweetheart,' Gavin told his stunned wife. 'I shouldn't be gone more than a week.' He pivoted with one boot still planted on the first stair. 'Would you like to come too?'

'No, I would not,' Sarah said crossly. 'This is too bad of you, Gavin. I thought we were to make plans for James's christening. You have not long arrived from London and now you say you want to go back?'

Gavin strode across the hall to cradle his wife's vexed countenance between his palms. 'I must go…I didn't want to worry you with the ins and outs, but…' he sighed in resignation '…Clayton has a bit of a problem to sort out.'

Sarah's jaw dropped and, unmollified, she flicked free of his touch. 'You are not about to tell me that you think Sir Clayton Powell unable to sort out his own problems?' she scoffed.

'He said much the same thing to me when I insisted on going with him.' Gavin's expression sobered. 'He's left for town already and you know I would not go after him unless it were a serious matter.'

'Now you are worrying me, Gavin.' Sarah's brows knitted together. She quickly came close to him and her small fingers gripped his forearm to hurry his answer. 'Has something happened to one of his houses or servants in his absence?'

Gavin drew his wife towards the library; once they were within the room he turned to gaze at her. He didn't relish telling Sarah that Clayton's mistress had stirred up such trouble behind his back that, if not skilfully defused, it might end in blood and crime.

If Pomfrey refused to listen to reason from Clayton or himself, then his friend would be obliged by honour to keep the dawn appointment. And Gavin would stand second for him. In truth, Gavin felt rather guilty for having dismissed Loretta's scheming as unimportant, and for having encouraged Clayton to view it in a similar vein. She'd obviously known exactly how to incite Pomfrey to suicidal recklessness. The note that Clayton had received challenging him to return to town and turn up at the appointed hour had been venomously concise.

If, despite efforts at conciliation, Loretta had done

her work too well and the duel went ahead, the protagonists could end in a courtroom. And that was assuming one or other of them survived. The outcome looked cut and dried—if pistols were used, Pomfrey should miss his target, allowing Clayton to delope. If swords were chosen, Clayton should be able to disarm Pomfrey within minutes. But fate was impossible to predict and accidents happened. A nick from a rapier or a graze from a bullet could be deadlier than it at first seemed if infection set in. There were instances to cite of nice fellows who had allowed a petty grievance to put a premature end to their otherwise healthy and blameless lives.

An impatient sigh from Sarah cut into Gavin's troubled brooding. An anxious, entreating look from her settled the matter. Clayton was a close friend, but Sarah was his wife and no secrets were allowed between them. He told her everything.

'Trollop!' Sarah fumed.

'I know,' Gavin concurred. 'But he will keep company with such people.'

Sarah's eyes narrowed on her husband at the self-mockery in his tone. A few years ago, before they'd met, her beloved husband had kept company with just such people.

'How stupid you gentlemen can be at times! The hussy is not worth taking a small scratch for! Go at once! Clayton might be stabbed or shot to death.'

'Unlikely…unless Pomfrey's employed an assassin to impersonate him.' Gavin hoped his light tone might reassure Sarah, for she looked close to tears. He thrust his hands into his pockets and strode away a few paces. 'Pomfrey, the blasted fool, can't use a gun or a sword, whereas Clayton…can,' he concluded with masterly understatement. He thought it unnecessary to add that his friend's military background had furnished him with quite deadly and awe-inspiring combat skills.

'You must start to pack…' Sarah insisted and started urgently towards the exit.

'Will you come and join me later in the week?' Gavin caught at her arm to arrest her mid-flight and gently draw her close. 'Bring whoever you want with you to Lansdowne Crescent. Let's make the most of a bad situation. We haven't spent much time in town during a Season. James is much better, is he not, and up to the journey?'

Sarah nodded while frowning. 'I had wanted to spend some time here with Ruth. I haven't seen her for so long.'

'Why not ask her to accompany you?' Gavin suggested innocently. 'I'm sure she would like a change of scenery and to put a little distance between herself and the doctor.' He added wryly, 'The poor chap looks distinctly lovelorn around her. And she looks a little embarrassed by it.'

'She hasn't completely dismissed the idea of becoming his wife, you know,' Sarah said. 'She simply needs time to weigh it all up. Marrying somebody when no love is present is a decision of great import.'

'Absence, they say, makes the heart grow fonder. If Ian Bryant is right for Ruth, she should know it by the time she returns.' Gavin opened the door for his wife and, arm in arm, they proceeded towards the stairs discussing the good sense in entering matrimony only after much inner debate.

'But *we* didn't,' Sarah pointed out, turning to her husband with a hand on the banisters.

He grinned and touched a kiss to the ivory knuckles he'd brought to his lips. 'Ah...but that was different. I knew straight away we were made for each other...and persuading you of it gave me great pleasure.'

'Well, if you won't come, then I won't go.'

'Don't be silly, Sarah,' Ruth chided as she bobbed little James on her lap. She was rewarded with a grin that displayed two tiny pearls embedded in the baby's bottom gum. Having planted a little kiss on James's silken crown, she said, 'Of course you must go. You will enjoy yourself in town. There is so much to do at this time of the year. The Season is just under way...'

'I shan't go without you,' Sarah declared adamantly. 'I came to Willowdene to spend time with you and I shall. I doubt Gavin will be gone long in any case if I refuse to join him in Lansdowne Crescent.'

Ruth sighed. 'You are doing a fine job of making me feel guilty.'

'Am I?' Sarah enquired brightly before looking chagrined. 'Sorry. It would never have occurred to me to go, but once Gavin had infuriatingly planted the idea in my head, I came to think it a very good suggestion.' She looked appealingly at Ruth. 'I think it would be very good for us both. You might benefit from having a little time away from here in order to think what you must do.'

Ruth continued to thread her fingers through little James's soft locks. She could not deny what Sarah had latterly said was true.

'Have you seen Ian since the night James was ill?'

Ruth shook her head and glanced at Sarah. 'I'm not sure if I am relieved or indignant at his absence.' Her lips slanted ruefully. 'It is simple vanity. I know he ought to transfer his attention to a more appreciative lady…but perhaps not too soon.'

'He will be back,' Sarah declared confidently. 'And it would be as well if you had your reply ready.'

'Indeed it would,' Ruth concurred.

'So it's best to put distance between the two of you till you have quite clear in your mind what you must say,' Sarah said triumphantly.

Ruth chuckled at her friend's tactics. 'I should like to visit London and think it all through while spending more time with you, but it is not practical.'

'Do you mean money?' Sarah asked bluntly.

'In part,' Ruth owned up. 'But it is not just that. It is a long time since I socialised amid the *ton*. I have become quite provincial. Sometimes I think I will end up talking with a pronounced country burr.'

'But mainly you are concerned about stylish dresses and bonnets and all those things we ladies must have if we are not to appear ridiculous out in polite society.'

'Yes,' Ruth said simply. It was crystallised truth. It did prick at her pride that she might be considered some quaint yokel visiting the metropolis with her fashionable friends. 'Why has Gavin gone so suddenly?' Ruth asked, for she sensed Sarah was about to offer to provide her with everything she might need for a sojourn in Mayfair. 'Why did you not travel together?'

'Oh, Clayton has a crisis in his life and has gone already back to London. Gavin insists he must also go to be of assistance.'

'Crisis?' Ruth echoed faintly, the blood seeping from her complexion. It was the first time Clayton's name had cropped up in their conversation, although thoughts and images of him were constantly infiltrating her mind. 'Has a calamity occurred? Is he ill?'

'No…it's a drama of his own making, for if he hadn't got involved with such a woman in the first place…but I shan't bore you with the sordid details.' Sarah abruptly decided to change the subject.

Before he set on the road Gavin had suggested it might be as well to keep Clayton's woes from Ruth. It would solve nothing, he'd said, to worry her with it. If Ruth found out Clayton might soon be embroiled in a great scandal, it was sure to deter her from taking a trip to town. And why should she miss out on the benefits to be had in escaping from Fernlea for a short while?

In fact the opposite was true. Having been quite sure she would remain where she was, Ruth felt a sudden strong compulsion to insist she must accompany Sarah to London.

'Is his wife causing him problems?' Ruth finally asked, her features puckered with tension as she awaited an answer.

'No…not his wife, his mistress,' Sarah admitted on a sigh. Despite Gavin's sensible cautions to keep mum, she would not lie to Ruth when asked a direct question. 'Gavin did not elaborate, but I gather that the hussy has been plotting outrageously to trap Clayton into marrying her while she is still betrothed to another chap. Loretta Vane has put it about that Clayton has browbeaten her into accepting his offer instead.' Sarah grimaced her disgust. 'Her fiancé, Ralph Pomfrey, naturally feels gravely insulted. He's taken it into his head to call Clayton out rather than taking the lying minx to task.'

Ruth shot to her feet, making little James, clasped

in her arms, catch his breath. Swiftly she handed Sarah her son. 'Clayton is to fight a duel?'

'Quite possibly.' Sarah frowned at Ruth's increased pallor and agitated dance on the spot. 'I admit I was fretting too when I first found out. But Gavin assures me that Pomfrey can't shoot straight and is probably hoping the gauntlet won't be picked up. He's a jilted fiancé with ruffled feathers and keener, I'll warrant, to protect his good name than his marriage prospects to such a woman.'

If he'd been unsure how much of Loretta's pernicious mischief had become common knowledge, it took just a couple of seconds to find out. Momentarily Clayton remained standing on the threshold of the Palm House gambling den. A hush rippled away into the room as conversation ceased and gentlemen began turning their faces his way.

Clayton started to stroll into an atmosphere murky with the odour of alcohol and tobacco smoke. He returned greetings from those fellows who offered one. With great ruefulness he noticed that a few acquaintances pretended not to notice him in order to avoid his eye.

A knot of Pomfrey's chums had congregated about a dice table and Clayton started in that direction despite being conscious of their hard stares designed to deter him.

'Is he due here this evening?' Clayton asked bluntly. He'd called at Pomfrey's house and been informed by the man's butler that he was out. In fact, he'd made the trip back and forth to Caledon Street several times over the past days since he'd arrived in town, and always received the same answer from his manservant. Any probing inquiries as to where his master might be found had been met with tight-lipped silence and a shake of the fellow's ancient head.

So far Clayton had kept away from places such as this, knowing that his presence was likely to evoke just such an atmosphere of morbid speculation. The only gentleman with whom he presently wanted to have a conversation on the confounded matter of the looming duel was Pomfrey. And, damn the man, he was nowhere to be found.

He looked from one to the other of the few men grouped by the dice table. Christopher Perkins and his younger brother John shuffled their feet before striking up an urgent whispered conversation about a sick relative.

Claude Potts was not a good friend of Pomfrey's. He was not a good friend of anybody's. He was the sort of preening dandy who flitted about on the fringes of various circles, but who invariably managed to wriggle into view when a drama was unfolding in order to strut in the limelight.

'You'll see Pomfrey soon enough,' Potts stated

loudly while keeping an eye on his audience. Many gentlemen seemed fascinated enough by the proceedings to have come closer. 'I'll wager a tidy sum it'll be a meeting at dawn light.'

'If you'd kept your mouth shut about the size of the loan you'd made him, it might not have come to this.' Clayton's remark transformed the smirk on Claude's face to ruddy embarrassment. Clayton immediately turned his back on the crushed fellow.

'You've gone too far this time, Powell,' Claude spat. He was furiously aware that the looks directed his way were now derisive. 'You think you can take whatever you want. Loretta Vane might be your mistress, but she was Pomfrey's future wife…'

'And still is, as far as I'm concerned.' Clayton continued to scan the area by the door for new arrivals.

'You're backing down?' Claude barked a jeering laugh and cast about glances that invited support. 'Are you saying you haven't tried to steal her for yourself?'

'Don't need to steal what's freely available,' a gentleman called from the back of the crowd and started in motion a roll of amusement among fellow spectators.

'Freely available?' another wag chipped in mournfully. 'I think not. The lady cost me a small fortune.'

'And went on her way when you were on your uppers,' was added by another fellow with comical sympathy in his voice.

'And now Pomfrey knows all about how that feels…' a different voice added mockingly. The general air of jollity faded a little. The gentlemen present were again aware that this was no laughing matter; it could be deadly serious.

Clayton started towards the door. He had no reason to protect Loretta's reputation; she'd blatantly lied and schemed in trying to trap him into marrying her. But he was a gentleman and as such not about to be drawn into contributing to the attack on her character, much as he might have liked to do so. Ruefully he realised that his reticence wasn't all noble in cause; he was cast in no better light than were the other gentlemen here who'd fallen foul of her grasping, mendacious nature. He'd known Lady Loretta Vane's reputation when he took her on, yet had succumbed to her seduction and kept her in style for the basest of reasons.

'Everybody knows Loretta's lying.' Clayton's friend, Keith Storey, had moved from the Palm House and into the street with him. They stopped beneath a gas lamp. 'I suspect Pomfrey does too, in his heart. Nobody has seen him for days. I'll wager he's already regretting his action.'

Clayton gave Keith a faint smile in appreciation of his support.

'He's been put in a damned awkward situation,'

Keith continued. 'Trouble is, I don't feel much sympathy for Pomfrey and nor does anybody else. The blockhead should never have proposed to the golddigger in the first place. It was obvious her sights were still set on you.' Keith blew out his lips, shook his head in dismay. 'As soon as it got around his pockets were to let, it was obvious it would end badly.'

Clayton grimaced agreement.

'You know I'll stand second for you if it comes to that.' Keith gripped Clayton's arm to reinforce his sincerity.

'I'm hoping it won't come to that,' Clayton returned quietly and, having clasped Keith by the shoulder to show his appreciation of the fellow's offer, turned and strode towards his carriage. About to climb in, he turned back. Keith was where he'd left him at the entrance to the Palm House.

A few slow steps brought Clayton back towards him. Even with the duel imminent, he couldn't quite banish Ruth from his thoughts.

'I believe you know Mrs Hayden. I made her acquaintance through the Tremaynes. She tells me she used to live with her parents in Willoughby Street and you and your family were neighbours.'

Keith frowned, tested the name in a murmur.

'Ruth Hayden…' Clayton said to jog his memory.

'Ah…Ruth Hayden, *née* Sanderson…' Keith's face split into a grin. 'Lovely girl. If that Hayden chap hadn't got to her first, I might have proposed to her myself.'

'Do you know she's now widowed?'

Keith nodded, his face grim. 'Poor little Ruth couldn't have been more than nineteen when her husband was shot. It broke her parents, you know, the scandal. By then they'd moved away from Willoughby Street and gone to live in the country.'

'Scandal?' Clayton echoed. 'He was killed in the war, surely?'

Keith nodded. 'He was shot during the war right enough, but not by the enemy. I knew Paul Hayden and a fellow less like a coward I can't imagine.'

'He was court-martialled?' Clayton sounded incredulous.

'I suppose it won't hurt to repeat the tale. It was a long time ago and the subject of gossip for a while. Captain Paul Hayden was executed for desertion from the army. It was in Belgium…1815. Ruth was there with him and heavily pregnant. He was named a coward for absconding to see her when she was gravely ill in childbed and expected to die with the baby inside her. She survived, but their baby was lost.' Keith shook his head. 'In my opinion, Paul had no choice but to do what he did. She was close by…too close perhaps. Had she been safe in England perhaps he'd still be alive. But as far as I see it, he had no choice but to go to her. It might have been the last opportunity he'd have to see his wife alive. I know what decision I'd have made in those circumstances.'

Clayton's shock kept him momentarily speechless. 'What of her husband's family? Did they not help her?' Clayton already knew the answer to that question. Colonel Hayden had not been rich, but when Clayton knew him he'd lived comfortably. It seemed none of that comfort was bestowed on his daughter-in-law. Ruth looked to be struggling to make ends meet.

'Disgraceful behaviour, in my opinion,' Keith muttered. 'The Haydens blamed her. They thought she'd sent a message to Paul demanding he come to her on the eve of battle. They continued to believe it even after one of Ruth's servants owned up to contacting Paul behind Ruth's back.'

'The Haydens will have nothing to do with her?' Clayton asked quietly.

'Nothing! The family disowned her…banished her as though she'd perished along with their son and grandchild. Disgraceful behaviour…' Keith repeated with quiet vehemence.

Chapter Twelve

On arriving back at Belgravia Place at close to ten o'clock in the evening, Clayton was informed sternly by Hughes that his best friend had called this afternoon three times in three hours. He learned too that the viscount had again come and gone just a short while since and on this occasion left a note. The disapproving droop to Hughes's clamped lips once they'd imparted the news caused Clayton to comprehend that his old retainer was feeling far from pleased at repeatedly having to tell Gavin that he was out and no message was to be had.

Clayton knew that over the past couple of days Gavin had called on him a total of nine times. He'd been actively avoiding his friend, and quite successfully, as he'd been out from dawn till dusk seeking somebody with the same zeal that Gavin was pursuing him. Clayton was quite relieved that no chance meeting had taken place between him and Gavin at one of their clubs.

Under normal circumstances Clayton would have been pleased to see his friend and would have paid Gavin an immediate return call. But circumstances were far from normal. Gavin sought to urgently confront him about the confounded mess in which he was now mired in order to insist he take up his offer of support. Knowing he had such a loyal and tenacious friend made Clayton feel humble…and guilty. But still he had no plans to go to Gavin's town house in Lansdowne Crescent and make his apologies for having been oddly aloof. The next time he saw Gavin, he intended to confidently declare his friend's assistance to be unnecessary. In short, Clayton wanted to resolve the problem between him and Pomfrey as soon as possible and without Gavin having been involved in it.

Gavin Stone was no longer a carefree bachelor. He was newly a peer of the realm and a doting husband and father. He had commitments and responsibilities that were too precious to be risked on the paltry altar of Loretta Vane's spite…or his regrettable lechery. For, no doubt about it, Clayton knew that he was partly to blame for the sorry situation in which he found himself.

Aware that Hughes was still waiting for him to take

the letter from the silver salver, Clayton obligingly picked it up and broke the seal. He scanned the parchment and his mouth formed a soundless laugh at the few sarcastic sentences that expressed—between expletives—Gavin's resentment at being ignored.

Having handed Hughes his coat, he gave the servant a conciliatory look before striding on towards his study.

Hughes was not mollified by half a smile. 'What shall I tell the viscount when he comes tomorrow, Sir Clayton?' he peevishly insisted on knowing.

'Tell him I'll soon go and see him,' Clayton sent back over a shoulder as he continued to cover the marble in long strides.

Once inside his cosy den, he headed towards the fire and warmed his palms on the yellow glow. He placed Gavin's note on the mantelpiece, then lifted his eyes to the huge gilt-framed mirror that soared above it. Solemnly he scrutinised his reflection until his lashes lowered, shielding eyes darkened by self-disgust.

He found the decanter and glass on the desk and poured a measure while trying to concentrate on places to go tomorrow in his search for Pomfrey. When that didn't work and his mind stubbornly strayed, he considered the thankless sacrifice Gavin had made in leaving his wife and son—a baby who had been so recently ill—to make the journey back to town to stand by his side. But pondering on the Tremaynes inevitably led him to reminisce on his recent stay in Willowdene and in turn that brought his thoughts circling back to Ruth. And try as he might, he could not find the energy to again wrestle free of the gentle memory of her.

What he had learned from Keith Storey about her husband's tragic execution, and her unfair ostracism by his family, had only served to make his present predicament seem yet more squalid and contemptible. Captain Paul Hayden had died for love of his wife and unborn child. Clayton could think of no more honourable death for a gentleman. Soon…this very week perhaps…he might risk his life…or take a life…and for what? The answer caused a nauseating sense of shame to sour his stomach. He'd become bewitched by Loretta's artful tricks. He'd known before he took her on that she was rumoured to be a sly wanton. As soon as she became his paramour, he knew it to be true and had mixed feelings about her. Her sensuality he encouraged, her lies repelled him. What Loretta had failed to grasp was that he gave little heed to her overspent allowance or her dalliances with gallants. He had money enough to be generous; he didn't care enough to be jealous. She'd had no need to constantly dissemble.

What he'd failed to grasp was that her deceit might very soon outweigh her allure. And he should have known it straight away. Her calculating nature should have prevented him getting involved with her at all. Lord knew he'd had experience of such a woman. He'd fought a duel over a mendacious harlot before. On that occasion she'd just happened to be his wife. Priscilla Winslow had been Loretta's equal in perfidiousness, if superior in looks and pedigree.

When he'd met Count Giovanni Montesso on Wimbledon Common the swordplay had been savage. He'd won, but not easily, and he had the physical scars as a lasting reminder of the ordeal that preceded his divorce. But he'd allowed the Italian to keep his life and his wife, much to Priscilla's indignation. The outcome of the fight and his unshakeable determination to divorce her had seemed to make him once again desirable in her eyes. But it was too late. After enduring ten months of pain and humiliation during which he had been constantly mocked by his wife and some of his peers as a cuckold, he felt nothing for her or her parade of lovers. When she left for the Continent with the count, he could not stir from apathy to even feel relief. It had been a wretched *mésalliance* from the start but, at a tender twenty-two years of age, he'd thought he was in love and ready to be a husband. No such tender emotion or honourable intent had been present in his liaison with Loretta. Now he pondered on it, he wasn't sure he had ever even liked her.

Clayton tipped back his head and sank what

remained in his glass. There was no satisfaction in knowing that he seemed able to detach his heart and mind so easily from his nether regions.

Ruth's exquisite countenance flitted unbidden into his mind and a moment of quiet heart-stopping insight presented itself. With his breath wedged in his throat and a whisky tumbler in a fist frozen in mid-air, he finally understood why he'd let her go when every part of his being had been urging him to stay and properly make love to her. His eyes closed and his irritation melted as he revelled in the phantom feel of her mouth merging with his, of the instinctive response of her warm flesh filling his hands. He could sense the soft silky texture of her luxuriant hair passing through his fingers, see velvet brown eyes sultry with desire… wanting him.

A tortured oath tore from his lips and was sent flying at the ceiling. He thumped his empty glass down on his desk before wheeling away to the fire. Double-handed, he gripped at the mantelshelf and dropped his head between rigid arms. For some minutes he remained in that stance, corded muscle in his shoulders visibly bunched beneath the fine cloth of his jacket. His breathing was as laboured as that of a man who had sprinted some distance.

In his absence she might accept Bryant, she might give her word…and never would she break that pledge, no matter what was offered in exchange. She was a woman of pure integrity and what grotesque an irony it would be if he returned to Willowdene to tell her how he felt about her only to find he was too late. For he'd willingly fight to the bitter end for her if need be. He'd meet the doctor tomorrow and honour and principle be damned if it meant having the woman he loved.

With a vicious shove he sent himself away from the fire and to an upright position. His fiery eyes were raised to the mirror and he twisted an acrid little smile. 'Are you ready to risk taking on the role of lovestruck lapdog again? Are you?' he taunted his reflection.

'Did you see him this time?' That breathless query was launched at Gavin as he strode into the blue salon in Lansdowne Crescent. Sarah had jumped to her feet and rushed towards her husband. Moments before she and Ruth had been idly playing a game of cards while awaiting Gavin's return from Belgravia Place with, they'd hoped, some news of Clayton's predicament.

'He was from home...or so Hughes said.' Gavin's features displayed his displeasure. 'When I catch up with him, he'll have some explaining to do. I've left messages for him to contact me at the clubs, too. I missed bumping into him by mere minutes in St James's, so I was told. Keith Storey has spoken to him and knows he is after Pomfrey.'

'Is he *deliberately* avoiding you, do you think? Why

would he do that?' Sarah had guessed what annoyed her husband and given voice to it. She turned her frowning countenance to Ruth to include her in this dialogue.

Ruth had been sitting listening earnestly to the exchange between husband and wife. Now she got to her feet and quickly approached. 'Has the duel gone ahead, do you think? Is Sir Clayton injured?' Her train of thought sped on into terrifying territory. 'If he is recovering at home, perhaps his butler has been instructed to keep secret his whereabouts as it is so grave and delicate a matter—'

'It hasn't yet gone ahead, you may rest easy on that score,' Gavin gently interrupted. He'd divined the agitation Ruth was striving to keep hidden behind a calm façade. He gained some contentment from knowing that Ruth appeared to be as captivated by Clayton as he was with her. There was obviously a bond between them, even if neither of them presently acknowledged its existence. Despite that small positive, his scowl had soon returned. He was not amused by Clayton's Scarlet Pimpernel act.

'Perhaps Clayton can't find Pomfrey because the man's come to his senses and is ashamed to show his face.' Sarah coupled an optimistic look with that observation.

'Perhaps,' Gavin agreed kindly. 'But now the matter is common knowledge, both gentlemen have their good names to consider.'

'I wish Pomfrey would withdraw.' The vehement plea broke from Ruth unbidden. A faint bloom lit her complexion as she realised that the phrase that had been rotating furiously in her head had actually escaped her lips.

'And so do I wish it,' Sarah declared helpfully.

Ruth returned to her chair and sat down, allowing a conversation between husband and wife to continue. She was obliquely aware of the gist of what was being said, but actual words washed over her. She'd heard all she needed to. There was no news of Clayton and, despite Gavin's reassurance that the duel hadn't yet taken place, a sense of dread had constricted her chest. She could no longer ignore the reason for her distress or her abrupt change of mind about coming to town.

She cared for Clayton...deeply...and wanted desperately to know he was safe. The thought of him mortally injured, or hurt in any way, made her whole being shiver and ache. Even the memory of their final, frosty parting, of his rejection of her, couldn't prick her pride into subduing her anxiety for his health and safety.

Besides, she'd had time since that fateful afternoon to see the incident more clearly rather than viewed through a veil of excruciating humiliation.

Would you truly have wanted me to continue? he'd asked when putting her clinging, willing body away from his. Yes...she had almost cried...*please*...had teetered on her lips as they'd pulsated still from his passionate kisses. In her mortification she'd believed he'd stopped because he was cruelly toying with her. But had she too quickly thought ill of him?

He was an urbane gentleman, but no doubt conscious that people were the same in town and country and loved to gossip. Had he simply kept a firmer grasp on his self-control than she'd managed to exert over her own senses? Had he, far from being cruel, been kind in attempting to protect her reputation? He was a stranger—a gentleman of obvious wealth and position—and the reason for his lengthy visit would have been obvious had he been spotted emerging from her cottage some hours after dark.

I would have risked further ostracism for him...I wish I had made him stay...I might not see him again to tell him so... The wild thoughts spun crazily in her mind until she whipped up a cool hand to soothe a burning cheek.

'Perhaps Pomfrey is hiding beneath the skirts of the trollop who started this nonsense in the first place,' Sarah stated pithily, focusing Ruth's attention on her.

'I think we have spent enough time and emotion on this matter.' Gavin took one of his wife's expressive hands and gave it a calming pat. 'If Clayton prefers to deal alone with this affair, then so be it. If he wants me, he knows where I'm to be found.' He gave Sarah a smile. 'We said, did we not, that if you joined me in town—and how very glad I am that you did—that we would make the best of a bad situation. It is time we enjoyed ourselves. Keith Storey has invited us to his home. He and his wife are holding a *musicale*. I think we should go and perhaps accept one or two of the other invitations we've received.'

'I wondered when you'd turn up.'

The Honourable Ralph Pomfrey halted just inside his mother's back parlour with his jaw lengthening towards his chest. He had journeyed through the night to reach Elkington Tower's Dower House in Sussex and had hoped to delightfully surprise his mama with his unsolicited visit. 'You were expecting me, ma'am?' he said, a trifle crestfallen.

'Of course I was expecting you,' she returned rather testily. 'Your brother wrote me a note to let me know of the shenanigans you've started in town.' Yvonne Pomfrey, Dowager Countess of Elkington, cast her knitting into her lap and sent her youngest son a beady look. 'It's all a ruse, isn't it? How much did you have to pay him?'

Ralph trudged closer, stooping to give his mother's withered cheek a peck. As he straightened he said, perplexed, 'How much did I pay Gerald? Why, nothing at all. I know we don't get on, but if he's intending to bill me for sending a note maligning me to me own mother, he can whistle for the expense of it.'

A raucous cackle burst through the old lady's desiccated lips. 'He would try that, too, if he thought he might get away with it,' she agreed. 'Gerald never writes to me on his own account, only ever to damage you.' She frowned, scouring her muddled mind for the gist of their conversation before being diverted to comment on Gerald Pomfrey's malice and meanness. 'I didn't mean him. Talk of a duel's a bluff, isn't it? How much did you pay Sir Clayton Powell to take that vixen off your hands? Clever move, m'boy…I'm impressed.' She endorsed her praise with a gap-toothed grin. 'Didn't think you had it in you. 'Course, if you'd given heed to my good advice, you'd have got yourself unhooked from that Vane woman months ago.'

Ralph coloured slightly. 'You're quite wrong on that head, Mama. I'm most put out that the cad has seen fit to steal Loretta away from me.'

'Fiddlesticks!' the old lady snapped. 'You're nothing of the sort if the truth be known. It's plain as the nose on your face that she's concocted the whole thing so she can drop you now you've no money.'

Her son's pink complexion took on a more fiery hue. It was the first time he'd heard anyone actually put into words what the whole *ton* was thinking and whispering behind his back.

'No good looking so sorry for yourself, m'boy,' the dowager said. 'You've come here for some straight talking and that's what you'll get. Now you've sobered up, you expect me to tell you how you may wriggle your way out of the hole you're in.'

'I want no such thing,' Ralph spluttered, unconvincingly.

'But you *were* drunk or in her bed when you agreed to this lunacy of calling out Sir Clayton?'

Ralph choked and his mouth worked for a moment like a beached fish. He'd learned over the years to remain impassive when confronted by his mother's forthright ways. What disconcerted him was that she'd guessed correctly...on both counts...the origins of the challenge he'd stupidly issued. The note to Clayton had been composed in a haze of champagne while he lay propped up on Loretta's perfumed pillows. The lady herself had been stretched out naked beside him and, from time to time, giving him just the encouragement he needed to keep going when reason penetrated the fog in his brain.

'I see,' his mother said in a dry tone of voice that told him she did indeed see only too well. And hardly surprising, was it, that she knew what power an attractive woman could wield. In her heyday she'd been a beauty and a duke's mistress. But Yvonne had never lost sight of her duty to her husband, the Earl of Elkington. She picked up her knitting. 'What's brought you here, then? The cost of your funeral?'

Ralph swallowed audibly and the blood suffusing his face drained away. 'I've a fair chance of winning. I've been practising at the range,' he croaked.

The dowager snorted and then cursed as she dropped a stitch. She fumbled with wool and needles, picking and poking at the shapeless mass as she said, 'If you're lucky, Sir Clayton will wing you. If you're not and he's fired up enough over this to feel mean...' She cocked a dark eye up at her son. 'You'd better hope he's not...'

'I should have called him to account months ago, when our betrothal was announced,' Ralph blustered. 'The man's a scoundrel to carry on with another fellow's fiancée.'

'He was carrying on with her before you proposed, and you knew it,' the dowager returned. 'Were you drunk and in her bed that time too?'

This time the dowager took pity on her blushing, gulping offspring. She dragged her knitting from her lap to eye it grimly, then cast it on to the floor. 'Call Simmons, will you?' She pulled her shawl about her. 'Now you're here I suppose we ought to have some tea. Are you staying long?' The tone of her voice indicated she hoped to hear a negative. 'I suppose you will.' She sighed. 'No doubt you'll be under my feet until the day of the duel's come and gone. Your father would be most upset to know you've skulked away from a fight. But I understand. What else can you do if you've a mind to see thirty?'

'I shall turn up for it,' Pomfrey squeaked in a way that made his mother scowl.

'Bloodbath,' she spat. 'You could pay him to take her off your hands,' she suddenly said with a wag of a bony digit. 'I'd stump up the necessary for that.'

It was Ralph's turn to snort derisively. 'Have you no idea just how much the infernal Powell estate is worth?'

'Of course I have,' the dowager shot back. 'But he might be in need of betting chips. A million in the bank don't mean it's there to be used. Sir Clayton might be glad of a bit of blunt.'

Ralph cast a jaundiced eye on his mother, then at her faded surroundings. She meant it too. She might not have a million, but she had funds tied up in stocks and bonds and property and no intention of letting go of one halfpenny of it.

With her gnarled fingers on the chair arms, the old lady levered herself upright. She came towards her son in a slow swinging gait and, on passing, patted his arm. 'All I can say, m'boy, is you'd best contact Sir Clayton as soon as may be and make your excuses. After that, you'd best see that scheming trollop and do likewise.'

Clayton strode the length of the cold spartan hallway, then turned and retraced his steps. He felt inclined to rub together his palms so chilly was the atmosphere, yet outside the spring day was bright and sunny. The butler approached again. 'You may wait for the Earl in the small saloon, Sir Clayton,' he said solicitously. 'There is a small fire…'

'Thank you, but no,' Clayton returned. 'My business will not take long.'

The butler withdrew at the same moment Gerald Pomfrey, Earl of Elkington, hove into view. 'Did the old cove not offer you a warmer spot to kick your heels, Powell?' he inquired jovially.

Clayton gave the man a thin smile. He was aware, as was the whole of the *ton*, that the Earl was a miser. He doubted that there was a warm spot in the whole of the house. 'He was most attentive,' he said shortly. 'I cannot stop long and apologise for calling unexpectedly. I simply want to know if you are aware of your brother's whereabouts.' Clayton had not approached this man sooner for news of Pomfrey as he was aware, as was the whole *ton*, that the only connection between Gerald and Ralph Pomfrey was an enduring hatred. But time was fast disappearing and he was now scraping the barrel and desperate for some information as to where Ralph might be found.

Gerald snorted a laugh. 'He don't keep me informed of his movements. Haven't seen the snivelling wretch for six months. Haven't spoken to him for six years.'

Clayton gave a curt nod that incorporated his thanks and his farewell and turned for the exit.

The butler sprang with surprising agility from the shadows to the door.

'But I know where he's sure to be.'

Clayton swung back and frowned fiercely at the Earl's smug expression.

'He'll be where every blue-eyed boy is to be found when he's in bad trouble. He's sure to be in Sussex, hiding beneath his dear mama's skirts.'

Chapter Thirteen

'Mrs Hayden!'

On hearing that enthusiastic greeting Ruth turned about and her eyes flitted over unfamiliar faces before settling on one. A rush of recognition put a smile on her lips and a becoming blush in her cheeks.

A short while ago she had entered an elegant town house in Berkeley Square to enjoy Mr. and Mrs Storeys' *musicale*. Gavin, ever the perfect escort, had treated Ruth to the same solicitous courtesy as he did his wife. As soon as they'd alighted from his sleek dress coach he had tucked her hand on to his sleeve and, with Sarah similarly positioned on his other side, they'd ascended together the grand sweep of steps that led to their hosts' mansion.

Many eyes had followed the progress of the attractive trio. Ruth's rich dark beauty was in startling contrast to Sarah's fair loveliness and, of course, the distinguished gentleman between them had long set ladies swooning with his easy charm.

Once mingling with the other guests in the first-floor drawing room, Gavin and Sarah had been at subtle pains to introduce Ruth to some of their friends and include her in their conversations. Ruth had moments ago exchanged cordialities with the Earl and Countess of Morganston who had an estate close to Tremayne Park in Surrey. The Countess had a little girl who was about the same age as James and, as the conversation had turned to the wonder and worry of babies, Ruth had given the new mothers a fond smile and taken a step away to glance appreciatively at her opulent surroundings.

Now, having been spotted by her host and feeling quite overwhelmed by the genuine pleasure lighting Keith's eyes, Ruth gladly went to meet him. Oddly she'd recognised her childhood friend straight away despite the fact that almost a decade had passed since they'd last spoken. His chestnut hair was now shorter and neater than it had been when he was a gangly youth, but his hazel eyes and bluff friendliness were exactly as she remembered.

Keith Storey held out his hands and as Ruth's fingers touched his they were enclosed in a warm firm grasp. 'Mr. Storey indeed!' he gently mocked her formal address, then raised her small digits to his lips.

'It has been far too long since we had an opportunity to chat, but I would have recognised you anywhere. You look no different, you know, than you did at eighteen…just as captivating. And I recall clearly that you and I used the names Keith and Ruth in those days.' A chuckle burst from him as a fond memory surfaced in his mind. 'Do you recall what horrors we could be? I shall never forget the late summer afternoons we spent scrumping apples in the vicar's orchard. And that scoundrel of a cousin of yours would come with us sometimes. What was his name now…?' He frowned, private laughter still curving his mouth as he revelled in the reminiscence.

'Jake…' Ruth supplied with a faraway look as momentarily she wallowed in those carefree times. She bucked up to say, 'But hush, sir. No mention, please, of my hoydenish ways in such fine company. You will have your guests think me incorrigibly wayward.' Her humour faded. Of course, there was a far greater scandal in her past to be uncovered than her tomboy antics, and Ruth wondered who here might already know of it. She was sure Keith must be aware that her husband had been executed, leaving her stranded in the shadow of his undeserved disgrace. Her parents had recently resided in Willoughby Road at the time of the horrible episode and had been friendly with Keith's parents.

'I was so very sorry to hear about the death of your

husband,' Keith said gently, correctly interpreting her slight withdrawal. 'And I believe your cousin, Jake, also did not come home from the war. I heard that your aunt and uncle moved to the Continent and now live close to where their son perished.'

Ruth gave a single nod, a ghost of a smile. 'It was a harsh unforgiving time…for so many people…for so many reasons… You have a very fine house.' She immediately launched into that gruff observation as emotion thickened her throat. 'You have done very nicely since you left Willoughby Road and got married…' Ruth frowned her regret. In her eagerness to talk about something more cheerful and less sensitive, she'd been very tactless and very insensitive. And she felt dreadfully churlish about that, considering Keith's kindness to her.

On the way to Berkeley Square this evening Gavin had told his wife and Ruth a little about the couple they were visiting. They'd learned that Keith Storey had married Susannah Vincent, an heiress who was also a baron's daughter. Keith had greatly prospered by the match, Gavin had said, and the couple were considered by polite society to be extremely popular people. It was from that recalled dialogue that her blurted reference to Keith's advantageous marriage had originated.

'That…that didn't sound as I meant it to…' Ruth stuttered apologetically and put a gloved hand to one of her tingling cheeks to shield her chagrin.

'I have indeed done very well for myself, Ruth.' Keith inclined a little towards her to add gently, 'And I'm always the first to admit it. Every day I give thanks for my good fortune…twice…because Susannah not only brought me great riches, but great happiness too. I shall not be a hypocrite and say we would be as blissful living in a hovel as we are in this fine mansion. Of course we would not. But my wife is the sweetest soul imaginable and I doubt I would have resisted her if she hadn't two ha'pennies to rub together. I love her dearly, you see.'

'Then you are, indeed, a very lucky gentleman,' Ruth said, adopting his wry tone.

'I should like to introduce you to Susannah. Might I steal you from your friends for a while? I believe Susannah is in the music room.

'I understand we have a mutual acquaintance,' Keith said as they strolled.

Ruth slanted up at him an enquiring look.

'Sir Clayton Powell,' Keith concisely informed her. 'I saw him recently. He told me he'd been staying with the Tremaynes and said he'd seen you.'

Ruth felt her stomach somersault at the mention of the gentleman who, even on a diverting occasion such as this, was continually disturbing her thoughts. 'I…yes…we both are very good friends of the Tremaynes and recently were their house guests at Willowdene Manor. I live close by, but the bad snowfall left us stranded at the Manor for some days.' With barely a pause Ruth asked, 'Do you know where he is?'

'Sir Clayton? I imagine he is still stalking Pomfrey in the hope of talking some sense into the chump.' Keith cleared his throat. It was not the done thing to talk to ladies—other than perhaps one's wife—about a delicate issue such as a duel, especially when a scheming trollop was the cause of the dispute. 'Ah…here she is,' Keith said quickly and with some relief as he spotted his spouse. He speedily introduced the ladies.

Susannah Storey was a petite redhead who warmly welcomed Ruth to her home and seemed genuinely engrossed when her husband launched again into an animated reminiscence about his and Ruth's escapades in Willoughby Road. Susannah's lively green eyes crinkled with genuine amusement as she heard about the plunder of the vicar's fruit.

'We had a huge old apple tree in York,' she interjected in to the conversation. 'Our head gardener made us a wonderful swing. As children we would have fine times and Mama says that it is as sturdy today as it was fifteen years ago…' Susannah's anecdote trailed away and a perplexed look creased her brow. A moment later her expression had hardened to encompass shock and annoyance.

Keith, disturbed by the change in his wife's mood,

immediately cast a look in the same direction as Susannah was gazing. His subsequent consternation mirrored that of his wife.

'What in…!' The rest of the expletive was hastily muffled as Keith remembered where he was.

'I'm so sorry, Mrs Hayden.' Susannah gave Ruth an apologetic look. 'You must think us the rudest people to suddenly appear so out of humour. But…' Unable to contain her anger she ended in a suffocated voice, 'I cannot believe that Lord Graves has seen fit to bring that…that dreadful woman to my house after what she has done.'

'The lady was certainly not invited here on her own account,' Keith added grimly.

'Indeed she was not!' his wife endorsed in a forceful mutter. 'Lady Vane has sneaked her way in on the arm of that silly old cove.'

'He meant no harm by it, Susannah,' Keith quietly soothed his vexed spouse. 'Graves's problem is that he sees no harm in anybody, and never has.'

Susannah gave her husband a brief smile and a little nod. She knew, as did everybody acquainted with the elderly widower, that he was kind hearted to a fault and apt to have advantage taken of him because of it.

Even before she'd heard the name of the unwelcome female guest, Ruth had had an inkling of who it could be. She turned her head just a little, not wanting to appear too eager to scrutinise Clayton's mistress, the woman who was trying to trap him into marriage and into fighting a duel over her.

Immediately Ruth noticed that she wasn't the only person taking peeks at the couple just entering the anteroom. Loretta Vane and her elderly escort were certainly arousing a great deal of inquisitiveness and scandalised looks. Once she'd located the object of her curiosity, Ruth found it difficult to tear away her gaze.

Lady Vane might be a shameless minx, but she was also exceedingly beautiful. Her raven hair was styled to one side so that it draped in ringlets to a milky shoulder. A low-cut bodice exposed more pale voluptuous flesh and beneath the diaphanous dress were visible long lissom limbs.

'I'll have a word with Graves.' Keith's features were set in a stony mask. 'The infernal woman could at least have found the manners to dress decently.'

Immediately Susannah put a restraining hand on her husband's arm. 'No…I have a feeling it is what the hussy wants—to cause a stir and be the centre of attention. I'll not allow her to spoil this evening. Just ignore her. Hopefully if she feels the frost in the air she might get him to take her elsewhere.'

As Loretta haughtily tilted her chin and set a contented slant to her rouged lips, Ruth comprehended that Susannah had given her husband wise advice. It seemed it was indeed the widow's intention to draw all eyes as she paraded into the room on the arm of her portly partner. As several of the other guests followed their hosts' suit and turned their backs on the couple, Ruth noticed a perceptible transformation in Loretta's demeanour. Indignation was starting to skew her pretty features.

Having decided on their course of action, Keith and Susannah clung fast to it. They went about the business of encouraging the invited company to be seated to enjoy the evening's entertainment. Solicitously Keith found Ruth a chair situated in a prime spot to enjoy the music.

'I shall reserve these two chairs beside you for the Tremaynes,' he told Ruth and was then off to politely attend to the comfort of others.

A moment or two later Sarah slipped on to the seat next to Ruth. 'Have you seen that baggage?' she hissed to Ruth in a low, scandalised tone. 'Everybody is talking about her. The nerve of the woman, to turn up uninvited knowing that the *ton* is scandalised by the mischief she's concocted.'

A small smile tilted Ruth's lips. 'She *is* very audacious...very pretty, too,' she added ruefully.

'Powder and paint!' Sarah dismissed with uncharacteristic cattishness. 'Whereas you,' she said to Ruth, 'are a most naturally beautiful brunette.'

'Thank you,' Ruth said.

'You're very welcome,' Sarah returned, adopting the same wry tone.

As the company quietened, and the first poignantly sombre notes of a viola trembled in the air, Ruth glanced down at her superb gown. She passed a hand lightly over the lavender-blue satin skirt. She did feel pleased with her appearance this evening and had seen genuine, if platonic, male admiration in Gavin's eyes when he first clapped eyes on her in his hallway earlier that evening.

When Sarah had initially tried to persuade her to accompany them to London, Ruth had felt uncomfortable with the thought of having all necessary garments for the trip donated to her by her friend. But once she'd learned of the severity of Clayton's troubles, any idea of standing on ceremony over it had dispersed. Clayton was in danger of being killed or injured and the thought of quibbling over sensibilities with a friend she loved as deeply as she might have loved a sister seemed ludicrously petty. She simply wanted to go immediately to London and be satisfied he was safe.

Thus Ruth had accepted Sarah's idly presented gifts and loans with muted appreciation so as not to offend, and had arrived in Lansdowne Crescent with several portmanteaux filled with all manner of stylish silk, satin and lace.

Ruth put up her head and listened to the soulful serenade before slanting a glance at Sarah's profile. A quietly fierce affection radiated from her and, as though Sarah felt it she momentarily covered one of Ruth's hands with a small soft palm before returning it to her own lap.

'This folly will do Bernard Graves no good at all. Does he not realise that he is likely to be blacklisted for the entire Season by all the hostesses?'

'And little wonder at it. I feel very sorry for Susannah. I certainly would not want the trollop under my roof.'

Ruth and Sarah exchanged a knowing look on overhearing a conversation between the Countess of Morganston and her sister, Joanna Peebles.

They'd just entered the ladies' withdrawing room. It was a sanctuary set aside by their hosts so that female guests could rest and refresh themselves during the many hours of entertainment. Bright candle flame illuminated sofas and tables adorned with potpourri and bowls of daffodil trumpets that mingled their delicate fragrance with the ladies' French perfume.

The countess, on spotting the newcomers, beckoned them closer to whisper conspiratorially, 'We were just discussing whether that silly old fool Bernard Graves might rue succumbing to Loretta's charms.'

Sarah's expressive grimace indicated she thought it very possible. But she made no comment as she took a seat on the sofa next to Ruth. Both Ruth and Sarah began to idly tidy their coiffures while glancing at their reflections in the mirrors ranged along one wall.

'What do you say, Mrs Hayden?' the countess probed, obviously not yet done with the subject. 'I know you're also one of Sir Clayton's friends. Sarah said you've recently all been spending a nice time together. Are you aware that Lady Vane has gone to such wicked lengths to try to trap him into marrying her?'

Tucking a dark curl behind an ear, Ruth raised her eyes, meeting in the glass those of the countess. She'd no wish to become embroiled in any gossip over Clayton's mistress and she guessed that Sarah had held back her opinion for the same reason. Clayton was, after all, Gavin's closest friend and loyalty to him was paramount. Loretta Vane probably deserved every bad word that was said about her but, by association, Clayton must also be criticised for his poor choice of mistress. Worried as she was for his safety, Ruth realised she'd tell him so if the opportunity arose. He'd impertinently quizzed her over Ian Bryant and implied he didn't like the doctor. Why should she not return him her opinion on the dreadful woman with whom he was involved?

Aware of Ruth hesitating to comment on such an indelicate matter to people she'd just met, Sarah piped up, 'Ruth is too diplomatic to say what she thinks, so

I shall do so. Gavin and I are to hold a party next month. We will invite Lord Graves, but stipulate on his card that he must bring Maude if he's to gain entry.'

A chorus of laughter from the sisters met that information. Everyone knew of Maude Graves. She was Bernard's spinster sister, a decade younger than her brother, and a committed puritan. It was doubtful she could be lured to take part in any such wicked self-indulgence and the countess and Joanna Peebles knew it.

'How very righteous you sound, Miss Marchant… oh, beg pardon, I forgot. You're now married to Sir Clayton's friend. It's most enterprising of you to have got Viscount Tremayne to make an honest woman of you. I'm impressed, and equally ambitious, you know.'

The four ladies, momentarily shocked into paralysis at what they'd just heard, finally turned, as one, to look at the entrance to the retiring room and see Loretta posing on the threshold.

Her piercing blue eyes darted belligerently over the assembled female company and she looked undaunted at being outranked by two members. If she noticed Sarah's complexion had turned chalk white at her cruel comment, it moved her not one jot. She relinquished her languid posture, one hand on her hip, one toying with an ebony ringlet, and swayed further in to the room. 'You're not so different to me, Lady Tremayne, although it's true I was not sixteen or a spinster when I became a kept woman. I've always had the status and protection of my late husband's name. But I promise I'll not shun you because of it.' Loretta gave a husky chuckle as Sarah jumped to her feet, then immediately sat down again as though her legs wouldn't support her. 'How nice it'll be when I am Sir Clayton's wife. We'll take tea together, dear Lady Tremayne, and our husbands will be so pleased that we get on.'

While listening to this outrageous and vicious attack on her friend, Ruth had blenched, too, but more in fury than in shock. She feared that this might not be the end of Loretta's spite. Perhaps the cat was simply sharpening her claws in readiness for another strike, and Sarah already looked to be close to tears.

Ruth calmly stood up. 'I think that you are deluded, Lady Vane.' Her voice was level, yet cold as ice. 'And I think you must apologise to the viscountess for your appalling insults.'

Loretta turned deliberately towards the exit, ignoring Ruth as though she were beneath her notice. Her smug expression displayed her contentment at the stupefaction she was leaving in her wake. The countess and Mrs Peebles had not altered position since she'd arrived. Both ladies were still drop-jawed and statue-like.

'Please don't ignore me or leave this room just yet or I'll have to ask my friend Mr. Storey to have you immediately ejected from his house.'

That did halt Loretta's triumphant retreat. She knew very well that the Storeys were itching to find an excuse to have her thrown out. She'd sooner go of her own accord than face the ignominy of being led away by a servant.

Loretta swished about and her eyes glittered in condescension at Ruth. 'And I think that you ought to mind your own business,' she snapped. 'Who are you and what, pray, has any of this to do with you?'

'I am Mrs Ruth Hayden,' Ruth introduced herself, although it took some effort to expel the words through her gritted teeth. Never had she condoned violence, but she presently felt sorely tempted to slap the smugness from Lady Vane's face. She desisted for one reason only: she sensed that Loretta would be glad to incite her to act in such a vulgar fashion. Instead, Ruth stooped to use another tactic that was normally foreign to her. She lied, and with convincing fluency. 'This matter is very much to do with me,' she said with admirable composure. 'I'm the viscountess's friend and I'm also Sir Clayton's fiancée. We're soon to be married and I must ask you to refrain from any further pathetic attempts to steal my future husband.'

Chapter Fourteen

'The harpy had no right to be so mean! I said not one bad word about her to the countess, despite being sorely tempted to do so!'

'Hush,' Ruth said and drew her agitated friend in to a comforting embrace. 'The vile woman has gone now. I expect she has quit the house of her own accord rather than be shown the door.'

'There will be mud raking about me…it will soil you, too…perhaps we should go home…'

'The mud raking here tonight will be about that spiteful cat, not you,' Ruth said. 'The countess and Mrs Peebles were shocked to the core by her disgraceful attack on you.'

Sarah hadn't received Loretta's apology, but she'd had the satisfaction of seeing her tormentor turn and flee from the withdrawing room with the smirk wiped from her face. When Loretta had made a dash for the exit, her complexion had looked as ashen as her victim's.

Lady Vane had been visibly shaken by what she'd heard. She'd not challenged Ruth's claim to be engaged to Clayton and Ruth knew why that was. No sane, genteel lady would disclose something so explosive in front of witnesses if it were untrue. The fact that Ruth had made her announcement while with the wife of Sir Clayton's best friend had polished its credibility. To top it all, it would be an act of social suicide to provoke the ire of Lady Morganston and Mrs Peebles—two of the *ton*'s foremost hostesses. The two women risked being made laughing stocks if they spread the tale she'd given them and it was later found to be false.

After breathlessly impressing on Sarah that she had their sympathy and support, the sisters had given Ruth startled smiles and breathy felicitations. Within a few moments they'd quit the retiring room hot on the heels of Loretta. Ruth guessed, with an awful pang, that only yards away chatter about her happy news was as lively as that about Loretta's atrocious behaviour. Within a very short while she feared talk about her engagement to Clayton would be spreading like wildfire throughout the *beau monde*.

Having supplied fresh succulent meat for the gossips to chew over, no real attention would be given to the facts of Sarah's past life as a fallen woman. It was already known that her father had been a cowardly embezzler who'd shot himself, leaving his children to fend for themselves. The general consensus of opinion, by all those people with a scrap of humanity, was that Sarah deserved sympathy for having stoically endured such a harrowing time. She'd been praised and admired for her intrepid, enterprising nature in protecting herself and her relatives and keeping them all from the poorhouse. When news of her marriage to Viscount Tremayne had been announced, even those ladies who'd harboured a yen for the rich aristocrat had admitted that Sarah Marchant deserved her good fortune.

'I must thank you for coming to my rescue. If I'd seen the attack coming, I'd have been ready for the strumpet.' A pugnacious glint fired Sarah's eyes. 'As it was, I was close to breaking down in front of her and I'd have hated that.' She pulled a handkerchief from her reticule and dabbed her nose and eyes. She gave a watery chuckle. 'It was priceless seeing her face when you announced you're to marry Clayton.'

'I know,' Ruth said and knuckled into submission a little hysterical giggle. 'I imagine watching Clayton's reaction when he hears about it will be less amusing.' A rueful expression slanted her soft mouth, but in no way reflected Ruth's inner turmoil. Her heart was battering painfully at her ribs and a quick glance in the mirror opposite alerted her to the fact that her guilt and apprehension showed in her appearance. Huge brown eyes stared back at her from a face that looked pale and peaky.

'I think Clayton's reaction might surprise us all.' It was Sarah's turn to offer comfort. Taking one of Ruth's lightly trembling hands, she gave it a squeeze.

'I'm certain he will be as furious as I am to know that you were subjected to such spite,' Ruth ventured optimistically. Whatever the present state of his relationship with his mistress Clayton must find abhorrent her meanness to Sarah. 'Thank Heavens he's at present keeping himself to himself,' Ruth mused and bucked up a little. 'At least while he's preoccupied with finding Pomfrey there's a little time to think of what to say to him…'

The last person Clayton had expected, or hoped, to see as he made to alight from his coach in Berkeley Square was Loretta. He knew that she wasn't friendly with Susannah Storey and unlikely to have secured an invitation to her home. As an elderly gentleman appeared in the open doorway to join her on the threshold, Clayton understood how she'd managed to gain entry to the *musicale*. Loretta had persuaded Lord Graves to act as her escort. As he watched her snatch at the elderly widower's arm and hurry him at a stumbling pace down the steps, her callous abuse of the nice old fellow deepened Clayton's disgust for her. It was due to him brooding on it that he omitted to think it odd that, having wangled her way in, Loretta had chosen to leave so early. Once the couple had crossed the road towards Lord Graves's vehicle, Clayton slammed shut his carriage door and strode towards the Storeys' house.

'So…you must have been privy to your good friend's happy news.' Lady Morganston's stage whisper was directed at Gavin's left ear. 'I know you've all recently been having a nice time in the country. Did Sir Clayton propose to Mrs Hayden while there? When is it to be made official?'

Gavin gave the woman a suave smile when she'd finished hissing at him. 'I'm sure you know I can't possibly comment on Sir Clayton's private affairs,' he answered disarmingly. 'You must ask him that question.'

'How annoying that he's taken himself off somewhere.' Lady Morganston frowned, for she was itching to know what had gone on to make the confirmed bachelor change his mind about once again becoming a husband. Everybody knew he'd vowed never to wed again thanks to the treachery of his first wife. His distinct disenchantment with the marital state had been one of the reasons that Loretta's scheme had always been doomed to stir scepticism.

The countess tried to catch Ruth's eye to no avail.

She sighed. The lucky lady who'd hooked Sir Clayton and softened his hard heart was as tight-lipped as a clam on how she'd achieved it. Of course, the fact that Sarah and Ruth were close friends had probably helped the match succeed. The viscountess must be delighted to know her husband's best friend was marrying her friend. The countess was also dying to know whether Sir Clayton had yet given Mrs Hayden a betrothal ring. No doubt it would be monstrously fine and she'd start to wear it once the announcement had been gazetted.

Having overheard Lady Morganston's dialogue, as of course it had been intended she should, Ruth inwardly squirmed beneath the countess's increasingly speculative looks. She knew that shortly there would be no escape. She took a glance about. Ladies were discreetly advancing on her from all sides. No one had rushed up to bombard her with impertinent questions when she and Sarah had, with an air of admirable insouciance, rejoined Gavin in the drawing room. Of course, the assembled company was far too well bred to do so. But slowly they were hemming her in. Inquisitive eyes were constantly on her and she sensed her looks, her attire, her manner and bearing were all under intense scrutiny. And soon…very soon…there would be subtle prying in to her past. She was a widow…who had been her late husband? What sort of a man had he been?

Up went Ruth's chin and she made a gay response to Gavin's comment on the fine concert they'd enjoyed earlier. Of course, he knew what stress she was now under and that she'd taken on that burden to defend his wife. In turn, he was doing his utmost to put her at her ease and keep the talk pleasantly neutral.

A movement at one side of her alerted Ruth to the fact that two middle-aged ladies sporting plumed turbans had manoeuvred themselves close enough to butt in to the conversation. No matter her outward calm, Ruth's heart was drumming erratically. She knew the newcomers were simply waiting for an opportunity to slide a question her way. She spied Sarah at a distance, close to the drawing-room doors, talking to their hostess.

'Mrs Hayden, is it not?' One of the matrons startled Ruth into attention as she made her opening gambit.

'Yes, I am Mrs Hayden…how do you do, ma'am,' Ruth replied. Before the lady could introduce a question, she pressed on mendaciously, 'Oh, if you will excuse me, I see that Viscountess Tremayne is beckoning me.' With an appealing glance Gavin's way, Ruth left the disappointed ladies to his patient courtesy. She began to head briskly towards the door of the drawing room. Briefly she stopped by Sarah and Susannah to exchange a few words with them. Despite her outward composure, her insides were painfully writhing and she knew she simply wanted to be alone with her turbulent thoughts to force them in to some sort of order.

What *had* she done! was the mantra that rotated in her head as she slipped out in to the quiet corridor, then kept going. She proceeded aimlessly, slid a palm over a pillar and felt it soothe her febrile skin. When she thought she'd put sufficient distance between herself and her would-be inquisitors, she came to a halt. Her forehead tipped forwards to sway soothingly against cool marble. But the refreshing sensation couldn't ease the torment in her mind. She knew very well what she'd done. She'd set dreadful trouble to brew.

You came to London because you were concerned about Clayton, but now you've caused more problems in his life. Loretta Vane tried to trap him into marriage. Now he'll think you are attempting to do so. He'll consider you to be no better than that scheming hussy. What on earth will you say to him? How can it all be remedied?

Her unsuspecting fiancé—when suspecting the worst—was sure to point out, in that sardonic way he had, that less extreme methods should have been used to send Loretta packing. The next thought to enter Ruth's mind was that it might be wise to immediately return to Fernlea while she pondered on it all and sheltered from Clayton's fury. She cringed on acknowledging how craven it would be to run away. Her friends might then suffer the brunt of the storm instead of her.

When they'd been at the Manor together, Clayton had initially, irascibly cast Sarah in the role of matchmaker. And if Ruth disappeared from town, it wouldn't prevent Sarah being bombarded with calling cards from *grandes dames* keen to discover more about Clayton's elusive future bride. No, Ruth decided she must stay and face the music. But that brave resolution couldn't prevent her eyes closing in sheer thankfulness that at least while Clayton was in blissful ignorance of it all she had a welcome reprieve…

As Clayton reached the top of the stairs, he turned right. He'd been friendly with Keith for many years and had been a frequent guest in this house. Even had he not known the layout of the property, a soft melody would have lured him in the right direction. But as he walked, he idly glanced across the void of the stairwell to the landing opposite. His pace slowed until he stopped and squinted through the wavering flames of a thousand candles shimmering amid crystal. His features displayed his astonishment before softening into an expression of pure pleasure. Retracing his steps, he reached the head of the stairs and proceeded along the other corridor.

'This is a most pleasant surprise.'

Ruth nearly started out of her skin at that husky

greeting. She twisted about to face Clayton, the blood already gone from her complexion, for she'd immediately recognised those well-known ironic tones. How could she not when his anticipated reprimands sounded constantly in her head? She clutched behind at the pillar in support, for her legs felt suddenly boneless.

Clayton frowned. They might have parted in Fernlea on bad terms, but he'd not expected when next they met Ruth would look anguished to see him.

'What's the matter? Did I startle you?'

Ruth swallowed, made to speak, but forcing words past the blockage in her throat was impossible. 'Yes…no…' she finally stuttered. 'Yes…you startled me,' she forced out through lips that felt frozen. 'Why are you here?' she softly wailed in a way that was distinctly unflattering.

'I received an invitation,' he returned drily as his eyes lowered to skim over the beautiful sight of her. He'd never seen her dressed so glamorously and his immediate urge was to take over where he'd left off in her little cottage. He wanted to reach for her, soothe her with a kiss, tell her there hadn't been an hour that'd passed since he'd left her on that day that he hadn't regretted his decision to go. He wanted to say that she'd been constantly in his thoughts despite the damnable business with Pomfrey. That she was here, in London, was an exquisite unexpected gift. He guessed that she'd accompanied Gavin and Sarah to town and, had he known about it, he would have returned Gavin's first call on him within the hour.

Clayton raised desire-darkened eyes from her face as a movement in the distance made his attention slew to the drawing-room doors. He noted with an indolent hike of one dark brow that they were being watched by a group of ladies who were congregating on the threshold. The consequence of being observed penetrated his mind and caused him to curse beneath his breath. The idea he'd had to slip with Ruth into one of the rooms close by was now dashed.

'It seems we're causing quite a stir. I suppose we should go in to stop rumours flying.'

'It's too late for that.' Her spontaneous response was followed by a sob of muffled hysteria and Ruth simply stared blindly at the hand he'd politely extended to her.

'Too late for what?' Clayton asked, returning his hand to his side. Ruth blinked at the marble pillar, her mind racing in an attempt to find an innocent answer. Of course there wasn't one and the rapidity of her breathing was straining tiny buttons fastened across her bosom. The lure was too great for Clayton to ignore. There'd been no release to the passion she'd aroused in him in Fernlea. During his lengthy search for Pomfrey he'd dissipated his frustration through mental and physical exertion and tiredness. But now he could smell the sweet scent of her skin, almost taste the shape of her mouth beneath his. The protracted pause between them was shattered as he repeated his question in a voice made harsh by unrelieved sensual tension, 'Too late for what, Ruth?'

Ruth recognised the sultry heat in his eyes and it caused her to feel a phantom touch of long fingers cupping her nude breasts. Her lips parted beneath the memory of a kiss bruising, then smoothing their softness. The blood that had fled her face returned with a vengeance and a small stifled noise rasped in her throat.

It was not a note of anguish this time; Clayton recognised its source only too well. With a soundless oath he realised her raw need equalled his own. One of his hands began to move as though to soothe the blush in her cheeks. He knew what memories she had. He had the same imagery in his mind and he would have given anything for a little privacy in order to prove to her how much he'd missed her. He glared at the drawing-room doors to see that one of the women had broken ranks and was on her way towards them.

'Please…don't go in there…not yet…please…' Ruth darted a beseeching gaze at him and inwardly cringed beneath a new shrewdness stifling the desire in his eyes.

A disturbing insight suddenly penetrated Clayton's passion-clouded mind. Ruth's anguish on seeing him had not been caused by their past clashes, but by something that had occurred here tonight. And then he remembered having seen Loretta leaving early and his expression became grimmer.

'Why should I not go in there?' he demanded quietly. 'Look at me, Ruth,' he added when she seemed unable to meet his eyes for even a second. 'What's the matter? And you'd best tell me straight away, because Lady Morganston is almost upon us.'

After a stunned second Ruth whipped about in a swish of lavender-blue silk to see that indeed the countess was just a few yards away. She raised frantic eyes to Clayton, a jumble of words cluttering on her tongue. She must tell him now…without delay. But how did one swiftly disclose to a gentleman who had vowed never again to take a wife that due to the terrible lie she'd told people expected him to soon again be a husband? Her husband…

'How clever of you to have persuaded Sir Clayton to attend this evening, Mrs Hayden.' Lady Morganston gave Ruth an arch look. 'He's devilish hard to secure as a guest, you know. But now, of course, we know how to make him come.'

Over the top of the countess's head, Clayton's eyes met Ruth's and a glimmer of suspicion made his grey gaze hold very thoughtfully still on her.

'I felt quite hot,' Ruth burbled. 'I came into the corridor for a little air. It is much cooler out here.' With that she took a step back towards the drawing room. 'Are the musicians making ready to again perform? Was it not a wonderful concert?'

For the entire time it took the three of them to stroll to the drawing room—probably mere minutes that seemed to Ruth to drag like an hour—Ruth kept up a constant chatter in order to prevent the countess hinting she knew of her companions' secret betrothal.

Of course, had Ruth lived longer in London and known but a little more of *ton* etiquette, she would have realised that the countess was too polite to openly make mention to the prospective groom of an engagement that he'd not yet made official. But after the little romantic tableau in the hallway, witnessed by so many people, no doubting Thomas remained to challenge Mrs Hayden's claim to be the future Lady Powell.

That said, the countess, along with everybody here this evening, knew that Sir Clayton had yet to play his proper part and gazette the notice introducing Mrs Hayden as his future wife. Everyone knew too that, but for that minx Loretta acting outrageously and forcing Mrs Hayden's hand, it would all still be a secret. So the consensus of whispered opinion was that they must respect the confidence into which they'd been delightfully plunged!

Chapter Fifteen

'Where in damnation have you been?'

'And it's good to see you too.' Clayton had issued Gavin a naturally ironic greeting while his grey eyes continued scanning the assembled company.

'I've been trying to pin you down since I arrived in town.'

'I know...sorry,' Clayton muttered but still his attention was elsewhere. Almost as soon as he'd set a foot inside the Storeys' drawing room he'd sensed that conversations had dwindled on his arrival. It seemed people were now happier to peep his way than talk and that fostered Clayton's suspicion that something had taken place here this evening that should concern him. He rarely attended such functions and he accepted, with cynicism rather than conceit, that his appearance was likely to stir excitement amongst the débutantes and their mamas. He knew too that the business with Pomfrey and Loretta had notched up his notoriety. But that had nothing to do with Ruth and instinctively he knew she was also involved in a drama that was, as yet, unknown to him.

On reaching the drawing room, Ruth had seemed keen to urge the countess to go with her to mingle with Sarah's circle of friends. She'd slipped immediately from his side, but Clayton had noticed her eyes frequently darting back to him. A smile was fixed on her sweet lips for her friends' benefit, but it couldn't conceal from Clayton her nervousness. There was only one person Clayton could bring to mind who might have upset her, though how Loretta might have guessed he was falling in love and wanted Ruth as his mistress was beyond him. Nobody knew about it except Gavin, and it was ludicrous to suppose that his friend had spilled the beans. Of course, Ruth was certainly aware that he wanted her despite his proposition remaining unspoken. It was equally silly to suppose she would have taunted Loretta. But if some sort of catfight had taken place, it would explain why Loretta had left so early and why he and Ruth—and their interaction—seemed to be under constant surveillance.

'Has Loretta been stirring the pot in my absence?' Clayton asked Gavin. 'I caught sight of her outside with Bernard Graves. I imagine Susannah had her thrown out.'

Gavin drew Clayton towards an alcove where they might talk more privately. He'd watched Clayton inwardly weighing up hints and clues to the cause of the crackling atmosphere he could sense. During those few minutes of amicable quiet that had cocooned them, Gavin had been attempting to assess how much Ruth might have confessed to Clayton in the corridor. From Clayton's question, and Ruth's fawn-like stance, he now suspected that Ruth hadn't found the time or the temerity to tell him much at all. Inwardly he smiled. In Gavin's opinion, Ruth had no need to fret. Clayton was in love with her, and would eventually realise he wanted to marry her. His friend simply needed a little longer to believe in the miracle: Ruth was every bit as perfect as she seemed.

Clayton frowned on realising his question had gone unanswered. 'Has Loretta caused trouble tonight?' he repeated impatiently.

'Indeed she has.'

'What did she do?' Clayton demanded to know, his expression thunderous. 'Did she insult Ruth for some reason?'

'No, she insulted Sarah.'

'Insulted Sarah?' Clayton echoed in bewilderment. 'Why on earth would she do that?'

'Because she's a spiteful vixen, I suspect,' Gavin replied flatly.

Clayton gazed fiercely at Sarah as though searching for some sign of the hurt done to her.

'Oh…you needn't fret that Sarah is much bothered by it. She's far too strong to be bested by someone such as Loretta.'

Gavin wasn't as angry as people might have imagined him to be on hearing of his wife's ordeal. Gavin knew Sarah for an intrepid little fighter. If she could survive bearing the scars of a harrowing childhood, followed by several years of service as an innocent courtesan, a woman of Loretta's stamp would never bring her down. He had nothing but contempt for Loretta; nevertheless, he wasn't about to act the hypocrite and castigate Clayton over his choice of paramour. Before he'd met Sarah, Gavin had been a libertine too and had sometimes chosen a mistress simply for salacious reasons.

'Are you sure Sarah is all right?' Clayton asked in concern. 'Should I speak to her…apologise…?'

'There's no need,' Gavin said mildly. 'If you want to apologise to anyone, you should do so to Ruth.'

Clayton's eyes whipped back to his friend. 'To Ruth?' he echoed. 'Loretta insulted her as well?' He sounded incensed.

'I'm not sure; possibly she did. She seems to be indiscriminate with her malice.'

'God's teeth! What are you keeping back?' Clayton gritted out. 'Tell me what has gone on, dammit.'

Gavin overlooked his friend's churlishness. He recalled well enough that when he'd been pursuing Sarah he'd often acted cantankerously and Clayton had borne it with equanimity. 'Loretta raked up Sarah's past in front of Lady Morganston and her sister. Ruth jumped to Sarah's defence and put Loretta to flight.'

On knowing the fitting finale to Loretta's spite Clayton's strengthening smile deepened in to a chuckle. Admiration was smouldering in the look he was directing Ruth's way. 'Did she, now?' he murmured with throaty contentment.

'Indeed she did,' Gavin said. A rueful inflection in his voice betrayed that Gavin was also impressed by Ruth's heroics.

'Ruth always seems so calm and collected…well, not always…' Clayton added as an afterthought as though talking to himself and dwelling pleasurably on how wildly she'd responded to his lovemaking. Suddenly conscious of Gavin's repressed amusement, he stuck his hands in his pockets and examined his shoes. 'I'm surprised Loretta was sent packing. She can be quite thick-skinned.'

'Ruth used a very clever tactic.'

When no explanation was immediately forthcoming, Clayton prompted, 'And that was?'

'She said she was your fiancée.'

For a moment Clayton's countenance remained unaltered, his features still shaped by affection and humour. Slowly those emotions ebbed away, leaving his expression blank. He glanced up at Gavin. 'She said what?'

'She said you were to be married.'

After a silent moment Clayton turned again to look at Ruth.

Ruth knew the exact moment that Gavin told him. As soon as she'd seen the two men move to hug the wall, she'd watched with bated breath for it, dreading its cruel inevitability.

Beneath that pitiless stare directed her way she felt herself quake. Clayton's anger and astonishment might not be obvious to others, concealed as it was behind an impenetrable mask of suave civility, but she felt it like a physical blow. Could he divine the apology that was trembling, unspoken, on her tongue? She guessed not, for his unyielding stance hadn't altered one jot. The steady stare went on, no scrap of understanding or forgiveness apparent in it. And then he moved and she knew he was coming for her.

With no mind given to appearing craven, Ruth moved too. Following a murmured excuse to her companions about a visit to the withdrawing room, she headed hastily in that direction. A darted glance through milling people told her that he'd altered direction and was now walking parallel to her on the opposite side of the room. She knew she had nothing to match his long easy stride and at any time he could accelerate and traverse the crowd to cut off her escape route. But he was in no hurry; he was toying with her, allowing her to almost reach her sanctuary before surely denying it to her. She might have spontaneously tried to avoid him, but she wouldn't give him the satisfaction of intimidating her in to ungainly flight.

Valiantly she kept her chin up and forced her wobbly legs to keep to a steady pace. But the moment long fingers closed on her skin, forcing her inexorably to a halt just a yard from her target, she emitted a startled gasp.

'Let me go,' she squeaked in an underbreath, conscious of watching eyes.

'Only if you return the favour, sweetheart,' he shot back with deadly sarcasm. 'But you know that's not possible, don't you?'

'It is…*it is*,' Ruth stressed in a whisper as her complexion glowed with mortification at his damning words. 'I'm sorry…truly. But after a suitable time has elapsed we can call it all off…'

A low harsh laugh curtailed her desperate solution to the dilemma into which she'd driven them both.

'I'll let you apologise properly later,' he said silkily. 'Right now I think it's time I took my fiancée home.'

Ruth jerked her arm in an attempt to free it and this time her eyes clashed proudly on his. 'I shall leave in the same manner as I arrived—with Gavin and Sarah, in their coach.'

'You will leave with me now, willing or unwilling.'

The mutinous look she gave him told Clayton she'd opted for the latter.

'I'm sure I needn't tell you that if you leave here over my shoulder it's likely to deprive you of dignity and provide these fine ladies—those who don't swoon, that is—with yet more scandal to tattle over this evening.'

'You wouldn't dare,' Ruth said, her wide sepia eyes bright with shock.

He didn't answer for a moment, but his quiet, coarse laugh chilled her to the core. Finally he said gently, 'I expect you think I've never done it before.'

Ruth's eyes remained captured by his ruthless stare. Somehow she found that softly scoffing utterance more wounding than his righteous anger. Momentarily bravado deserted her; her voice quavered and her eyes glittered traitorously. 'I doubt you care about any woman's dignity. I believe you capable of it, and much more besides.'

'Good…that's settled, then,' he said dulcetly. 'Let's find our hosts and thank them for a wonderful evening.'

She had expected he might unleash his fury as soon as they were private in his coach, but she was mistaken. Having assisted her into the coach, he sprang aboard and threw himself down on the opposite seat in a way that displayed his bitter mood far more eloquently than any words could. After a leisurely piercing stare from beneath his brows, that sent her back into a corner, he kept his gaze through the window to one side of him and his lips thrust cynically aslant.

Ruth imagined his intention was to impress upon her how contemptible he found her. So contemptible, in fact, that he couldn't bear to look at her or speak to her. For some time she gazed at the starry night, too, while the carriage clattered through the dusky streets. But finally her insides had knotted so tightly that she felt quite ill. Unable to endure it longer, she burst out, 'I'm sorry. I know I've said and done a very reckless thing tonight. If I could undo it I would. But it will come right. Engagements end all the time…'

'Not mine,' he said, his eyes still on the stars.

She had expected he might snap off her head when he did speak, but he might have been commenting mildly on the weather. A little encouraged by his moderate tone, she ventured, 'What do you mean…not yours? Your marriage was brought to an end so why not—?'

'That's what I mean,' he interrupted her, still deceptively subdued. 'One failed marriage is enough.'

'We…we don't need to actually marry.'

'We're expected to. Every club in St. James's will be running a book on the date of the wedding by tomorrow morning. Every hostess in Mayfair will be debating with her friends how you'll suit ivory lace by tomorrow evening.' He shot a damning look at her. 'Some people are no doubt already wagering on whether it'll last.'

Ruth's small teeth worried at her lower lip. He'd sounded so poignantly bitter that she felt tempted to comfort him by saying she'd never be unfaithful or leave him. How dreadfully inappropriate that would have been! He didn't care about keeping her; he cared that he might not find a way to slip free of her clutches. And there was no denying the veracity of what he'd said about the *beau monde*'s fascination with this affair. 'Still, it can be put to rights.' It sounded more a hesitant question than the confident statement she'd intended.

Clayton brought his hard mocking eyes to hers and left them there till she squirmed and snapped, 'You are not without blame in this, you know, sir.'

'Is that right?'

'Yes, it most certainly is right!' Ruth spluttered. 'It was your…your *lady* friend who started it all. Had she not been so vile and mean as to almost make Sarah cry—when she'd done nothing to deserve it—none of this would have come about. I was goaded beyond endurance at seeing my best friend so upset.'

'So to ease your temper you declared to all and sundry that I had asked you to marry me. Did it make you feel better?'

'It certainly made Sarah feel better when the spiteful cat ran off.' It was a snappish rejoinder uttered while she twisted her hands in her lap. 'You were not there! You do not know what went on!'

That seemed to give him food for thought, for he remained quiet for several seconds, his shadowy features inscrutable.

'Why did you come to London?'

'What?' Ruth murmured, still gathering breath after her fluent outburst.

'Why did you come to London? Did you come to see me?'

'No,' Ruth whispered, but something in her stilted response caused a corner of his mouth to lift.

'Were you worried about me? Did you find out that I was to fight a duel?'

'Sarah asked me to accompany her to town,' Ruth quickly returned. Her cheeks had become quite hot and she was glad of the cool shadowy interior of the coach neutralising her blush.

'I don't think you would have quit your home without a pressing reason.'

'I had a pressing reason. I needed some time away from Willowdene to think about important decisions I must make.' It was a truthful prevarication, and she was pleased to have remembered it.

'Ah…the upstanding pillar of Willowdene society. Has the doctor proposed again?'

A glare met his drawled mockery. 'Ian might live in the countryside, but he is a mannerly gentleman. I doubt he would threaten to throw a woman over his shoulder and carry her out of a drawing room,' Ruth said sourly.

'I imagine you're right,' Clayton returned as though it were to the fellow's detriment. 'Perhaps with him you manage to curb your provocative nature. Whereas with me…you certainly don't,' he finished with soft insinuation.

Ruth knew what it was that he'd left unsaid, just as he intended she should. That he would wave her lapse into wantonness in her face at such a time made her choke out, 'If I'm provocative with you it's because you intentionally make me so.'

'It wasn't wholly a complaint, sweetheart,' Clayton said softly. 'But you know that, don't you?'

Ruth swung her face away and stared sightlessly at the sombre sky. A throb of tension was now between them and Ruth was as keenly aware of that as she was of him. The shadowy coach interior helped him conceal his expression, but she knew a glimmer of lust now mingled with the anger in his eyes. He might be repulsed by what he saw as her naked ambition to be his wife, but having her naked was still his ambition.

'If Bryant has proposed again, I take it you've no intention of accepting him just yet…not while your hopes are pinned on me.'

'How dare you!' Ruth swung her livid face towards him. In her heart she'd cherished a hope that he would never class her with the Loretta Vanes of the world. 'I'd far sooner marry the doctor than you. Just because I've told a lie to protect a friend doesn't mean I wanted to do so, but…'

'But you're glad you did,' Clayton jeered softly. 'Because you think you've got me hooked.'

That was enough! Ruth shot to the front of the seat, her small hands balled in to fists that looked primed and ready to strike. Her furious indignation prevented her noticing the glint of triumph that lurked behind Clayton's dropped lashes or the fact that a muscle in his clenched jaw had pulled his mouth aslant in a dangerous smile.

'You are the most abominably conceited man. I'm not surprised your wife left you and ran off with someone else!' Ruth fumed. 'I wouldn't marry you if my life depended upon it and tomorrow I shall make that very clear to anyone who cares to listen.'

'Methinks that the lady doth protest too much…'

The lazy goading spurred Ruth into immediate action. With a little cry she lunged a slap, then another, at his arrogant head.

A lazy hand deflected the blows, then imprisoned her arm before Ruth could snatch it back. With a light tug she was off balance and lay spreadeagled against a broad hard-muscled chest.

'I suppose I should make it clear that I expect my fiancée to act with decorum at all times. I'll let you know if I want you to play the wench for me. So…no more catfights over me, or with me for that matter.' Having delivered that in a sardonic tone, Clayton forked his hand over her chin and forced her evasive face up to his. 'Let's see if you can still provoke me in a way I like…'

Ruth became very still, her eyes huge and glossy with shock. Despite her indignation at his rough treatment, she could feel traitorous heat flowing in her veins simply because she anticipated his mouth soon on hers. Her breasts were heaving and every breath she gasped in rasped her taut nipples against his chest.

In the moment between his anger and his punishment Ruth was obliquely aware that the coach was rocking over ruts and bumping her body against him in a most erotic manner. And then his mouth swooped to take hers in a savage punishing kiss while a hand plunged into a mass of silky dark hair. Long fingers gripped her scalp, keeping her face hard against his.

Ruth struggled in earnest to be free of the strong arms around her and sit upright. But treacherous warmth had stirred immediately to life low in her belly as his mouth covered hers and was defeating her defences. Despite the aggression between them, her body had responded instinctively to his touch. Of its own volition her mouth was softening beneath the pressure of his probing tongue. She knew he had every right to be angry at what she'd done, but she didn't deserve this humiliation and she feared it was his plan to bring her down.

With that thought helping to subdue her languor, she continued to struggle for her dignity, quite ineffectually, and that was why she felt startled when suddenly Clayton changed tack. The bruising weight of his mouth was lifted from hers. Instead she felt a soft moist caress touch her cheek before it trailed tormentingly slowly to bury behind her ear. The hard grip on her scalp relaxed and his fingers slid to straddle her nape, moving with slow rhythm against the sensitive skin there while the play of his lips continued to tantalise her.

'Let me go,' Ruth gasped even as her eyes closed and she angled back against the soothing feel of his fingers.

Clayton's response was to bring his mouth back to hers. With gentle yet inexorable insistence his lips slid artfully against hers, persuading her to part her mouth. The stroking thumb continued working its sorcery on her nape, stoking the hunger in her to revel in the sweet sensuality he was offering. The clamped line of her lips was slackening, yet he didn't immediately take advantage. His kiss remained teasingly courteous, tempting her to crave more…invite more from him. And she did. Ruth kissed him back. Her bunched fists unfurled against his chest, clutched at his jacket for support as they pulled to his shoulders and anchored there. Her back arched instinctively as his hands girdled, massaged the slender bones below her thrusting breasts. Beneath this powerful onslaught the vehicle added its weight to her seduction, swaying her body seductively side to side as it negotiated bends and turns in the road. A gasp broke gutturally in her throat and, as though it was the signal Clayton had been waiting for, he deepened the kiss. His tongue plunged and withdrew with slow determined rhythm, coaxing her to widen for him. Ruth surrendered herself to abandonment. When his skilful fingers opened her bodice and cupped a breast, she sighed pleasure in to his mouth. When his thumb rotated over a turgid nipple, she thrust further towards his hand.

With a groan Clayton dragged his mouth from hers and lowered his head. He tantalised the tight little nub with tongue and teeth until her squirming was invitation enough and he drew hungrily.

The pulse in Clayton's loins was a nagging agony and, in a reserved part of his mind that was crumbling to searing desire, he cursed himself for a fool. He'd wanted to punish her for what she'd done. God knew the shock of it was still reverberating in his mind. Ruth had resurrected all the hurt and humiliation he associated with marriage and having a wife. But Ruth wasn't Priscilla or Loretta. She was sweet, beautiful

Ruth. He was falling in love with her. Was he going to insult her and tumble her quickly in a carriage because she'd rammed back into his mind the hell and emotional torment Priscilla had put him through? Ruth deserved nightlong loving in luxurious surroundings and his deepest respect. She deserved affection and adoration and he knew he could give it…in time. He'd been so close to revitalising that withered part of his soul that he thought was for ever lost to him. But she'd forced his hand too soon, made him panic…and, coward that he was, he'd taken his revenge in the only way he knew how. It was the second time he'd started with Ruth something his conscience wouldn't allow him to finish. In a few more seconds he'd be lost in her passionate response to him and there'd be no way back. And how she'd hate him tomorrow for it!

Chapter Sixteen

With a little moan Ruth plunged her mouth up, desperately seeking Clayton's to demand he kiss her back. The slide of his artful hands on her feverish skin had kept at bay the memory of her dreadful lie and the hostility between them. Sweetly she strove to entice him with little nipping kisses and tongue touches until she sensed his lips form a smile against hers.

'Are you trying to seduce me, Mrs Hayden?'

His teasing was tender, but nevertheless embarrassment cluttered Ruth's throat. 'If I am, it seems I am unsuccessful,' she breathed in a suffocated voice.

'If only that were true,' Clayton returned on a sigh of self-mockery. He was tempted to kiss her to soothe her, but knew that if he did all his honourable intentions were doomed. Five fingers threaded though her long, soft hair to gently curve on her scalp. 'If things had been different...if I'd met you sooner...' He stopped and frowned. He'd spoken aloud his thoughts and didn't know now where next to take them.

A faint hope that had valiantly flickered in Ruth's breast extinguished as she listened to his gruff regrets. Now she accepted that the wounds he bore from his first marriage would never heal. He would never break free of the web of bitterness in which Priscilla had bound him. Her eyes closed and she garnered strength enough to swiftly sit upright and smoothly steal away. She settled opposite him again and clutched her silk cloak tightly about her open bodice rather than fumble with its fastenings. 'Surely we are nearly at Lansdowne Crescent?' she said in almost a normal tone. 'The journey seems endless...'

'Ruth...'

'Please don't say anything,' Ruth curtailed him in a brittle voice. Her eyes flew back to the window. She leaned towards it. 'Am I nearly home?'

'Yes.'

A nod of thankfulness met that confirmation, for she could not soon enough escape the leaden tension that once more had wedged them apart. A relieved sigh scraped her throat as the coach drew smoothly to a kerb. Immediately one of Ruth's hands darted to the handle. It was covered by one of Clayton's.

'I want you, but I don't want a wife,' he said hoarsely, apologetically.

'I don't want you as my husband,' she quickly countered and felt peaceful as soon as she'd found the truth in it. Heaven only knew she would sooner live out her life as a widow than be a wife to a reluctant, resentful man. 'I'm sorry I did such a senseless thing tonight,' Ruth blurted and slipped her fingers from beneath his. She was again composed and she met his eyes steadily. She would not crumble beneath his rejection or from knowing that a monstrous problem must be solved. Obviously he must now immediately contrive a plan to undo the mess she'd made and break their engagement.

Clayton shifted on the seat and leaned towards her. He planted his forearms on his knees and raised his eyes to lock his gaze with hers. 'A lengthy betrothal might have benefits for both of us.'

Ruth's tongue tip darted moisture to lips that still pulsed from his kisses. Eventually she asked, 'What benefits am I to have from such an arrangement, sir?'

'The protection of my name and my status. You may buy whatever you wish on my accounts and draw an unlimited cash allowance for anything else you want. You will be welcomed everywhere as my intended wife.'

'And yet I am not your intended wife and the whole affair is a sham.'

'Much of what goes on in polite society is not what it seems.'

'And what benefits are you to have?'

'I'll have the protection of your name and status,' he said softly, wry amusement glittering in his eyes. 'Your position as my betrothed will keep all the débutantes at arm's length.'

'I think you know that if you don't marry me within a reasonable time, people will presume I am your mistress.'

'People already presume that you are my mistress, Ruth.'

Ruth's eyes widened on him in astonishment but after a moment of frantic reflection she realised he'd probably spoken the truth. It was known that recently they'd both been guests at Willowdene Manor. They'd slept beneath the same roof in what was probably deemed to be a cosy arrangement with their friends, the Tremaynes. It was also obvious that she was a widow in her late twenties, not an innocent damsel. Now that she'd broadcast that a romantic attachment existed between them, of course sophisticated people would immediately think they were lovers.

'And what do you presume?' she asked huskily. 'That I will sleep with you in return for your money?'

'I assume that we will become lovers because it is what we both want,' Clayton differed very gently.

Ruth turned her face away. Was she about to act the hypocrite and say she didn't want that? She'd just again promised, in a way words could never equal, what a willing bed partner she would be. She couldn't deny she wanted his kisses and caresses. But what else did she want? Did she want to turn her back on the chance of meeting a man who would cherish her as his wife? How long would Clayton want her? Till her looks faded and her chance of marrying and having children were gone too? Perhaps in time he might fall in love again and manage to curb his contempt for the marital state. Perhaps he might change his rakish ways for his new wife's sake. What would become of her then? Did she want to risk conceiving and rearing children on her own? But most of all…did she want to love him, in and out of bed, knowing that he felt no such deep or enduring emotion for her?

Ruth looked back at him to see he was watching her intently. If she denied him, he would simply seduce her properly this time and she knew, to her shame, she wouldn't summon the will-power to stop him. 'I'm sorry I acted stupidly tonight. If needs be, I will admit I lied in order to help you end the dreadful farce of it. Goodnight.' She shook from her wrist the fingers that had immediately sprung to restrain her and, flinging open the door, stumbled out of the coach. She no longer cared that he saw her run from him and within seconds she was up the stone steps and rapping on the door of the Tremaynes' house in Lansdowne Crescent.

The following morning Ruth was started from a sound dreamless sleep by a knocking on her chamber door. A moment later Sarah had entered the room. Without ceremony, her friend settled on the edge of Ruth's bed.

'Did I wake you? Sorry…but I couldn't wait longer to find out what went on between you and Clayton.' Sarah's eyes were wide with a mingling of concern and curiosity. She pulled her wrap about her and, lifting her legs, curled them beneath her on the coverlet. 'I've been so worried that you and Clayton are now at dreadful loggerheads…and all because of me.'

Ruth pushed herself up on to her elbows and blinked at her friend. 'What time is it?' She gathered back a fistful of thick cocoa-coloured hair from where it flowed over her sleepy eyes.

'About nine o'clock. I'm glad you slept so well. I've barely shut my eyes for fretting. Did Clayton give you a dreadful roasting over it all?' Without waiting for a response, Sarah launched into, 'At first, I believed…oddly, I suppose…that he'd be quite glad you'd claimed to be engaged to him. It's obvious he has a deep fancy for you and I imagined he might need just such a nudge to stop him sulking over that harlot he married. Gavin has noticed, too, that he can't keep his eyes from you.' Sarah paused, nibbled at a lip, then a thumbnail. 'But then when you left the *musicale* early with him, he looked so furious and you looked so scared…'

'Was it obvious that I was scared?' Ruth interjected, jerked from her drowsy state by chagrin. She hated the idea that she might have appeared cowed by him.

'I know you both well and could tell you were apprehensive and Clayton was angry. But outwardly you both seemed remarkably composed. Clayton is always able to maintain a pleasant façade no matter what mood he is in.'

'Oh, yes…' Ruth agreed with quiet bitterness.

On hearing her friend's acrid tone Sarah's small teeth began to whittle her thumbnail again. Suddenly she clasped together her hands. 'It was so good of you to jump to my defence in the way you did. But I wish you had not. You've landed yourself in an awful pickle. He won't marry you, will he?'

'You cannot blame him, Sarah,' Ruth said. 'No gentleman would want to be forced to propose to a woman in such circumstances. When one considers his past misfortune with his first wife…'

'You've had past misfortune with your late husband,' Sarah interrupted. 'You've not allowed it to sour your view on marriage.'

Ruth managed a small smile and sat up properly in bed. As she moved, a luxuriant tumble of tresses settled about the shoulders of her crumpled white nightgown. 'I loved Paul and have fond memories as well as dark ones of being his wife.' Her slender fingers pleated the coverlet absently as she stared in to space. 'If Clayton gained nothing but deep unhappiness from once being a husband, then it is not surprising he refuses to take another wife.'

'I think you're too kind and understanding. He shouldn't make it so obvious he's smitten by you if he's not prepared to do the decent thing.'

'I don't want him to do the decent thing,' Ruth objected wryly. 'I have an equal aversion to being tolerated as a wife as he has to being forced in to the role of husband. In other words, I don't want to be married to him any more than he does to me.' Ruth put a hand on her dejected friend's arm and gave it a little squeeze. 'It will come right. It will be a scandal too for a while, I know. But I shall return to Fernlea once the truth is out. When I've gone away, the talk will dwindle, for there'll be no target for the gossips' scorn. Clayton will no doubt be showered with sympathy when it's generally known that another hussy lied to hook him. I suppose it's what he deserves.'

Sarah grimaced temporary defeat. She got up and paced to the window and looked at the bright sun behind the curtain she'd twitched aside. 'Gavin has said he'll take me for a drive in the park after breakfast. Will you come with us?'

Ruth shook her head, and, finding her slippers and dressing gown, she joined Sarah in gazing quietly at a bright new day.

'Do come,' Sarah said, turning from the light. 'I

don't like to think of you here on your own, fretting on it all.'

'I shall like to be here on my own. I must pack and be ready to return home. I won't go, of course, until I know the matter with Clayton is settled. I've said I'll own up and do what I can to help him unravel the tangle if he wants me to.'

'I'll lend you one of my finest carriage dresses to wear if you'll come for a ride,' Sarah cajoled. In her eyes stood tears of frustration; there was nothing she could think of to do that might help Ruth out of the quandary she was in. And her friend was only in trouble for selflessly rushing to her aid!

'I *adore* the dresses you've already given me,' Ruth said softly. 'And I adore all the other lovely things you've been so very kind enough to donate to me for this trip.'

'You're my best friend, why would I not share with you?' Sarah said solemnly.

'I think, though, I must not share your husband… not all the time.'

'Oh, Gavin doesn't mind if you join us again on an outing,' Sarah said, snuffling on her sleeve.

'Of course he doesn't mind,' Ruth concurred. 'He's too much of a fine gentleman ever to be discourteous, even in thought.' Ruth smiled. 'But I mind. I mind that you both have had very little time to yourselves since we arrived in London. Shall we find some breakfast?'

she suggested in the hope of bucking Sarah up despite the fact she felt too wretchedly queasy to enjoy a morsel.

'I can't eat anything. Take it away.'

With a dip of her mobcap the maid collected the breakfast tray and hastily obeyed her irritated mistress.

Loretta Vane picked up the note that had been delivered early that morning and her eyes again scanned the two concise paragraphs. Shock and disbelief were again shaping her features as she desperately tried to find some ambiguity in Ralph Pomfrey's prose.

But it was perfectly apparent that her official fiancé was eager to free her from their betrothal. He also no longer deemed it his duty to protect her honour by risking his life in a duel. She might marry whomsoever she pleased, he'd written as his parting shot before signing the parchment with a flourish.

Loretta let the paper drop to settle amid the debris of bottles and boxes on her dresser. She'd not seen Ralph for some while. Neither had she seen Clayton. She'd heard on the grapevine that Clayton was back in town and looking for Pomfrey to talk some sense in to him. Loretta had vainly believed she'd provided Pomfrey with adequate incentive to keep him hooked and hankering after her. It was galling to know Ralph had so soon been dissuaded from acting as her champion.

As soon as Loretta had learned of Clayton's arrival

in Mayfair, she'd sent a note to his house, begging him to come and see her. He'd not even acknowledged the letter, but she'd drawn some meagre comfort from the fact that nobody else had seen or heard much of him either.

But Pomfrey had seen him. It was obvious to Loretta that the two gentlemen had settled the differences she'd engineered for them. She felt resentment tightening her chest. She'd been made to look a fool at the Storeys' last night. She'd made her audacious intrusion on Bernard Graves's arm in the hope of seeing Clayton there and persuading him to take her back. He'd not even been present. But his wretched fiancée had been there.

Clayton was to be married and now, when it leaked out that Pomfrey had rejected her too, she'd be a risible figure of fun. Loretta knew she could probably preserve a little dignity by extracting a proposal from that old fool Bernard Graves…but…a shiver of revulsion passed through her as she recalled his ice-cold hands and the spittle that had flecked his bluish lips as she'd drawn his face towards hers to tempt him to kiss her.

'A visitor for you, madam.' The young maid managed to keep amusement from curling her mouth at madam's excitement on learning that news. 'It is a lady…Mrs Beauvoir,' the girl announced maliciously.

Loretta sighed disappointment. Obviously the woman was the first of her few friends who'd be calling to feign commiserations on her humiliation yesterday evening. Christine Beauvoir was more an ally than a confidante. Although Loretta considered herself to be vastly superior in status, having netted a title, the two women had remarkably similar lives. Both had been widowed quite young and subsequently lived as kept women. There were other similarities, too—neither Christine nor Loretta were particularly well liked. They were accepted by polite society under the mantle of protection bestowed by a current lover. The higher the fellow's rank and wealth, the better were their prospects. Now, with no lover and no fiancé, and her bank balance plummeting, Loretta had been left in a very vulnerable position. And she didn't relish it one bit. The *ton* liked its brazen temptresses to show humility in defeat. And that was certainly not *her* way.

About to tell her maid to send the woman away, for she felt in no mood to field Christine's barbs, Loretta suddenly recollected something about her visitor that greatly buoyed her mood. Momentarily lost in thought, she began to tap at her lips with a long shapely fingernail. 'Ask Mrs Beauvoir to wait in the Rose Salon; soon I will be down to receive her,' she eventually directed her maid.

With a thin smile Christine Beauvoir accepted the news that her ladyship had agreed to see her. She flounced to a chair and sat down. After an impatient moment tapping her well-shod feet against timber, she was again standing. She moved to a window to scour the street scene. But she could not stay irritable for long, not when such delightful news continued to bubble away inside of her. And one person should be greatly indebted to her for kindly sharing her information. Christine would be sure to remind her ladyship of that fact when she needed taking down a peg or two.

'Did my maid not fetch you tea? I shall ring for some,' Loretta said on sweeping regally into the Rose Salon.

'Perhaps once we've had a little chat, you might call for something stronger. Champagne might suit…'

Immediately intrigued by her visitor's opening gambit, Loretta became alert to Christine's excitement. She indicated that her friend sit beside her on the sofa.

'Have you received news from that bumpkin town you used to live in? Willowdene, isn't it?' Loretta knew very well that Ruth Hayden and her friend Viscountess Tremayne came from that part of the country.

Christine pursed her lips, quite put out that Loretta was some way towards spoiling the effect of her revelation.

'As I recall,' Loretta pressed on, unwilling to wait for Christine to come out of her sulk and spill all the beans, 'you used to be on *intimate* terms with the brother of Viscount Tremayne.' Loretta leaned forwards to archly smile at her friend.

'I was indeed Eddie Stone's dear friend for many years until he died.' Christine twirled a chestnut curl with a finger. Her ambition had been to become Gavin Stone's dear friend after his brother died, but Gavin had quite brusquely declined her offer. The humiliation of it still rankled and was the main reason Christine felt she had a score of her own to settle with the viscount and his kith and kin. 'I still have contacts in the town and know all the gossip about what goes on there,' Christine resumed. 'Recently some gossip concerning Mrs Ruth Hayden reached my ears.'

Loretta's eyes sharpened to blue slits on hearing her rival's name linked to gossip. 'I take it you've heard that Sir Clayton is betrothed to her,' she said. 'The brazen hussy broadcast it last night despite the fact he has not yet made it official.'

'Talk is spreading already,' Christine said. 'I was in Williamson's drapery this morning when Joanna Peebles entered the shop with the Belmont sisters. They spoke of nothing else, I can tell you, but when the wedding will take place and how fine they imagine it all will be.' Christine's lips curved in a little spiteful smile as she saw the effect her words were having on Loretta. 'How dreadful for you to hear of Clayton's marriage in such a way.'

'What gossip have you heard about her?' Loretta

demanded to know, her astute mind already turning over possibilities.

'She's very friendly with the viscountess. And of course you know Sarah's history, for I was the one who told you of it.'

Loretta wished now she'd not known of Sarah's history. She'd used that information in pique and had it backfire on her. 'Never mind about her,' she dismissed impatiently. 'What do you know about Ruth Hayden?'

'She lives close to Willowdene and is shunned by the townsfolk because of the manner of her late husband's death. He was court-martialled and executed for cowardice in the war.' Christine took a deep breath before delivering her *pièce de résistance*. 'As she is ostracised locally it was considered by most people to be extraordinary when a respectable and eligible gentleman proposed to her. Doctor Bryant is said to be smitten with the widow and the consensus of opinion is that he presumes she will agree to marry him.'

Loretta sat back, disappointed. What cared she for knowing that? The doctor might presume all he liked, but any sensible woman would snatch at the marriage proposal from a wealthy aristocrat rather than settle for the local leech.

Christine understood her friend's sour expression and added slyly, 'When Clayton was in Willowdene recently with his friends, he met the doctor. Ian Bryant went to the Manor and, rumour has it, was invited to dine with them all. If the fellow believed Ruth to be engaged to Clayton, why would he pursue her here to town to renew his proposal?'

'He is here?'

Christine nodded. 'He is not without connections and cash, you know. Ian Bryant's maternal grandfather was a baron and, although he couldn't pass on to Ian his title, he gave him a portion of his wealth and a town house in Connaught Street.'

'So…you think that Ruth Hayden is being a cruel tease to the doctor? Or is she trying to play them off against each other?'

'I doubt she has it in her,' Christine said flatly. 'I also heard the ladies in the drapery discussing Clayton's arrival and swift departure from the *musicale* last night.'

'He turned up?' Loretta spat in annoyance.

'He did, and he left almost straight away with Mrs Hayden. The ladies guessed that some sort of tiff between them might have occurred because she'd let the cat out of the bag about their betrothal.' Christine paused. 'In my opinion, there was no cat to let out of the bag. I know how very close Ruth and Sarah are. I know you were horrible to her friend and I know Ruth would act on impulse to protect Sarah.' After a deep breath she delivered her damning verdict. 'I think Mrs

Hayden told a wicked lie last night in saying she was Sir Clayton's fiancée and I doubt that Dr Bryant will be any more pleased than Clayton was on finding out about it.'

Chapter Seventeen

'Where did you eventually run Pomfrey to ground?'

Gavin had been on his way home from his attorney's when he'd spied Clayton strolling along St James's. His friend had looked to be deep in thought with his head down, shoulders hunched and hands thrust deep into his pockets. The elements had been whipping his flaxen locks to obscure his features, but the buffeting hadn't disturbed Clayton's air of preoccupation. Having rapped for his driver to halt, Gavin had sprung from his coach to accost Clayton and bark out his question.

Yesterday evening there'd been no opportunity for them to talk about the business with Pomfrey. The commotion between the ladies had precluded all other conversation. But Gavin had seen one of Pomfrey's friends in the park earlier when out driving with Sarah.

Christopher Perkins had ridden over specifically to tell him, with courteous brevity as Sarah was with him, that the duel was off. Gavin therefore had gained no insight to the whys and wherefores and was now keen to get some.

With his eyebrows slanted to a quizzical angle, Clayton came to a halt outside White's. Gavin grimaced an apathetic acceptance to Clayton's wordless suggestion, and they entered the gentlemen's club.

'Brighton…he was staying with his mother,' Clayton eventually replied while dragging five neatening fingers through the knots in his hair.

'Was he in hiding?'

'He knows better than to go there for sanctuary.' Clayton grunted a laugh. 'The old lady had more of a mind to shoot him than me.' A signal at the steward requested drinks before he resumed the tale. 'She gave Ralph the choice of shaking hands with me, or wrestling away from her the keys to the gun cabinet. She looked peeved enough over it all to carry out the threat to put a bullet in him.'

'I remember she was always a game old bird.' Gavin chuckled. 'I doubt Loretta will be pleased to know that Ralph is further beneath his mother's thumb than hers.'

Clayton's eyes clouded with distaste at the mention of his erstwhile mistress. 'Ralph knows he's been a fool…' His voice trailed away but what he'd left unspoken was easily guessed.

'And he's not the only one,' Gavin supplied the words.

Clayton scowled and muttered about the steward's tardiness in bringing a bottle of cognac. He slumped into a chair at a table and immediately picked up a pack of cards. He thumbed them idly, then fanned them into a semi-circle on the baize.

'Are you going to take a guess at why I think you're an equal fool to Pomfrey? I'll give you a clue—on this occasion it has nothing to do with Loretta.'

'No,' Clayton said harshly and forcefully flipped the cards into a stack.

'Well, I'll tell you anyway. Yesterday Ruth acted with immense selflessness and courage and you—'

'I know,' Clayton whipped across Gavin's quiet lauding of Ruth. 'You don't have to say more. I know it's all my fault.' He stabbed a glance at his friend from beneath close brows. 'There's no need to worry. I'll take care of Ruth.'

'How?' Gavin demanded. But no matter what other probing looks and questions he used, his friend refused to disclose any more. They played a half-hearted game of rummy. When various acquaintances ambled over to grip Clayton by the shoulder and mutter gruff congratulations, Clayton remained stoically polite but uncommunicative. When Pomfrey turned up in White's and made a point of sauntering over to their table for a significant show of solidarity, Clayton barely quit brooding long enough to join in the charade. Just half an hour later he abruptly took his leave and Gavin knew better than to delay him and ask where he was going.

'A gentleman is here to see you, ma'am. He's waiting in the parlour.' Having delivered her message, the maidservant withdrew almost immediately from Ruth's bedchamber. Ruth quickly came to a sitting position on her bed. She'd been idly lounging there, flicking through a journal while awaiting Clayton's arrival. Not that she'd received word from him that he would call this afternoon. But she'd had an instinct that he'd come at some point during the day. In fact, so sure of it had she been that she'd turned down an invitation to take tea with Susannah Storey simply so she wouldn't miss his visit. Sarah had accepted the invitation and taken little James with her for Susannah to coo over.

But now the moment had finally arrived, Ruth sensed her chest constrict with a combination of exhilaration and dread. She wanted to see him despite knowing the atmosphere between them was sure to be thick with friction. Urgent and important matters needed to be resolved between them. What had he decided to do? What had *she* decided to do? Since waking that morning, whenever she'd attempted to calmly assess her predicament, a jumble of emotion had muddled her thoughts. All she knew for sure was that she loved him. But was that a good or a bad thing?

The maid had seemed a little apprehensive on announcing she had a visitor. From that Ruth had guessed that *the gentleman* did not look to be in the best of tempers. Her heart fluttered against her ribs, making her feel quite queasy. So Clayton was still angry. At least she had an indication of what lay in store for her. She *was* ready to admit she'd lied; it hadn't been an idle boast given last night to escape his dangerous virility. If he'd come to tell her that she must own up to her deceit, then so be it. With a last look at her reflection and with her stomach feeling as tight as a vice, she went downstairs.

'Doctor Bryant!'

Ruth had halted in astonishment on the threshold of the parlour. Recovering her composure, she quickly entered the room and closed the door. In a reversal of the incident that had occurred at her cottage in Fernlea, she'd today been sure her caller was Clayton. The other time she'd expected Dr Bryant's visit. On neither occasion had she taken the wise precaution of checking on the gentleman's identity.

'You are surprised to see me,' Ian stated in a voice that hinted at acrid humour.

'Why…yes…I own I am, sir. I had no idea you

were coming to town,' Ruth returned in as pleasant a tone as her confusion would allow.

'And I had no idea that *you* were coming to town, Mrs Hayden,' Ian drawled her words back at her. 'Ignorant as I was of your plans to visit London, I'm no longer ignorant of the reasons for them.'

For a long moment Ruth remained quiet, a small frown marring her smooth brow. She sensed that beneath Ian's dialogue was a violent ire he was striving to subdue. 'If you're hoping to provoke me into demanding an explanation to a riddle, you're to be disappointed, sir,' Ruth answered levelly.

'I'm quite used to being disappointed by you, madam,' Ian retorted with heavy insinuation. 'Yet at one time you led me to believe that you'd more than satisfy all my expectations.'

Ruth sensed her spine stiffening and her hackles rising. She knew to what incident he'd referred just as he'd intended she should. But he wouldn't make her feel she'd done wrong in rushing into his embrace on the day her father died. She'd wanted platonic comfort from him. If he'd been too mean to allow her it, he should feel ashamed, not her. With a flash of insight Ruth realised what had prompted his resentment and his visit. She imagined that here before her was the proof that snippets of last night's brouhaha at the Storeys' *musicale* were already circulating.

'Have you been in town long, sir?' It was a leading

question and she wasn't surprised when it drew from him a sour smile.

'Long enough to be apprised of some disturbing news concerning you.'

'Will you enlighten me further?' It was purely prevarication; Ruth was well aware of what talk he'd heard.

'I understand you are to be the rake's wife, not mine,' Ian spat out.

'I don't recall ever having hinted that I might become your wife.' Ruth elevated her chin to a proud angle. 'I do recall unequivocally turning down your proposal.'

Two angry strides brought Ian to Ruth's side and a grip on her upper arm jerked her close. His lips hovered an inch above her pale cheek. 'And I knew you regretted doing so. I knew eventually you would have me. And, by Christ, I would have you. You've been a fire in my blood since the day you pressed your body against mine, and you've known it.'

Ruth attempted to jerk free, but his fingers bit deeper into her soft flesh and he moved his mouth so his exasperation effectively steamed on her skin.

'Tell me now that you did not expect me to again propose to you.'

A flood of blood beneath Ruth's complexion answered that question.

'And, by God, you would have accepted me, would you not, but for Powell arriving on the scene?'

The flame in Ruth's face burnt yet brighter. She *had* expected the doctor to shortly renew his proposal and she *had* been giving consideration to the benefits of being his wife.

'You're so desperate to net Powell you've acted like a vulgar wanton. You've broadcast he'll marry you before he's made it official. What everybody's wondering is…has he any intention of ever making it official?'

Ruth shrank her face back from the bitterness blazing in his eyes. 'I had not taken you for a gentleman who'd listen to tattlers,' she whispered. 'You might have asked me to explain—'

'Explain?' he savagely curtailed her. 'Would you care to tell me if you were acting the whore for him under the Tremaynes' roof?' His fingers snaked tighter about her arm. 'No?' he jeered. 'I thought you might not. Then tell me instead why you chased after him to town when he'd done with you. Was it to pester him for a proposal?' Ian furiously demanded to know. 'Tell me…have you cornered the rake well enough to get him up the aisle or is he likely to slip your clutches?'

Ruth pushed violently at Ian's chest and momentarily gained liberation, but within seconds he'd renewed his grip on her arm and swung her back to face him.

'One of our neighbours from Willowdene paid me a visit earlier. Christine Beauvoir brought with her a friend. Lady Vane's disappointment equals my own.

It seems she anticipated becoming betrothed to Powell before you put paid to her ambitions.'

'Did she also tell you that she's another man's fiancée? Did she say she's caused untold problems pursuing her ambition through outright lies?' Ruth could tell from Ian's abruptly shuttered expression that he knew nothing of Loretta's duplicity.

Beneath the onslaught of Ian's spite and censure Ruth felt her whole being trembling. She knew his frustration was powerful enough to make him act crazed. In turn she sensed her disgust for him deepening with every passing second. If soon he didn't let her go, she'd fight him with fists and fingernails. Yet she felt a similar disgust for herself. She had contemplated marrying a man capable of violent jealousy because of material benefits to be gained and without truly knowing his character. And how could she condemn Loretta Vane for falsely claiming to be Clayton's fiancée? She'd told the exact same outright lie.

'Let me go and please leave at once.' Ruth strove to keep a tremor from her voice. 'I don't want to create a scene in the viscount's house. But if you make it necessary, I will.'

'Making a scene is something you seem to like to do,' Ian mocked and brought his mouth menacingly close to hers. 'I'll go and gladly, madam, now I know you for what you are. You're nothing but a common tease. But before I leave I think you owe me something—'

'At which point I believe it's my duty to say unhand my fiancée or suffer the consequences,' drawled a lethal voice.

A startled silence fell on the grappling couple. Ruth twisted her face from Ian's pursuing lips and looked up. Clayton was standing with his back against the closed door, as though moments ago he'd quietly entered the room.

Ian shot him a purely poisonous glare, but his need and his opportunity were too great to deny. With a tortured oath he jerked Ruth's face back to his and rammed his mouth home.

The ordeal lasted no more than a second or two. The next thing Ruth was aware of was Ian being dragged by his collar from the floor, where he'd been sprawled. She watched in a daze, one hand pressed against her bruised mouth, the other steadying herself against the sofa as Clayton shoved the doctor tottering back against the wall.

Ian fell spreadeagled against the paneling, a fist planted either side of him. Then one moved and pressed against his mouth. It came away bloodied and Ruth realised that Clayton had at some point swiftly and efficiently hit him.

'She's all yours,' Ian sneered. He looked at his blood, then at Clayton. 'I've taken as much as I want. I'm satisfied.'

'But I'm not,' Clayton said with perilous calm.

'Find yourself a second to stand for you. Your choice of weapons. Beech Common at dawn tomorrow. I'll arrange for a doctor to attend,' he added with a glimmer of mordant humour.

'As you wish,' Ian muttered hoarsely, but his complexion had turned pallid.

'No!' Ruth breathed so quietly that at first neither gentleman heard her heartfelt plea. 'No!' The word tore from her throat with greater volume this time. 'You can't. It doesn't matter...' She flew towards Clayton and was immediately caught and anchored to his side by a powerful arm.

'How touching...' Ian sneered. Without a farewell of any sort he straightened his dishevelled attire and strode from the room.

'Did he hurt you?' Clayton asked in a voice so controlled it sounded stilted.

Ruth shook her head and gazed up at him. The grey of his eyes was lost to black, so huge were his pupils. 'He didn't hurt me, I swear. You must go after him and tell him you didn't mean what you said about the duel.'

'I can't do that, Ruth,' Clayton said quietly.

'Yes...yes, you can,' she urged hysterically. 'I won't have you fight over something so...so trivial. Ian was consumed with bitterness because he's heard we're to be married.' Her briny eyes were raised to his. 'And it's not even true,' she finished in a whisper. 'Is a man to die for a lie?'

'I won't kill him,' Clayton promised gently. 'In any case, he might wound me,' he pointed out, his grim amusement barely perceptible.

Ruth shook her head frantically. 'You know he will not…cannot do so. He's not trained as you are in weaponry. And if either of you are wounded, there is a chance it might be a fatal injury. Please, Clayton…' her arms spontaneously hugged about his waist to stress that he must do as she wanted '…go after him and say you didn't mean to challenge him…'

Clayton's hands immediately sank into her soft hair to keep her close, but within a moment the soothing had stopped.

'Are you concerned because you care for him?' Clayton asked very quietly. He moved her back from him so he might see her expression. 'Look at me, Ruth,' he demanded. 'What did I interrupt just now? Was it a lover's tiff? Was it arranged that he would come to visit you in London?'

Ruth's glistening gaze shot upwards to merge with his. Her wet lashes were blinked rapidly as she strove to subdue her astonishment and answer him. 'Of course not,' she finally choked out. 'I was stunned to see him. He's enraged because your mistress and Mrs Beauvoir paid him a visit. I'm sure you can guess their motive for doing so,' Ruth finished sharply.

Two bluish lines bracketed Clayton's mouth as his lips compressed into a hard line. He wheeled away from her and went to the window to plant his fists against the frame. 'I can guess at something else too. Bryant came to London to look for you and renew his proposal.' He shot Ruth a fierce look. 'If nothing had happened last night, what would have been your answer?'

'Do you think I would consider marrying a man capable of such...such vile behaviour?' Ruth took a step towards him, her features crumpled by hurt.

'If nothing had happened last night, Bryant wouldn't have received a visit from two mischief-making women. He wouldn't have been provoked into showing his true colours. So, believing him an up-standing fellow, and a pillar of Willowdene society, what answer would you have given him, Ruth?' Clayton persisted.

Ruth made a hopeless gesture. 'I don't know,' she said, too truthful. 'I admit he has shocked me by behaving in such a way. I admit too that at one time...some years ago...I considered him to be a friend.'

'A friend?' Clayton echoed and slanted at her a trenchant stare.

'He was present when my father died. He offered me comfort and I took it,' Ruth said quietly. 'When I allowed him to hold me, he mistook my reasons and my feelings for him.'

'Ah...' Clayton murmured. 'And at the time you

believed him too fine a gentleman to embrace a beautiful woman and later find an opportunity in it.'

Ruth snapped up her head, her temper beginning to simmer beneath his barbs. 'Perhaps you should not judge every gentleman by your own standards, sir.'

'Perhaps I should not,' Clayton concurred coolly. 'And at that time…when your father died…I take it the doctor was still married as he has an infant son.'

Ruth nodded and her eyes did not flinch from his, although she'd guessed his next words.

'He asked you to be his mistress.'

'Yes,' Ruth said hoarsely.

'And were you?'

'No,' Ruth breathed. 'I've said he mistook my feelings for him. Besides, I'm sure I need not point out to a sophisticate such as yourself that, had I acquiesced to an informal arrangement with the doctor, he probably wouldn't have bothered to improve upon it.'

A subtle smile touched Clayton's lips and lingered there. 'Indeed, you're coming to know me,' he murmured.

'And I do not like all I know,' Ruth returned in a whisper.

'Then I'm glad to have some qualities you find irresistible,' Clayton said and started back towards her. 'We'll always find common ground, Ruth. Perhaps we should settle for that…'

'Oh…um…sorry…'

Ruth shot a startled glance at the door to see that Gavin was hovering on the threshold.

'I was looking for Sarah,' he said apologetically. 'Never mind, I'll just see if she's…um…somewhere else…'

'Sarah went to Susannah's for tea,' Ruth informed him huskily. She darted a look at Clayton to see he was giving his friend a fearsome stare. Gavin responded with a barely perceptible gesture of regret.

On cue, Sarah's voice could be heard in the hallway. A moment later she appeared in the doorway with James in her arms. Her bright smile faded and her eyes immediately sought Ruth's with earnest enquiry.

'Sir Clayton has challenged Dr Bryant to a duel,' Ruth announced into the expectant quiet.

Chapter Eighteen

'What on earth has happened?' Sarah gasped.

Ruth sank into an armchair and her head dropped to rest in her quivering palms. For some minutes she seemed incapable of marshalling her thoughts well enough to answer Sarah's frantic question. Her friend knelt down beside her chair and hugged her, prompting salty tears to slide down Ruth's cheeks.

Shortly after Ruth had made her shocking announcement, Clayton had gone from the house with Gavin hot on his heels. But before Clayton had left he had quite tenderly drawn one of Ruth's hands to his lips in farewell. She'd feared he might be furious that her daze had caused her to spontaneously blurt out about the duel. A glimmer of exasperation had been at the backs of his eyes, but he had not reprimanded her by either harsh look or word.

Sarah rang for tea while Ruth, true to her word that in a moment she would be fine, dried her eyes and composed herself. A few minutes later, after Ruth had related all that had gone on, Sarah rattled her cup back on to its saucer. 'Hateful man!' she spat in disgust. 'And who would have thought it of him?'

'Not me, that's for sure,' Ruth said, smiling weakly.

'It is as well he is a capable doctor, for he certainly has no other commendable qualities,' Sarah returned pithily. She looked up urgently as her husband came back in to the room.

'He is in no mood to discuss the matter and has gone,' Gavin announced gloomily. 'I shall stand second for him. He can refuse me all he wants, it will make no difference. I shall be there.'

Sarah jumped to her feet. 'It is ridiculous!' she exploded. 'The meeting with Pomfrey has not been aborted for one whole day before Clayton gets involved in a different fight.'

'It's my fault,' Ruth said miserably.

'No, it is not!' A chorus of vehement denial issued from the couple.

'It is not, Ruth,' Gavin stressed softly. 'And if Clayton wanted me to know anything at all about what went on, it was that you are innocent of any blame.' Gavin came towards Ruth and took her hands in his in reassurance. 'He impressed that fact on me more than once and you must believe it.'

* * *

The idea of flouting etiquette to such a degree and visiting him at home would once have been beyond Ruth's scope of conduct. But with such damage to her reputation as had already been done, and might soon be added to, what did it matter? What value did a reputation have when set against a human life? There was an awful chance of a man being mortally wounded. Clayton and her friends wanted to shield her from the truth, but she knew she was the catalyst to an imminent tragedy. And her conscience could not bear it.

When she had told Gavin and Sarah that she wanted no dinner and must go out, she had noticed the bleak look that passed between them. But they had offered no demurral, although sweetly Sarah offered to accompany her. Ruth's insistence that she must go alone had then drawn a small sad smile and a nod of comprehension from her friend. When Gavin had quietly forced on her transport from his coach house, Ruth had accepted.

So, at seven o'clock in the evening she had set out for Belgravia Place in a sleek coach bearing the Tremayne crest. Sharing its luxurious comforts was one of Sarah's maids, seated opposite her. But now their journey was done.

Having told the young serving maid to wait where she was as she would not be long, Ruth now placed hesitant fingers on the door handle. She looked up at the imposing town house and fiercely quashed the temptation to tell the driver to set off back to Lansdowne Crescent. Nothing as paltry as faintheartedness was allowed to distract her from the vital task in front of her. She opened the door and got out.

'Ah, Mrs Hayden. Sir Clayton said you might come.'

Thoroughly unnerved by that polite yet very unexpected welcome, Ruth stared witlessly with huge dark eyes at the butler. 'Sir Clayton is expecting me?' she finally echoed faintly.

Hughes simply smiled and stepped aside, indicating that Ruth should come into the warm for the wind was strong enough to sway her on the top step and force her to snatch at her bonnet.

'Come along to the library. I believe Sir Clayton is to be found in there. I saw him enter the room not long ago.'

With her heart racing, Ruth followed the manservant. Darting glances roved the hallway, alighting on cool white marble and rich mahogany surfaces. Her fiancé's house was tastefully and expensively equipped, yet as Ruth walked amid Clayton's possessions she doubted she would ever be chatelaine of such splendour. She drew level with a magnificent gilt-framed mirror and, just before passing it, slipped a glance sideways. Her reflection startled and dismayed her—her huge dark eyes looked to be set in a complexion so pale as to be wraithlike. And then Hughes stopped and opened a door.

'Ah…he is not here,' the butler said with a frown, retreating from the room. Despite that setback, he ushered Ruth over the threshold of the library. 'If you would care to wait within, Mrs Hayden, I shall go and find Sir Clayton. I know he has not gone out.'

'Thank you,' Ruth murmured.

'Would you like some refreshment, ma'am?' Hughes remembered to ask before he fully closed the door.

Ruth shook her head and managed to murmur a polite declination.

Once alone, she loosened her bonnet and removed it, then took a few faltering steps over polished boards. She stepped on to a claret-coloured rug, then pivoted slowly about on the spot so she might fully see the grandeur of her surroundings. Her sepia eyes soared up and over the cased books. There were thousands, she guessed, ranging from tomes that looked to be over two feet tall and almost as wide, to tiny hide-bound booklets that refused to stand upright. Along the centre of the room were three sturdy library tables. Bulbous legs of turned oak supported leather tops of the same rich red hue as the rug she trod upon. Two of them bore a few scattered titles as though somebody had chosen them, finished with them, but not yet bothered to slide them home. Ruth's dark eyes flitted to the third table. There were no books, but it had on it an open wooden case…

Ruth felt her heart cease its erratic hammering and vault to her throat. She had seen such a box before. Her papa had owned a set of pistols.

Her clammy palms were dried on her skirts as swift steps took her closer to see if her fears were realised. She gazed down and, even to her inexperienced eye, guessed the guns were awesomely expensive duelling weapons. She extended a finger and touched the deadly cold metal, wonderfully chased in silver, before she slid her palm over polished wood and lifted one from where it innocently nestled.

'Are you going to use that?'

Ruth swished about with the weapon still gripped in her hand. Her denial was wordless and barely perceptible, yet set her dark tresses to trembling.

'Are you going to use it on Dr Bryant?' she returned in a whisper.

He didn't reply immediately; as he came towards her, she obliquely studied his appearance. She'd never seen him look so casually attired in buff breeches and a white linen shirt, agape at the throat, with the sleeves shoved back on solid muscle. When he reached her he removed the gun from her hand. His grey eyes roved her features with such solemn yet vivid desire that Ruth felt tempted to sway against him and let him erase all her anguish with draining kisses.

Ashamed that she could crave passion at such a time, she repeated breathily, 'Are you intending to use these tomorrow?'

'He's chosen swords,' Clayton said and replaced the pistol in the box.

Spontaneous heat scalded the backs of Ruth's eyes, making her blink rapidly. 'Close combat?' she croaked, almost to herself. 'Why?'

'I'm not sure,' Clayton answered with quiet truthfulness. 'But as a doctor he would know what damage a lodged bullet can do.'

'And a stab wound is harmless?' Ruth choked out in fierce frustration. 'This is madness.' Her tone was thick with despair. 'You knew I would come here and ask you not to fight. Your butler said you were expecting me.'

'Did he?' Clayton muttered. 'He's got too much to say for himself.'

'And what have you got to say?' Ruth begged to know in a husky choke. 'Please tell me you won't do this. I know it is a great deal to ask of you. I know honour and ego and all those things that gentlemen find so very difficult to deny are at stake…but surely you can see the disgrace in it, too?'

When he remained silent, she spontaneously grabbed at his jaw and jerked his face so he must look at her. As though startled by her audacity, and by the sensation of his angular abrasive flesh beneath her fingers, she just as quickly let him go. 'Can you bear to have on your conscience that tomorrow you might make a motherless little boy an orphan?' she demanded brokenly. 'I know I cannot. Joseph Bryant is only a year old…'

'I won't kill Bryant…I swear that to you.'

'But you are going to keep the appointment.'

'I must.'

'Why? Why must you? You have a choice,' she burst out in exasperation.

'Name it,' he said gently.

'Withdraw…please. Ian forced a kiss on me. I am the injured party and I ask you to forget what happened, as I have.'

'He insulted you. I heard him,' Clayton said.

'I have forgotten that too,' Ruth lied again.

'I haven't,' Clayton returned in the same placid tone. He stared down at the boxed weapons as he said softly, 'I've fought over a faithless wife and, had Pomfrey not seen sense, I would have fought over a scheming mistress. By God, I'll fight for you, Ruth, or know myself for the worst type of fool.'

'But I don't expect or want you to fight for me,' Ruth reasoned swiftly.

'I know, sweetheart…that's why I must.'

She could tell from his quiet steady tone that he wouldn't be swayed from what he'd decided. He might have issued the challenge to Ian on the spur of the moment, but it was obvious that, on reflection, his conscience was clear over it all.

'If you want to prove something to me, and please me…give me what I want,' she said huskily and came closer to him. 'I want the future you promised me.' Her slender hands rose to his shoulders, splayed over contoured muscle sheathed in cambric. Her head tilted to a perfect angle to tempt his mouth, her eyelids lowering in innate seductiveness. From beneath an inky web of lashes she could see the need start to smoulder at the backs of his eyes. 'I know you're an experienced duellist but…terrible accidents can happen. I might lose you.' Her warning was impressed on him as her straying fingers straddled his forearms. Abruptly she tossed her pride to the wind. 'How then will you give me that common ground we like to share, or a lengthy engagement?'

Clayton smiled slowly and with a hint of rueful humour. 'That's not what you want, Ruth. Nor should you,' he said gently, his grey gaze merging with her profoundly soulful eyes. He lowered his head and touched his mouth very lightly, very briefly to hers before moving away from the lure of her warm lush body. 'Go home, Ruth,' he said hoarsely. 'I swear to you Joseph will soon have his wretched papa back in one piece.'

Frost was glittering on the grass when the coach stopped and two men got out.

The vehicle scrunched away to halt beneath an arc

of trees hemming a small clearing on Beech Common. Gavin immediately ran a booted foot back and forth, testing the white surface beneath it. 'Icy as hell,' he said and tossed Clayton a bleak look.

Clayton grimaced, then pivoted to look towards the sound of an approaching vehicle. The ghostly outline of a carriage emerged from the wispy mist. 'It's Francis Wells,' he told Gavin as his friend continued to walk back and forth over the treacherous turf, searching incessantly for a less perilous patch. But the yellow orb in the east had barely quit the horizon and was in no position to disperse the rime with its weak rays.

Gavin extended a hand as the surgeon marched over solid ground towards them. 'Gentlemen,' Francis intoned in solemn greeting, and shook hands with them both. 'Pistols or swords?' He looked at Clayton sharply for an answer.

'Swords,' Clayton informed him. 'But, unless Bryant's a master fencer, I wouldn't be surprised to hear him change his mind.'

'It's a foolish choice indeed,' Francis Wells said disapprovingly. 'Every morning this week has seen severe hoarfrost. It's not easy walking on such terrain. It would need to be a fool indeed who'd choose to fence on it.' He sent a grim gaze to rove over the crisp white environment.

Clayton smiled thinly. 'It obviously didn't occur to

Bryant to take into account prevailing weather conditions. I think the doctor is probably inexperienced in these matters.'

'Whereas you are not.' Francis cast on him a jaundiced eye.

The sound of hooves and a creaking axle precluded any further debate. Another carriage loomed into view from beyond the screening trees.

It came to a stop on the opposite side of the clearing. Ian Bryant got out and shot a long stare Clayton's way. A dandified-looking fellow jumped down after him and immediately blew in his cupped hands to warm them.

'I didn't know Ian Bryant was on friendly terms with Claude Potts.' Gavin made that observation as he stuck his hands into his coat pockets to protect them from the sting in the air.

'I doubt he is,' Clayton returned. 'I'd heard Christine Beauvoir has recently become Claude's mistress. Perhaps she thought it her duty to persuade him to offer his services to the doctor as she's helped to embroil him in this mess.'

'There's no chance of the matter being kept quiet now,' Gavin grimly remarked. 'Potts is the worst sort of blabbermouth. I doubt Bryant knows that about him, or much else. I'll warrant he'll not be pleased to discover all and sundry might soon know his business.'

Clayton didn't respond. He was watching the two men as they talked earnestly in between casting glances at their surroundings. Clayton had already guessed the outcome to their debate. A moment later Claude Potts picked a path across the hazardous terrain towards them and promptly confirmed Clayton's suspicions.

'Gentlemen,' he said and flourished a deep bow. 'My principal has asked that, if Sir Clayton is agreeable, weapons should be changed to pistols. The ground appears treacherous for fencing…' He slid an indicative look sideways.

'I make no objection to that,' Clayton agreed. 'Have you brought pistols?'

Already aglow from the cold, Potts's cheeks became brighter. He'd recognised immediately the light irony in Clayton's tone. 'I believe Dr Bryant was wondering…that is…have you brought a pair with you? We did not anticipate…'

'Clever fellows,' Clayton commented caustically.

'We'll settle for swords, if you have not,' Potts snapped. He knew, as the doctor's second, he should have thought to cover all eventualities. He knew too that, if something untoward were to occur, he could be called on to fight in the doctor's stead. The idea of combat of any sort with Clayton Powell as his adversary was enough to make beads of cold sweat decorate Claude's bony forehead.

'I've a pair of pistols in the coach.' Clayton took pity on his blushing confusion.

Potts swallowed squeakily in relief. Having executed a less flamboyant bow, he started off treading daintily back across the frost.

Before Claude had reached the doctor's side, the assembled company were distracted by the noise of another coach. In seconds it was thundering into view through the mist. The horses were snorting from exertion and the vehicle shuddered to a halt in the middle of the clearing. Several gentlemen tumbled out, looking rather the worse for a night's roistering. The coachman then got off his perch and it was as he shoved his hat back on his head that Clayton recognised him.

'What in damnation…!' he expostulated in sheer exasperation.

'I said Potts has got a big mouth…' Gavin ejected through his teeth.

Ralph Pomfrey was already striding across the grass towards Clayton. He grabbed at his hand and pumped it up and down. 'Rum do, this, Powell. Any support needed…glad to give it, you know…'

Clayton snatched back his fingers and looked past Ralph to his spectator chums. He knew that they were simply rounding off a night's entertainment by coming here to watch the spectacle. 'If you want to be of use,' he enunciated curtly, 'keep them quiet and out of the way.' He turned to Gavin and they started to walk back towards their coach. 'Let's get this under way before the authorities turn up.'

'This is turning in to a farce,' Gavin muttered.

'Indeed...but make no mistake about it. Bryant is deadly serious and out for my blood.'

'And you?' Gavin asked shrewdly.

'Fetch the pistols,' Clayton said.

Chapter Nineteen

'Have you been sitting there all night?' Sarah asked softly on seeing Ruth's still figure perched fully clothed on the edge of a chair.

Ruth stirred her numb mind enough to give Sarah an answer. 'I woke about an hour ago.'

'You managed to get some sleep?' Sarah asked gently. She came further into Ruth's bedchamber.

Ruth nodded. 'A little.' She'd surprised herself by falling in to a deep dreamless sleep for a few hours before waking with a start and blinking at the darkness. Then the ghastly memories had crowded in on her and no further rest had been possible. She'd washed and dressed, with nausea rolling in the pit of her stomach, then sat down to wait for the dawn and news of the duel. But sunrise had come many hours ago and still there was no word of what had happened.

Again her eyes were drawn to the small mantel clock. It was after eight o'clock.

'Is Gavin back yet?'

Sarah shook her head. 'I doubt he'll be long now… unless…' She hesitated to say any more.

'Unless something terrible has occurred.' Ruth sprang to her feet and paced to and fro. Her dread that a disaster had caused Gavin's tardiness prompted angry futile words to explode from her lips. 'Men are such arrogant, egotistical brutes!'

'Indeed,' Sarah wryly agreed. 'Yet still we love them…'

Ruth's silence was answer enough, but Sarah probed gently, 'You do love him, don't you?'

'I hate him, too, for doing this.'

'The feeling won't last,' Sarah advised gently. 'There were things that occurred between Gavin and me that I thought too serious to be forgiven or put right.'

'But…if he is dead…or badly hurt…how can that be put right?' Ruth asked with a sob in her voice.

Sarah was about to attempt an answer when the noise of a vehicle in the street sent her rushing to the window instead.

'It's Gavin!'

Ruth collapsed back in to the chair, her face ashen. 'Is he alone?' she whispered.

After a moment Sarah answered, 'Yes…he is…'

Sarah let the curtain drop and turned to Ruth. 'Will you come downstairs and hear the news or would you rather I—?'

'I'll come with you now,' Ruth interrupted in little above a whisper.

As they entered the parlour they came upon Gavin agitatedly prowling the room. His grim features made Ruth's heart thump with such force that she felt momentarily suffocated and unable to speak. 'Is he dead?' she finally gasped out.

'No,' Gavin answered quickly. 'But he is wounded… though not fatally,' he added immediately on seeing Ruth clutch a chair for support and turn so pale that he feared she might swoon. 'We've taken him back to the surgeon's house. Francis has stopped the bleeding and luckily the bullet did not lodge. The wound is clean.' His features tautened in ferocious anger. 'Bryant shot before the signal, then ran with his tail between his legs. He didn't even have the decency to offer to assist the surgeon in attending to Clayton's wound. He'd no idea what damage he'd caused and made no move to find out.'

'Was Clayton not able to get his shot in before the coward fled?' Sarah demanded, sounding as incensed as her husband.

'Oh…Clayton got a shot in. He put a bullet in the tree behind Bryant. It must have passed the caitiff's head with an inch to spare.'

'Thank God he missed him,' Ruth muttered so faintly the comment was almost inaudible.

'Clayton doesn't miss,' Gavin told her with bleak humour. 'He deloped. And why I'll never know. The fellow deserved some damage for what he'd done. At least he was frightened witless on knowing what he might get next time.' It was scant consolation and Gavin knew it. 'I have just come to put your minds at ease. I knew you would be desperately worried.' He passed a hand over his stubbly jaw. 'I must go back. Pomfrey is with Francis Wells and eager to assist. As soon as Clayton is fit to make the journey, we'll get him home and straight to bed.'

Ruth opened her mouth to speak, moistened her lips, desperately trying to think of some heartfelt message to send with Gavin. In the end all she could manage to croak out was, 'Please tell him I wish him well.'

'The gentleman's here, ma'am.'

Ruth turned from where she'd been sorting and labelling tubs and bottles in her larder. She gave Cissie a puzzled look while wiping flour from her hands on to her pinafore.

'The gentleman…you know…the one from London you said as might come back,' Cissie whispered, her eyes round as saucers.

Ruth froze in to immobility for a moment. She'd not expected him to come so soon. She'd thought that perhaps in a month, when he was well enough, he might visit her. But it was not yet a week since she'd left Mayfair on the afternoon of the day of the duel. The Tremaynes had not tried to persuade her to stay, but had put every comfort at her disposal for the return trip to Willowdene. The parting from Sarah had been quiet, but intensely tactile and emotional.

Quickly Ruth started from her daze. She snatched off her pinafore and dropped it on to the table. 'Where is he?' she gulped.

'In the front sitting room, ma'am. I didn't know where you'd want him took…'

Ruth forced a smile. Her panic had transferred to Cissie and the poor girl looked quite scared. 'Thank you, Cissie, you may go home.'

Cissie nodded, but made no move to leave. Suddenly she darted to a row of hooks, grabbed her cloak and slipped out of the kitchen door.

It was too late to wish she'd chosen another afternoon to spring clean her kitchen cupboards. Ruth looked down ruefully at her dowdy attire. Since she'd returned home she'd plunged into energetic occupation, in and out of doors, simply to keep her troubles from tormenting her mind. And now the cause of her frantic daily activity was here…too soon. In no way was she prepared to see him yet. But desire to see him she most certainly did. With an inspiriting deep breath, and a nervous hand fiddling with wisps of glossy dark hair, she quit the kitchen.

He looked the same; the fine cloth of his charcoal-grey jacket fitted snugly to a back as wonderfully broad as she remembered it to be. His long athletic legs looked to be as sturdy following his ordeal. As he turned towards her she searched his dear profile for signs of any lingering pain but found nothing to concern her. He was facing her now and her eyes slipped shyly over him. Had she no knowledge of his recent threat to carry her struggling out of the Storeys' drawing room or to fight a duel over her, such assertions about his behaviour would have seemed preposterous. He looked cool civility incarnate and the picture of health and vitality.

'You look well,' she remarked and forced her hungry gaze away from him.

'So do you,' Clayton returned softly and brought an immediate blush to her cheeks. He watched as she self-consciously brushed a slender hand over the work dress she wore.

'You must excuse my appearance,' Ruth said on a little laugh. 'I didn't expect you to come so soon.'

'But you were expecting me, your maid told me so.'

Ruth's colour increased. 'She's got too much to say for herself,' she said lightly.

Clayton smiled; he knew she was echoing his words about his servant, spoken on the last occasion they'd met.

The expectant quiet lengthened, so she told him what she was sure he was politely waiting to hear. 'I knew you'd come as there is important unfinished business between us.' She frowned slightly. 'The matter of the engagement is still unresolved.'

Again her eyes darted to his body, seeking clues as to his injury. 'Has your wound healed so soon?'

Clayton pressed a few fingers to his right side and winced very slightly. 'It's well enough…'

'Well enough?' Ruth echoed, aghast. 'You have travelled so far with a bullet wound that still pains you?'

His eyes merged with hers. 'I wanted to see you,' he said gruffly. 'I couldn't wait any longer.'

'You want to know if I meant what I said, about…a lengthy engagement.' Ruth raised limpid dark eyes to his face. 'I did…and, if it's still what you want, I'm willing—'

'It isn't what I want,' Clayton interrupted in a voice that sounded harsher than he'd intended.

Ruth's eyes slanted immediately to his, her heart squeezing in anguish. He was rejecting her. He had come to end things between them and do it as quickly and courteously as he could. 'I see,' she finally choked out.

'I don't think you do, Ruth.' Clayton came a little closer to her. He made to reach for her then dropped tightly furled fists to his sides. 'If a man may be known by the company he keeps…what do you know about me? Tell me what you think of a man who has kept in style Loretta Vane, then considered you suitable as her replacement.'

Ruth felt a flush stealing under her skin. Within a moment of studying him she realised he wasn't waiting to hear that she could equal any service Loretta had provided. His expression and stance were bashful, boyishly endearing. He still wanted her good opinion and he thought his association with Loretta had ruined the chance of having it.

'Do you want my forgiveness?' she asked quietly.

'Yes, and more besides.'

'Is she in your past now?'

'She's been in my past since the day I travelled through snow to Willowdene Manor with Gavin. I swear it to you,' he added gruffly on seeing scepticism cloud Ruth's eyes.

'Then I think your past is your affair,' she said simply. 'I also think you astonishingly honourable and brave. You allowed Dr Bryant to go home, unharmed, to his son despite his despicable cheating. Once I considered that cheat a worthy man, and a friend. I considered accepting his proposal to improve my lot in life. What do you think of a woman so easily duped, so easily bought?'

'Do you want my forgiveness?'

'Yes…and more besides,' Ruth echoed his words wistfully.

'Name it. It's yours.'

Ruth allowed her lids to fall and felt the words teeter on her tongue tip. But pride kept them there for the moment. She wouldn't beg him to say he loved her any more than she'd demand he give her that lengthy engagement he'd offered. 'I'm so sorry,' she blurted. 'I haven't offered you refreshment and you've travelled far.' Her lack of manners made her feel worryingly inhospitable. Immediately she went to the decanter of port and, whether or not he wanted it, poured him a glass of rich ruby wine.

'I thought you were to use swords. Yet you have a bullet wound,' she said as she placed the glass on a table close to him.

'The ground was hard and slippery. Bryant changed his mind.'

'And you let him?' she said in wonder.

'It made no difference to me.'

'Because you knew you would not fight back whatever weapon he chose,' Ruth said with strengthening perspicacity.

'Something like that,' Clayton said diffidently. He picked up the glass of port and took a sip.

'The coward shot you, yet you deloped and allowed Joseph to have his papa back in one piece. You did it for me, because you'd promised me you would.'

There was no need for him to give a reply. The solemn intensity in his eyes, the stillness in him, told her the truth. He'd been intolerably lenient for her rather than for Joseph.

'Did you name your daughter?' Clayton asked

huskily as though his mind tracked hers and he knew she thought of infants.

For a moment silence throbbed between them. Since that worrying evening at the Manor when little James had been poorly and Ruth had told him about her daughter, the matter had never again been mentioned between them. Her soulful dark eyes flicked up to him. 'Yes,' she eventually murmured. 'I named her Elizabeth.'

'Did your husband know her name before he died?'

Ruth swallowed, but the blockage remained in her throat so she nodded a reply. That was another matter that had remained unspoken between them. Yet instinctively she'd known he'd spoken to Keith Storey about the manner of Paul's death. 'Paul held Elizabeth before she was buried. He went back to his regiment of his own volition,' Ruth quietly volunteered. 'I didn't want him to leave. I feared what they might do to him. And so did he. But honour was everything to him, too. It was nothing to me but another body to bury. He was only twenty-two.'

'A man might live for his three score years and ten and never be as fortunate,' Clayton said softly. 'He had you. And you loved him.'

Ruth felt tears welling in her eyes at his quiet comfort. 'Did you want children?' she asked huskily.

'No,' Clayton said immediately. 'A child should have a good mother. A good father, too.'

'You would be a good father!' she cried spontaneously, then pressed together her lips. 'I'm sorry, I didn't mean to pry.'

'I want you to,' Clayton said with a coarse laugh. 'I want you to demand that I tell you why I've so long been wallowing in bitterness and unwilling to escape the shadow of a doomed marriage.'

'You don't need to tell me,' Ruth replied. 'I know it must have been a miserable time for you...' Suddenly the hurt she'd dammed behind pride and politeness exploded in harsh words. 'I don't want to know about her! I hate her! You're mine now! Why don't you want me now?' she keened in frustration. 'Is it because I tried to trap you to marry me?'

'Did you?' Clayton asked, but the wonderment in his face was put there by hope, not censure.

Already Ruth regretted what she'd done. She'd crumbled her own defences and the last bastions of her pride. Slowly she nodded and a watery little laugh bubbled in her throat. 'I didn't realise it at first. I thought I'd done it nobly for Sarah's sake. And of course I wanted to wipe the smirk from the face of that awful mistress of yours. But mainly I did it for me. I said we were to be married because I wanted it to be true.' She began to raise her head, feeling shy and apologetic. But by the time their eyes merged hers were vivid with challenge. She knew she had no bridges left to burn.

'So…you really don't mind that your affianced husband was once a maudlin idiot with very poor taste in women?' Clayton said gently. 'You don't mind that he was so sunk in self-pity he thought never in his miserable life would he have a chance with a woman as fine and beautiful as you?'

She shook her head, unable to speak for the wedge of emotion blocking her throat.

'Come here…' he ordered huskily and held out his arms.

Ruth stood rooted to the spot as tears spilled on to her lashes.

'I love you, Ruth. Please come here…' he begged huskily.

She flew across the room to him to hug him about the waist, then sprang back as she felt him wince. Immediately he drew her back against him and buried his lips in the scented mass of her hair.

'I'll take that pain and more just to have you in the same room as me,' he said hoarsely. 'God, I love you, Ruth. I love you so much.'

She lifted her watery countenance to his and touched a hand to his face. 'And I love you, Clayton.'

As though it was what he'd been waiting to hear his mouth plunged to hers with urgent need, sliding silkily back and forth. Ruth responded immediately, parting her soft lips beneath his sweet savagery. As his hands moved on her body she touched him back. Her fingers slid inside his coat, gently investigating. She felt the padding covering the wound and with infinite tenderness cupped her hand over it as though to protect him from any further hurt. Burying her face in the cosy nook beneath his shoulder, she asked with a throb of uncertainty, 'Do you want me as wife or mistress?'

'Both. I want only you. Will you marry me, Ruth?' he asked huskily.

'Are you sure it's what you want…?'

'Yes…and here's the proof.' He'd gently curtailed her anxieties while reaching in to a pocket and withdrawing a small box. With his arms about her, he opened it and turned the small casket to show her his gift. 'I came here, to beg on my knees if necessary, and make you have me and this ring. It belonged to my mother and now it's yours.'

Ruth gazed in awe at the fabulous round diamond. The shoulders of the shank were also encrusted with brilliant rectangular stones. 'Did Priscilla give it back?' she asked in amazement. It was the sort of gem any woman would be reluctant to part with.

'Priscilla?' He gave a bark of grim laughter. 'She didn't have it. My mother was still alive then and would never have allowed her to have it. She never liked Priscilla. I should have listened to her from the start.' His mouth touched her crown of silken dark hair. 'My mother would have adored you. She would be overjoyed to know she has at last a daughter-in-law to be proud of.'

'I'm most happy to accept it, and you,' Ruth said in a voice husky with tears. She took the ring then and slipped it on her finger, moving her hand to let the fading light in the room catch the stone and fire it to life. 'It's so very beautiful…I wish I had something equally precious to give you…' As her thanks faded, her cheeks blossomed beneath the sultry heat blazing in his eyes.

'I think there's something…' he suggested wryly and dipped his mouth to seduce at the corner of hers.

She could sense the sweet wine on his breath, feel the heat of his desire warming her cheek.

'What about your injury?' she said softly, but turned her lips so they were ready to quickly couple with his.

'I trust you to be gentle with me,' he said and, with his mouth pressed to hers, took her towards the sofa.

Chapter Twenty

'There's somebody knocking on your door.'

Ruth stirred. She felt cosy and comfortable nestling against Clayton. His seduction had been wonderfully long and luxuriant and had culminated in a fiery ecstasy that had left her blissfully languid. Now she reluctantly lifted her head fractionally away from his warm chest and listened. There was an unmistakable sound of her knocker again being used. She squirmed against him to look into his eyes.

A groan escaped Clayton as she innocently tormented his hard sensitive body. Gathering back from her rosy face a fistful of tumbled chocolate-brown hair, he gently drew her face close and touched his mouth to the bruised bow of her lips.

'Did anybody see you arrive earlier?' Ruth whispered against his skin.

'Two women were in the street. They were stationed there last time I called on you,' he whispered back in amusement. 'Does this mean I must make good on my promise to marry you…or ruin your reputation?'

Ruth nodded. 'It does, I'm afraid.' She started slightly as the knocking became more insistent. In a flurry of petticoats, and tapping away Clayton's restraining hands, she scrambled to her feet. In a moment she'd smoothed down her crumpled skirts and arrived at the door to open it a fraction.

'Mrs Brewer…Mrs Stern,' she greeted breathily, thankfully unaware of the ravishing sight she made. Her bodice buttons were undone and displaying a creamy uncorseted cleavage. Her cheeks were flushed, her mouth plump and purple from Clayton's kisses and her rich dark hair waved about her face in artless disarray.

The two women goggled at her, then slid a speaking look at each other. Mrs Hayden might be unaware of how she appeared, but it was nevertheless quite obvious to them what she'd been about.

'We…we wondered…that is, we saw your gentleman visitor arrive some while ago and were concerned…' Mrs Brewer spluttered.

'Did you hear something?' Ruth asked, cringing from the possibility that her sighs and moans had been loud enough to travel through the wall.

'Why…no, Mrs Hayden. We could hear nothing at all,' Mrs Stern said disappointedly. 'So we decided to knock and make sure you were not in need of anything.'

'I have everything I need,' Ruth said with a simple serenity. Aware of the direction of Mrs Stern's gaze, she began to fasten her bodice.

The diamond flashed blindingly at the women, making their jaws simultaneously drop.

If Ruth had not known from a subtle caress on her hip that Clayton now stood behind her, the gawping ladies would have given the game away.

'You have not met my fiancé,' Ruth said with quiet pride. 'Sir Clayton Powell.' She turned against Clayton's body unable even now, under observation, to resist bodily contact with him.

'Sir Clayton…these ladies are two of my neighbours…Mrs Brewer and Mrs Stern.'

Clayton politely inclined his blond head and murmured an impeccably polite greeting, coupled with a farewell as he quietly closed the door. Just behind it he trapped Ruth against the wall and, placing a finger over her laughing mouth, trailed kisses on her joyous face from brow to jaw.

'Thank you for rescuing me,' she bubbled.

'Do you like me now?' he asked with a hint of gravity belying the wryness in his tone.

Ruth went on to tiptoe and brushed her mouth on his. 'I love you now. I also like you very much. In fact you have qualities I find irresistible, but you've always known that, haven't you?' she added softly.

'I'm equally captivated, sweetheart,' Clayton returned before transforming her gentle teasing of his lips into a deeply passionate kiss.

'Are you hungry? I can cook, you know,' Ruth finally said when their mouths parted. She cradled his hard handsome face between her soft palms. 'Would you like some dinner?'

'I'm hungry and tired. What shall we do first? Sleep or eat?' he asked hoarsely.

Ruth's eyes coupled with his. Gently, sweetly he had courted her on the sofa with kisses and caresses and tormented himself in the doing of it. Selflessly he had bestowed on her unbelievable pleasure while his own need went unrelieved. Wordlessly she gave her answer by slipping her arms about his neck and laying her head on his shoulder. She gasped as he swung her up into his arms as though she were featherlight.

'Have you truly carried a woman out of a drawing room over your shoulder?'

'She was more a girl than a woman,' he answered as he took the first stair.

'Who was she?' Ruth asked, steeling to keep jealousy from her voice.

'My sister, Rosemary. She was sixteen and professed to be desperately in love with a young poet. He'd written some ditties for her and she insisted on sharing them with the assembled company despite requests not to.'

'Did she marry him?' Ruth asked as she slipped sinuously sideways to scoop up the sconce from its holder and light their way.

'No…she married a Devon farmer without a romantic bone in his body.'

'Poor Rosemary.' Ruth sighed. 'Every woman needs a little romance in her life.'

'The poet's her lover,' Clayton said drily.

Ruth clasped his shady chin so he must look at her. 'Truly?'

'Truly.'

'Can you write poetry?' Ruth asked impishly.

'If I need to,' Clayton growled. 'But first let me show you an irresistible way I know of being romantic…'

'Did you see that diamond?'

'Did you see that gentleman?'

Mrs Stern and Mrs Brewer exchanged a look as they hesitated by the gate of Ruth's cottage.

'*Now* I understand those rumours I've heard about Dr Bryant going away.' Mrs Brewer crossed her arms over her chest.

'I said from the start he was going off to sunnier climes for his own good, not the boy's,' Mrs Stern added. 'Joseph looks to be a bonny little lad to me.'

'The doctor must be feeling most put out at being turned down by Mrs Hayden to go to such extremes!'

'It's a queer do, right enough.' Mrs Brewer huffed. 'She waits ten years for a decent man to happen by and two turn up at once.'

'Sons are the same,' Mrs Stern said darkly. 'I saw six daughters arrive before Stanley was born. Then Benjamin after him in less than eleven months.

'Look at that.' Mrs Stern nodded her head at the outline of the racing curricle gleaming in the dusk.

'Mayfair and devilish rich, I'd say,' Mrs Brewer whispered in awe.

'Devilish in every way, I'd say.' Mrs Stern dug her companion in the ribs and gave a scandalised gasp. 'It's as well Mrs Hayden will be moving away. She'd set tongues wagging doing *that* when it's not yet properly dark!'

The women watched as a wavering candle flame disappeared from the hall, only to reappear on the landing. As they waited with bated breath, it flared in the front bedchamber before being extinguished.

'You can't deny he is devilish handsome, too,' Mrs Brewer said charitably and cackled a laugh.

'I suppose she'd need to be a nun not to...' Mrs Stern generously agreed and, linking arms, they walked on home.